For Mickey —
I think you'll like this.

FLIGHT FROM FEAR

by SARAH BYRN RICKMAN

Sarah Byrn Rickman
WASP Permission
Oct. 4, 2002
fellow FOW

Flight From Fear

This original work published by arrangement with the author.
Published by Disc-Us Books, Inc., Santa Fe, NM, USA
Printed in the USA

Cover Credits:
Cover illustration by Steve Long
                    Long's Graphic Design, Centerville, OH
Cover layout and design by G.V. Pulli

PUBLISHER'S NOTE:
This is a work of fiction. Names, characters, places, and incidents either are the product of the author's imagination or are used fictitiously, and any resemblance to actual persons, living or dead, events, or locales is entirely coincidental.

For more information contact:
                    Disc-Us Books, Inc.
                    Santa Fe, NM
                    Email: books@disc-us.com

www.disc-us.com

Dedication

To Nadine, Caro, Kaddy and Emma —

Thank you for sharing what is in your hearts and your very souls,
your love for a special time in your young lives,
and for an organization of which
there will never be more than 1102 members.

Through this book, may some of that spirit live on. . .

ONE

Lacy Stearns noted the lettering on the weathered door as she pushed it open. McDermott Aviation, Flight Base Operator, Lamar, Colorado. The mingled aromas of aviation fuel, motor oil, solvent, aging leather and dust greeted her. She swallowed the little lump of hesitation that stuck in her throat and squared her shoulders inside her faded jeans jacket.

Behind the counter, a stocky man with a salt and pepper crew cut sat at a cluttered desk working over a ledger. At the sound of the door closing, he looked up. Clear blue eyes gazed out from a face bronzed and lined by too much Colorado sunshine. "Yes, Ma'am. What can I do for you?"

"Are you Shorty McDermott?"

"That's me." He stood, revealing why he carried the name. He was maybe five feet five with a burly chest and thick, muscled arms that looked like they belonged on a wrestler. A ruff of graying hair peeked from his open-necked plaid shirt. A chaw of tobacco in his left cheek gave him the look of an aging chipmunk. "Who might you be?"

"I'm Lacy Stearns." She stuck out her right hand, not flinching at his bone-crushing grip, but returning it with every bit of strength and assurance she could muster. "I believe you know my uncle, Ike Jernigan."

"Ike and I go back a long ways," Shorty said, letting go of her hand. "What can I do for you, little lady?"

"I want to learn to fly."

The man stared at her.

Lacy fingered the long brown braid that hung over her right shoulder. She knew the braids made her look younger than her twenty-three years, but they were convenient for riding horseback so, she reasoned, surely they would be convenient for flying.

"You wanna take flying lessons?"

"Yes."

The stare had turned to a scowl. "Why? With this war on and fuel restrictions, it'll be years before you do any real flying. No joy ridin' with the boy friend."

Lacy's chin came up. She tamped down the urge to tell him that there was no boy friend. That her flyer husband, John, was dead. That a mere three months ago, his wounded B-24 had crashed returning from a bombing run over German submarine bases on the coast of France. That she had this crazy notion she could make a difference in this war by putting on a uniform and flying for her country.

She dared not tell him the real reason for fear he'd laugh at her. Even if he had heard about the women already ferrying airplanes for the Army, he'd think she was crazy.

So instead, she said, "I teach fifth grade down in Two Buttes. I've got the money and the time. I want to do it while I can."

McDermott cocked his head to one side, sizing her up. Lacy felt color rising in her cheeks.

"I never taught a woman to fly," he growled. "The country needs men flyin' right now, not women."

"My money's as good as any man's," Lacy said, and drew herself up to her full five feet ten inches. She remembered to smile when she said it, but more doubts raced through her mind. John always told her pilots were an egotistical bunch and the worst were the short guys who thought they had something to prove. She towered over this man.

"You're barely more than a girl," he said.

Her gray eyes flashed. "I'm twenty-three," she said, jaw clenched, and she looked him in the eye as she said it. She refused to look away for fear of losing her nerve.

"Women got no business flyin' airplanes. Little ladies don't have the muscle. . ."

"I'm not little." She fought the urge to add *as you may have noticed.* "And my father raised me just like he did my brothers. I can ride and rope and brand cattle with any man."

A flush had crept up the man's thick neck and onto his cheeks, making his blue eyes even brighter. "Ya gotta have it in here," Shorty said, punching his ample belly with his fist.

"Guts, Mr. McDermott? I've got plenty of that and I've got the ability to read a compass and plot a true course and do all those other calculations necessary to fly cross country from one point on the charts to another." She stared at him, head high, jaw thrust out.

He met her gaze then looked down at the open ledger on the desk.

Lacy sensed movement. Was it in her favor or not? She dared not breathe.

"Well," he said, running his finger down the left hand column. "I'm not exactly overrun with students right now. You won't last long, but what the h. . ." He paused, glared at her again. "When would you want to start?"

"Right now," she answered, exhaling slightly, as she reached back and pulled her wallet out of her jeans pocket.

"Whoa! Put your money up for a minute. Slow down. Let's talk about what-all learning to fly calls for — how quickly you want to do it, that sort of thing."

"OK," she said, "but I want to do it as soon as possible. I've got a deadline."

He shifted the chaw of tobacco to the other cheek and worked it while he chewed on that information for a minute. "Can you fly three times a week?"

"I can fly weekends now through the end of May." She glanced at the wall calendar behind his desk. "After school's out, May 28, I can fly every day if you'll let me."

"Well, that'll certainly speed up the process, provided you're a quick learner. You ever flown in one of these before?" He jerked his head toward the window.

Two yellow J-3 Cubs sat on the grass beside the hangar. The small, high-winged trainers were just like the one John had taken her up in — three years, a lifetime, and a world war ago.

"Once," she said, "as a passenger."

"Come on," Shorty said, and pushed open the door that led out to the airplanes. Lacy followed.

A man in coveralls, clipboard in hand, stood erect beneath the leading edge of the wing of one of the Cubs. Lacy remembered that her six-foot-four-inch husband had to duck his head to walk under the airplane's wing and climb into the pilot's seat at the rear of the enclosed cockpit.

The sweet and the bittersweet surfaced and tugged for an instant at her resolve and she closed her eyes — picturing John that day in 1940 before the world fell apart. When Lacy opened her eyes, the two Cubs were still there and Shorty now stood under the wing beside the man in coveralls, scowling with obvious impatience, waiting for her to catch up.

She hurried after him.

"Tell you what. Let's go for a spin and let you be a passenger one more time just to be sure you really want to learn to fly one of these things yourself. But first I'm gonna do what we call a pre-flight. I want you to watch everything I do 'cause you're gonna do it every time you get in an airplane from now on."

The cool April morning air stirred the loose strands of hair at the back of her neck. She put her hand back and smoothed them, a useless gesture she realized as the ever present high plains wind continued to toss them about. But she had to do something with her clammy hands.

Shorty handed her a clipboard with a checklist. She watched him closely and made a mental note of what he did and how he did it.

"Any questions?" he asked, when he was finished.

Lacy shook her head. She knew eventually she would have many, but the only one that came to mind was directed at herself, not him. *Why*, she thought, a hint of the familiar panic rising once again in her stomach, *why on earth did I get myself into this?*

"OK, let's go then."

And just like that came the tingling excitement Lacy always felt when embarking on something new — from the day she jumped from the haymow on her brother Kenny's dare, to the first time she made love with John, to the day she stepped into that J-3 Cub to fly with him the first and only time.

Today, April 24, 1943, was a new beginning.

TWO

At eight o'clock the following Saturday morning, Lacy headed for the airport in her battered black '35 Plymouth coupé. The fields of winter wheat rippled in the light morning air. The budding branches of the cottonwoods along the creek already sported their spring mantle of iridescent green.

She stopped at the turn onto the main highway. Through the open window she heard the trill of a meadowlark and saw him perched on a fence post across the road. Lacy watched as he took flight and landed on another post farther down the fence line that stretched away to the south.

The tires seemed barely to touch the road as she headed north for Lamar and the airport. The flight of the songbird captivated her as never before because she knew that in an hour or so she, too, would take flight. Butterflies of anticipation danced in her stomach. She fought the urge to press the accelerator all the way to the floor. Nothing would spoil a beautiful flying day like an earthbound ticket for speeding.

Shorty watched her as she made her way painstakingly through the pre-flight. She checked nuts, bolts and cotter pins, inspected the leading edge of the wooden propeller, the fabric wings for snags and tears, the tail. She made sure no bird had ill-advisedly begun to build a nest in the nose cowling. The fuel tank was full. The wire gauge, attached to the cork bobber inside the tank, was standing tall. She drained a half cup of the pale blue fluid into a glass bottle looking for sediment and water.

Everything was checked out and she was ready to climb into the cockpit when a tiny, trim woman with curly silver-blonde hair appeared at the door to the office. She beckoned to Lacy.

"I'm Clara, Shorty's wife," the woman said, smiling and extending her small, surprisingly strong hand, her blue eyes looking up at Lacy from beneath whitish lashes. "He's never had a woman student before. Always sent 'em to Marty Boswell in La Junta. Doesn't think women belong in the cockpit. Somehow, I think you just might change his mind," she said, looking Lacy up and down.

"Anyway, he won't think to remind you to make a pit stop before you go up. Men don't think of such things because they carry relief tubes in the aircraft should the need arise, but, as you probably know, that doesn't work too well for us gals. Besides, gruff as he makes out to be, he's a marshmallow inside and wouldn't dare mention such a delicate subject, particularly to a pretty young woman."

Lacy blushed. "Thank you, Clara. My name's Lacy Stearns."

"I know who you are. You're Ike Jernigan's niece. Now hurry, don't keep him waiting. As you may have guessed, he tends to be the impatient type."

Moments later, Lacy and Shorty climbed through the split door on the right side of the yellow Cub. He took the front seat, she sat in the seat behind. He pulled the bottom half of the door up and fastened it, leaving the top open to the air. Then he began to walk her through the start-up procedure.

The cockpit had little room to spare. The fuselage, made of fabric-covered steel tubing, gave Lacy the feeling she was enclosed in a cotton-covered tin can. The airplane sat high in the front on two large front wheels and rested low in the back on a pigmy-sized tail wheel.

Shorty's mechanic, the man she had seen standing under the wing inspecting the plane on her first visit to the airport, stood by the propeller and awaited the signal to hand rotate the prop to start the engine. When Shorty nodded, the man gave the blade a mighty pull through. On the second try, the engine caught and roared, sending a throb of excitement through Lacy's tense body.

Lacy couldn't see the instrument panel because Shorty's bulk was in the way, but she had a set of controls — a stick between her knees, a hand throttle to her left, and rudder pedals beneath her feet.

"Use the rudders to steer," he shouted back to her over the racket of the rotating prop. "Heels on the brakes, for what little use they are," and he laughed. "In case you've forgotten, they're under the rudders. You'll have to push down hard to get 'em to work." He paused.

Lacy waited.

"You're in control. Take her out."

The trip down the taxiway to the runway was next to disastrous. She could see nothing beyond the windscreen because of the cant and swell of the engine cowling. She tried to taxi the plane in a series of gentle S-curves, the way Shorty had showed her, but the rudders took on a life of their own, her feet the unwilling instruments of their rebellion. The plane careened from side to side.

When they reached the runway, he had her traverse the entire

1900-foot length to practice steering with her feet. She headed first for the wheat field on the right and then for the wind tee on the left. Their progress more resembled that of a drunken sailor than a well-maintained flight trainer. It took her several runs up and down, followed at each end by a 180-degree turn — hard right rudder — to get it under control.

Then they were at the end of Runway Four, the wind coming at them out of the northeast. Shorty went through the engine runup and takeoff procedure one more time. He had to yell to be heard over the noise of the prop. "Full power. When you feel the plane start to lift, pull back gently on the stick and bring the nose up." He paused. "Whenever you're ready."

"You want me to do the takeoff?" Lacy heard her voice croak. Her mouth was dry and she tried to swallow.

"You can do it. I have the same controls you do. I'm here if you need me."

Right hand on the stick, feet shoved against the rudder pedals, Lacy pushed the throttle forward with her left hand. All the sensations she had felt on the takeoff three years ago with John came back — the vibration as the rpm's built, the roar, felt as much as heard, generated by the single 65 horse-power engine, the release of its harnessed energy. She felt the plane surge forward. The tail wheel lifted and no longer was she looking at the engine cowling, but straight down the runway.

"Right rudder," Shorty yelled, just as she realized she was veering left. He had warned her that the torque of the rotating prop blade would pull her left. She applied a touch of right rudder and prayed that her feet would steer her true through takeoff as the little plane gathered speed.

It'll never get off, she thought. But then, as if by magic, the wind caught under the cloth-covered wings and lifted the tiny airplane. Lacy sensed its readiness to fly, pulled gently back on the stick, just as Shorty had showed her the first time they went aloft, and there they were — airborne.

She looked up and saw only blue sky and a few wisps of white clouds in front of her. To the sides, she watched the ground fall away beneath her and marveled at how free she felt. The throb of the engine echoed somewhere deep inside her and the wind through the open window pulled at her hair. She looked over her shoulder and saw the runway receding into the distance.

I did it! I did it! I did it! sang in her heart.

The little plane climbed.

"Now, keep your hands and feet on the controls, but I'll move them," and Shorty led her through a turn — left pressure on the stick, left rudder, and the plane began a shallow bank to the left. When he had negotiated a ninety-degree turn, he returned the stick and rudders to the neutral position, leveled out and continued climbing to cruising altitude.

"I want you to feel what I'm doing and see what happens," he yelled.

She felt the stick move frontwards and backwards in her hand and the plane's nose alternately climb and lower. "That's the elevators. Feel it?" He turned and looked at her.

She nodded.

Then the stick waggled from side to side and the wings gently rocked up and down in concert with his movements. "Ailerons," he said. "Now rudders." She felt him alternately tap the rudders and the little plane scooted and danced in the air. "Don't worry. The airplane won't fall out of the sky."

"Let me try," Lacy said, and laughed when the plane danced as she tapped the rudders.

"Now let's try a stall. I'll do one first. Follow my movements."

As the nose began to move higher in the sky, Lacy felt the stick come back in her hand. The sensation of falling backwards came on her, just like it had with John. The familiar queasiness crept over her. She looked out the open right window, fixed her eyes on the distant horizon and concentrated on keeping her breathing steady and her stomach from rising into her throat. She felt the plane shudder ever so slightly and then settle as the stick moved forward. And they were flying level again.

"You try it," he said.

Heart pounding, she pulled back on the stick between her knees. She thought of her mare Dusty, and riding her at a full gallop across the rangeland 2,000 feet below, her legs wrapped around the mare's middle, knees pressed in, heels down, fanny tucked under and sitting light and tall in the saddle.

Now, instead of watching the ground come at her between Dusty's laid-back ears, she watched the nose of the airplane climb the sky. When the controls felt mushy, she eased the stick forward. The plane settled back. She gulped, willing her fluttering stomach to relax and enjoy the ride.

"Another one," Shorty ordered.

This time she held the stick back a fraction of a second too long and the little plane kicked and dropped off to the left. Her heart stopped in mid beat.

"Drop the nose," Shorty yelled.

She pushed the stick forward, the plane shuddered and started to dive.

"Not too much," he shouted. "Pull back!" Then in a voice that was clipped but calm in contrast to her racing pulse and shallow breathing, "That's it."

Lacy tasted the metallic saliva of fear in her mouth. She tried to swallow, couldn't at first, had to work at it, gulping. Gradually, her calm came back. But she had felt it, the difference between the kinesthetic pull in her stomach when she did it right, and the lurching fear when she did it wrong. Now she knew what she had to master.

"OK, we're going to do a spin," he said. "Tighten your seatbelt."

The word spin caught her unawares, but there wasn't time to object. She pulled her belt tighter as she felt the nose start to come up, and up, and up. Then the nose dropped and she felt Shorty kick the left rudder and they were falling off to the left, rotating down. She was looking straight down at the Arkansas River and it was spinning around, coming up to meet her. Her heart lodged in her throat.

After what seemed an eternity, Shorty stopped the spin by kicking the opposite rudder and popping the stick forward. The airplane began to dive. Gradually, he eased the stick back and the Cub leveled out.

Lacy's heart was pounding, but she had felt it again. She knew what she had to do to get that feeling.

"Let's take her in. You can try your first landing."

When she was lined up straight for Runway Four, the grassy ribbon extending directly in front of her, narrowing into the distance, he shouted, "Back on the power!"

She pulled back on the throttle.

"Not too much!"

She fought to keep the wings level and tried not to think of John. When he made his ill-fated landing in England, it was on one wheel — reminiscent of the one-wheel landing he made the day she went flying with him. With her, in the J-3 Cub, the miscalculation had been brought on, she was convinced, by over-confidence and a tendency to show off for her. But on January 16, 1943, he was fighting for his life and the life of his crew, and he and his copilot had been unable to keep the wings of the wounded bomber level. One had dipped and struck the runway.

"Chop the power!"

She jerked herself back to the present and pulled the throttle back. The runway was rushing up to meet them.

"Nose up. . . a little more," he shouted.

She pulled the stick back still more.

The trees at the end of the runway were fingers reaching skyward, trying to snare the little yellow airplane and pull it abruptly to earth, but the craft cleared the tentacles, floated, and felt the gravitational pull of the ground coming up to meet it.

Thump. . . thump. . . they were down and rolling along the runway.

Lacy knew she had to stop the airplane. But it was already slowing. The tail wheel settled into the grass and she realized she had control. Joy erupted inside her all the way back to the hangar.

But as she stepped from the airplane onto solid ground, the waves of nausea returned and overwhelmed her. She ran from Shorty and heaved twice over the fence into the wheat field.

"You'll get over that," he said.

She hoped he was right.

THREE

That evening, following her first lesson with Shorty, Lacy sought out her Uncle Ike.

She was spending the night with him and her Aunt Virginia. Her father's brother and his wife lived on a ranch outside Lamar, fifty miles north of her family's ranch near tiny Two Buttes, in the far southeast corner of Colorado. The airport was three miles from Ike's spread. Planes flew over her uncle's rangeland all the time.

She found him sitting in his rocking chair on the wide verandah that encircled three sides of the small ranch house. The sun was low on the western horizon. A red-gold glow washed the weathered clapboard ranch house and out buildings, painting them a burnished copper. From the barn came the whinny of a horse and the thud of a hoof striking the stall. The air smelled sweet with hay and an overlay of dust from the warmth of the day

"Uncle Ike, I need to talk to you."

The rawboned man in Levi's, denim work shirt, and scarred brown leather boots, lit his pipe, drew on it until the round wad of tobacco glowed red-orange like the fiery round ball that was the setting sun. His bushy black eyebrows cast his eyes in shadow so she couldn't see them. But she knew they were gray like her father's. Like hers.

"Go ahead, I'm listening."

"After John died, and I was so lost and trying to find myself, you told me there were places to go and things to do that wouldn't be there for me when the war was over. And that I was free to do anything I wanted to do."

He drew on his pipe. "I said something like that, yes."

"At the time, I didn't understand what you meant. I was safe, with my teaching job and the ranch and Mother and Daddy. I just wanted to curl up in my little cocoon here and sleep the war away. Well, I've changed my mind."

Slowly, Lacy began to tell him her plan. "I was reading one of Mother's magazines and I found this article — about Jacqueline Cochran, the woman pilot who won all those flying trophies and who owns the cosmetics company. She's formed this organization for the

17

Army to teach women to fly airplanes for the war effort."

Lacy's voice revved like the engine on the little Cub when she pushed the throttle forward and let the power take her down the runway and into the air. "She says every woman who can ferry an airplane from the factory to New York or California frees up a man to fly in combat against the Germans or the Japs."

She noticed her uncle's pipe had gone out. But instead of relighting it, he held the bowl between his thumb and forefinger, the stem pointed at his chin, and watched her from those hooded eyes.

"I didn't pay much attention to it at first. I couldn't imagine a bunch of women flying around in war planes. All I could think of was how dangerous it would be. Look what happened to John flying airplanes. But the idea grew on me."

Her uncle fumbled for a match and fired up his pipe, sucking it to life again. He tossed the spent match into the ashtray on the wicker table next to his chair. "Go on."

She told him about Shorty and her first lesson earlier that day and her realization that she could do it. That she could earn her private pilot's license in a couple of months. And about the training facility Jacqueline Cochran had opened in Texas where women like her were learning to fly "the Army way."

"I want to fly planes for the Army and do my bit to help win the war."

Only the upper curve of the fire ball now was visible on the western horizon, painting the sky around it shades of pink and mauve and violet. The universe took a catch breath in the silence that hung between them there on the porch. Finally, her uncle spoke.

"Why flying, darlin'?"

"Because John flew. I haven't told this to anyone else, but before he shipped out, he asked me to 'go to war' in his place if he should die in battle. I can't fly combat like he did, but I can ferry airplanes."

"But you're not even sure you can qualify. Your efforts could all be for naught if this Miss Cochran doesn't accept you into her program."

"I have to believe she will. I'll never know unless I try."

Ike drew on his pipe. "I hear flyin's mighty expensive. I don't mean to pry, but do you have that kind of money? Your Daddy and Momma don't, that's for sure."

"I was giving them John's monthly allotment check to help out with the ranch. Now I plan to give them my widow's benefits. But

I've managed to save my teaching salary this year." Lacy looked down at her hands, two white wraiths in the growing darkness. "John and I planned to use it to buy a house — after the war."

She had fought to get those last words out. Now she swallowed hard and took a deep breath. "It's enough to pay for three months of flying."

"I'm sorry, Lacy," her uncle said. "I shouldn't have asked."

"No, it was a fair question." She paused again. "There are a couple of problems."

"What kind of problems?" he asked.

"Two things. After school's out, I'm going to be flying every day. I need to stay here with you and Aunt Virginia because you live close to the airport. If I try to do this from home, I have to drive a hundred miles round trip every day. Not only will the gas cost me more than I can afford, my gas rationing stamps won't stretch that far. Besides all that, Daddy says John's and my old car is barely reliable enough to get me back and forth to school. Making it to Lamar and back on a daily basis is probably out of the question."

"What else?"

This was the one she dreaded. She took a deep breath. "Mother and Daddy don't know about this yet."

Ike sighed. "Lacy, you're a grown woman. I respect your right to make your own decisions, but your parents deserve to know your plans. You've got to tell them."

"I can't do that just yet, Uncle Ike. Too much is uncertain. I've got to get a few lessons under my belt first — be sure I can do this. Then I'll tell them."

"Your mother was hoping you'd help your dad and brother work the ranch this summer while you're off from school."

"I know that," she said, staring at the fading line of light silhouetting the stand of cottonwoods along the distant creek bed that marked the western-most edge of her uncle's land. And Lacy felt that she, like the fleeting day, was on the brink of sinking into an inky darkness. Was it the oblivion of sameness that offered no escape or was it the chilling, isolating, impenetrable blackness that comes right before the newness of dawn?

"That was the hardest part of the decision," she heard herself saying. "Trying to live up to everybody else's expectations and still do what I feel I have to do."

"Flying is that important to you?"

Lacy raised her head and looked at the shadowy form that was her uncle. She needed him. She needed his support. His blessing. Without him, she knew she could not face the rest of the family, her father's hesitancy, and her mother's certain disapproval.

"Yes," she said, "it's that important to me. You'll let me stay with you, won't you?" And she held her breath because his answer would seal her fate.

As if sensing her veiled desperation, Ike answered immediately. "You know you're always welcome here, Lacy. Always have been."

She smiled, relief washing over her. "It'll be like it was when I was little and being the only girl on our spread got the best of me. Remember when I used to almost live here summers? Ginny and I were more like sisters than cousins."

Instantly, she hated herself for bringing her late cousin's name into the conversation. It had been nine years since Ginny, not only her cousin but her best friend, had died from head injuries received when her horse threw her. But her uncle seemed not to have heard. He was relighting his pipe.

"What if something happens to you — before you tell Jared and Janice?"

"I just need another week, Uncle Ike."

The light was gone. Only the glow of her uncle's pipe remained.

"Your mother won't like my interfering, and that's exactly what she'll call it."

"I won't move over here until school's out."

The silence sat comfortably between them while Ike finished his pipe. Then he rose. "Gettin' chilly out here. Time we went in. I'll tell your aunt you're comin' to stay with us again."

Before she went to bed, Lacy wrote her letter to Jacqueline Cochran asking to join the Women's Flying Training Detachment. She had been composing it in her mind for weeks now, waiting for her first flying lesson before she sent it off.

She dropped the letter at the Lamar Post Office the next afternoon, after her second lesson with Shorty and on her way back to her parents' ranch outside Two Buttes. She was due home for dinner and she had papers to grade before tomorrow's classes.

FOUR

"Flying!" Lacy's mother blurted out.

Janice Jernigan was a tall woman, almost as tall as her daughter. She carried no spare weight on her rangy frame and her faded print cotton dress, short waisted because of her height, hung loosely on her.

She was the daughter of pioneers who helped settle western Kansas in the 1880s and had come to Colorado with her cowboy husband to start a ranch in 1913. She had borne five children: Jared Jr., Jana who died of influenza the winter of 1918-19, Kenny, Lacy, and seventeen-year-old Norman.

The Jernigans had come out of the Great Depression and the Dust Bowl years of the Thirties, holding onto their small cattle ranch by sheer determination. Deep lines, put there by the unrelenting eastern Colorado wind and sun, by hard work and by harder worry, creased Janice's handsome face. Iron gray hair was pulled back into a tight, severe bun giving her piercing blue eyes an uncharacteristic slanted look for someone so obviously Anglo Saxon.

Lacy had asked her parents please to listen to what she had to say before they spoke, asked questions, made comments. "Mother, please hear me out," she asked again.

"Flying! You lost your husband to an airplane and now you want to go out and commit suicide, too?"

Jared Jernigan looked from his wife to his daughter. An angry red flush crept onto his weathered cheeks. "Janice, at least let the girl finish."

"Two of your brothers have gone to war," Janice said. "God knows if they'll come home. Your husband's dead. Isn't that enough?" Lacy's mother pressed a handkerchief to her thin lips.

Since she had come back home to the ranch the previous September, after John's squadron left for England, Lacy had watched the furrow between her mother's brows perceptibly deepen as the war dragged on. Jared Jr. was in the Pacific serving with the Marines and Kenny, just thirteen months older than Lacy and to whom she was the closest growing up, had been in the thick of the Allied invasion of North Africa in November under General Eisenhower. And now

Norman was less than a year away from the draft.

"This what you want to do, girl?" Her father looked at her hard. "You want to cause your mother grief?"

"You don't understand."

Her father sat, head set precariously on his leathered neck and pushed forward, turtle-fashion, his elbows propped on his denim-clad thighs, his big gnarled cowpuncher hands dangling between his knees. The knuckles already showed signs of the arthritis that, one day, would put an end to his active ranching. Though only fifty-three, he was gaunt and gray, like an old man. His gray eyes had an uncharacteristic film over them.

"Lacy," he said, gently, "I know you're still grievin' for John, but that's no reason to risk your own life. Besides, whoever heard of anythin' so foolish? Women flyin' around in war planes."

"Daddy, you never called it foolish when I broke a horse or roped a calf like the boys. You never said 'Lacy, you can't ride the range with me 'cause you're a girl.' Why would you start talking that way now?"

Her mother interrupted. "See, Jared. See how headstrong she is, since she was a little girl. It's your doin'. You wouldn't listen. You never could say no to her. You encouraged her. Let her do everything her brothers did. Now this. Now she wants to go out and get herself killed."

"Mother, he didn't 'let' me do those things. I wanted to do them. You've never understood that. And now I want to do this."

"But, Lacy," her father said, "airplanes. How?"

Lacy told them about Shorty and the lessons and about the program started by Jacqueline Cochran, and about the three hundred women already in Texas learning to fly "the Army way."

Her mother cut her off in mid sentence. "Oh, Lacy, no. You'll be thrown with all kinds — coarse women, loose women, bad women, women who aren't like us, maybe even women who like other women."

"Mother!"

"Jared, tell her she can't go."

Silence hung in the room and cloaked them in a pervasive dread of the unknown — the future. No one moved. No one spoke. Jared stared at his hands.

"Jared, you must tell her she can't go," she repeated.

Lacy stood, jaw set, fists clenched. "Mother, please try to

understand. My mind is made up. This is my life."

"It's wrong, Lacy. A woman should stay home and tend to her family."

They faced each other over a few feet of worn carpeting and a yawning gulf of wills, and dreams, and years.

"I don't have a family, Mother, not a family of my own. And I probably never will. My husband is dead." She paused and took a deep ragged breath. "But I'm still alive. I've got to live my life the way I think best. Otherwise, I might as well have died in that airplane with John."

She turned and started down the hall that led to her bedroom, then stopped. "I'm tired. We'll talk some more in the morning. Maybe you'll see then that this is something I have to do."

That night, as Lacy slept in her narrow childhood bed in her old room at the back of the rambling ranch house, the dream came again. She awoke in the deep, silent hours before dawn, gasping, her heart racing, the now familiar feeling of panic threatening to overwhelm her. She lay inert, fists clenched, and began to relive, as she always did when the dream faded, the day the telegram came from the War Department.

She watched for the hundredth time as the Army Air Forces major, who had known John and volunteered to deliver the news in person, got into his drab green staff car and drove off down the road toward the highway a quarter mile away. He had expressed concern at leaving her alone in the house, but she insisted that her mother was due home momentarily from work in town, that her father and brother were out working the north fence line, and that she was in complete control.

Standing at rigid attention, afraid she would crumble in a heap if she let go even a fraction of her control, she heard the gravel crunch and watched the dust cloud as the car drove away, turned right at the highway and headed west into the pale January sunshine. The thumb and finger that held the telegram seemed unconnected to the rest of her body. The limp yellow half sheet in her left hand stirred in the wind and threatened to blow out of her uneasy grip.

If only it were that simple, she thought. Let the wind have its way and take the grim message, the dreaded words, and with it the ache that had lodged in her heart when she saw the car drive up and the officer step from it with that maddeningly cool military assurance. She had seen that bearing in John and his classmates when, one by one, they stepped forward to receive their wings — assured in their ability to maneuver any of the Army's airplanes and come out of any mission alive.

Now the ache was like a balloon that grew bigger and rounder and tighter in her chest until it felt as if it was about to burst inside her.

The major had told her that John and his crew were returning to base following a mission, bombing German sub bases at St. Lorenz, France. The plane was hit by anti-aircraft fire over the English Channel. When John put the landing gear down, the right wheel failed to lock properly. He and the co-pilot tried to set the bomber down on the good left wheel and hoped the right would not buckle. It was that or run out of fuel and crash anyway, the co-pilot related from his hospital bed in Manchester where he was recuperating from a broken arm.

But the crippled right wheel strut did give way. Several of the crew sustained injuries, but John was the only one killed. He hit his head, apparently at the moment of impact, and died instantly. He had been buried in the cemetery at Cambridge, England.

Lacy was glad John didn't suffer, didn't burn up or get horribly mangled. A simple, but telling blow to the head was all it took.

Now, fully awake in the cold pre-dawn, she turned her face to see the clock beside her bed. Four forty-five. Streaks of light soon would appear out over the Kansas line, seventeen miles to the east, and the ranch would begin to stir to life as another working day began. Lacy felt as if she had not slept at all. She got up and moved soundlessly to the closet, opened the door, pushed aside her clothing and reached to the very back for the brown leather flying jacket that hung on a wall hook. She had given it to John the Christmas after he learned to fly.

Now, she held the jacket to her face and inhaled John's scent, still there more than a year after he had received his official Air Corps bomber jacket and left this one in her safekeeping pending his return from the war. Her throat constricted and the familiar ache returned. She swayed back and forth embracing the jacket, breathing him in.

Finally, realizing she was cold, she slipped her arms into the extra-long sleeves, hugged the warmth of the leather around her body, lay back down on her bed, and pulled the covers over her head. Minutes later, she was asleep. This time, there were no dreams.

At breakfast, Janice bustled about the kitchen as she always did, but the telltale circles under her eyes gave away that she, too, had cried herself to sleep. Lacy's father, just in from the morning chores, was stony faced. Norman was still out feeding the stock. Alone with her parents, still wearing John's jacket, Lacy sat down at the kitchen table beside her father and, once again, asked them to listen. Her mother sat down, too.

"We talked about it some more last night," her father said. "If that's what you want, daughter, then I hope you get it."

"I have to get my private pilot's license first, Daddy. That's what I'm working on with Shorty McDermott now. And I'll need additional hours after that. But I've come a long way. Shorty thinks I can solo soon."

Her mother had been silent, but now a smothered sob escaped. Lacy looked over at her and saw tears welling in her mother's eyes and the handkerchief, once again, was pressed to her lips. Lacy wasn't used to tears from her mother, but knew they were indicative of a deeper dread of what the war might yet inflict on her. Lacy was beyond that dread. To her, the worst had already happened.

"Mother, please try to understand."

"You're a grown woman, Lacy." Her mother's posture was ramrod straight in her equally straight-backed chair, but her voice was nearly breaking. "You've been married and you've lost your husband to this terrible war. I suppose you've earned the right to do what you want, but I think you're being selfish and I hope you'll come to your senses before it's too late. You can do just as much for the war effort, probably more, by staying here and teaching those children who so desperately need you, and by helping your father and Norman and me on the ranch. We need every hand we can get. We still could lose it, you know. But if you've got to go off for awhile and fly airplanes, then God keep you safe."

FIVE

Shorty seemed grouchier than usual when he climbed in the airplane that morning. A cross wind meant Lacy had to compensate — aileron into the wind and opposite rudder to keep the airplane straight. On each of the first three landings she made, she over-corrected. Each time he had to yell at her to ease up. Each time she bounced the wheels.

On the fourth try, finally, she managed a smooth landing. Shorty was silent. Lacy didn't know whether she had finally done it to his satisfaction or if he was just tired of yelling at her.

As the plane slowed, he told her to taxi over to the edge of the runway nearest the hangar. He popped the top door, pushed the bottom door open, got out, laid his seatbelt on the seat and fastened it so that it wouldn't slide down into the rudder pedals. He'd never done that before. Lacy didn't know what was wrong.

"Taxi out and do this by yourself. Go 'round in the pattern a couple of times then make three landings. Don't go gettin' yourself lost. By the way, it will take off sooner without me in the front seat." And then he shut the bottom door.

She was on her own.

Though her fingers had turned to ice the moment Shorty said "do this by yourself," by the time Lacy started her takeoff roll, her heart was singing. *I'm in an airplane by myself*, she thought. *By myself!*

Moments later, she was in the air, so engrossed in flying solo, she forgot to make her first turn in the pattern and when she looked up, the birds-eye view of the Pentland's barn that was supposed to be off her left wing, wasn't. Panic stabbed at her stomach and she scanned the horizon anxiously for a few seconds until she recognized, in the distance, the familiar landmark of the two buttes that gave their name to her home town. She put the tiny airplane into a 180-degree turn back to the northeast and soon spotted the familiar barn that marked the beginning of the downwind leg for Runway Two Two. She was back on course.

Her first two landings were smooth, but when she set the wheels of the little Cub down on the runway the third and final time, she bounced them badly. She stayed with the airplane, just like Shorty had taught her to, and kept them down and soon was rolling smoothly toward the hangar, experiencing the unparalleled elation of the first solo flight.

I will never be the same person again, she thought, as the little plane came to a stop.

Standing beside the airplane moments later, Lacy savored the feeling of triumph. She had soloed with eight hours and fifteen minutes air time recorded in her log book and no nausea had marred this morning's flight. She waited for Shorty's praise.

"What was that all about?" he yelled.

"What?"

"You took off southwest and just kept goin'. I thought maybe you had a hot date in Santa Fe or somethin'."

"I just wanted to stay up a few extra minutes, that's all. I flew down and looked at the buttes."

"I told you not to get lost," he said, his voice dripping with I-told-you-so.

"I wasn't lost. I knew exactly where I was."

"Don't get the big head, Stearns. Do you know the percentage of student pilots who crash on landing the second time they're in the air alone?"

"No," Lacy said, hesitantly, shaking her head, puzzled. Had that statistic been in her ground school lessons?

"I don't either," he said. What passed for a smile crossed his face and disappeared as quickly as it had come. "But if it happens to be you, it's a hundred percent. You bounced the wheels four of the last seven landings. Not only is that bad piloting, it's hard on the airplane. I got a mind not to let you fly solo again until you've put it down ten times without a bounce with me in there with you."

"That'll put us behind schedule," she said, and instantly wished she hadn't. By now she had told Shorty why she was learning to fly and, though outwardly he scoffed at the idea of women flying war planes, Lacy figured he saw some bragging rights with his too-old-for-service, cropduster buddies if he could place one of his students in the Women's Flying Training Detachment.

Clara had told her he already was letting it slip to his cronies that he had a "really special student." But Lacy saw none of it.

She started to move away from the airplane. Shorty stepped forward and blocked her way, trapped her in the corner where the wing met the fuselage. "Whose schedule? That Cochran woman's?

The Army's? You haven't even heard from her yet. You bounce the Army's planes like that more than once and they'll wash you out faster than piss out of a chamber pot."

He stopped, flushing beneath his tan. "Ah, sorry, got a little carried away there, Stearns. Not used to flyin' with women, but then I told you that. Where was I? Oh, yeah, schedules. Your schedule is the one I tell you you're on. If I say ten touch-and-goes without a bounce, then ten touch-and-goes it is. If I say fly to La Junta and back blindfolded, then La Junta blindfolded it is. I'll be the one who determines when you're behind, on, or ahead of schedule. Is that clear?"

Lacy, eyes wide, nodded.

He leaned his face close to hers, looking up, jaw jutting out like a drill sergeant. "What's the first thing I taught you, Stearns?"

"You've got to stall the plane to land it." Her voice was barely more than a whisper.

"Say it for me again, Stearns, and louder. 'You got to *stall* the plane to land it!'" He almost shouted the word "stall."

Startled, she blinked, then forced herself to look back into his flinty blue eyes. She lifted her chin, stuck out her own jaw, and found her voice. "Okay, you've got to *stall* the airplane to land it. Goddammit, I'll stall the airplane. Get in and I'll show you!"

"That's the way to talk," he said, the grin returning to his weather-beaten face.

In four more weeks, Lacy had mastered the basics. She completed ground school June 19, the day after she logged her required thirty-five hours to qualify for her license. On June 21, she and Shorty flew to Pueblo so that she could take both her checkride and her Civil Aeronautics Administration exam.

Coming home, flying away from the setting sun and in a hurry to land before dark, Lacy watched the shadow of the little airplane racing over the ground in front of her as she flew east over seas of ripening wheat alternating with scrub grazing land. Her newly issued private pilot's license rode easy in her wallet, secure in the back pocket of her jeans.

Shorty pointed out the occasional grass or dirt airstrip that belonged to a wealthy rancher or farmer. "If they can afford it, an air-plane gets 'em to town a whole lot faster than a car. Remember to look for them. Someday, you may be flying cross country and need to make one of those emergency landings we've practiced. And you may get lucky enough to find one of those strips instead of a field with trees, cows and arroyos in 'em."

The shadows were stretching long across the prairie when she passed over her uncle's ranch house. She put the Cub into a 360-degree turn, descending as she executed the maneuver. She knew the noise of the engine would draw him outside. And when she saw a figure emerge from the verandah and wave, she leveled off and waggled the Cub's wings.

Lacy located the airfield, a single grass strip cutting a diagonal swath across the checkerboard of southeastern Colorado's rangeland and cultivated fields, and turned into her downwind leg. Moments later, she made her final approach to Runway Two Two, the sinking sun of the summer solstice off her right shoulder.

"Nice," she heard Shorty murmur as the wheels kissed the grass and the aircraft slowed. It was the first praise she'd ever heard from his lips.

Lacy played the rudders, turned onto the taxiway and ran the plane back to the hangar. It was rote now; she didn't even have to think about her movements. When she alighted from the two-seater, her stomach no longer lurched or sent her running for the fence. Lacy knew, finally, she was in control.

That night, her mother called to tell her that a letter had come for her from Jacqueline Cochran.

The next afternoon, Lacy got to the house before Janice got home from her job as office manager at Bud Walton's farm insurance agency in Two Buttes. She had left the cream vellum envelope propped on the kitchen table. It bore a crest of wings and the inscription Jacqueline Cochran, Director of Women Pilots, United States Army Air Forces.

So much was riding on the response inside. The gutsy blonde aviatrix — who had set records flying in airplane races against the best male pilots in the country and who ran her own cosmetics empire with the same sure hand that she used on the controls of her airplane — held her, Lacy's, future in those same capable hands.

Though she was alone, Lacy went to her bedroom, closed the door and sat on her bed. She stared in fascination at the envelope, unable to commit to opening it. That envelope contained the key to her everything in the foreseeable future, as far as Lacy was concerned.

Either way, I'll have to begin a new life, she thought, and closed her eyes and dreamed of taking the controls of a newly manufactured P-40 Warhawk. Suddenly she was soaring above the clouds, ferrying it to its eastern terminus to be loaded aboard a warship bound for England. Then, in a flight of fancy, she was firing a salvo of aircraft machine gun ammo at Hitler's face.

Lacy opened her eyes and was almost surprised to find herself still in her own bedroom, not in the cockpit of a Warhawk. She gripped Miss Cochran's letter and took a couple of deep breaths. The rest of her life hung in the balance. If Miss Cochran didn't want her, what should she do? Stay in Two Buttes and continue to teach or join the Red Cross and do her level best to aid in the war effort wherever she was sent? The Red Cross would at least put her in uniform.

I want to wear a uniform. Isn't that silly? Well, so what —

She tore the envelope open and pulled out the letter. Two short paragraphs said everything. She was to report for an interview with Jacqueline Cochran at Lowry Field in Denver on July 12. If she was accepted, she was to report to Avenger Field in Sweetwater, Texas, on July 31 — "at her own expense." Her class designation would be 43-W-9.

July 12 was just three weeks away.

SIX

"Miss Cochran will see you now," said the Army Air Force sergeant.

Lacy had been waiting only fifteen minutes, but it seemed more like an hour and fifteen minutes. The freshly pressed linen handkerchief, taken from her small purse when she sat down to wait, was now a damp, twisted rag used to wipe her perspiring palms.

A young woman who, by Lacy's reckoning, could not possibly be the required twenty-one years of age, had just exited the office, smiling. Now it was her turn. The next few minutes were the key. Rejection meant going back to the little yellow airplane parked at the hangar next door to the administration building and taking what would prove to be her last flight as a pilot. Her flight home.

Her savings were nearly spent. Only enough remained for the additional hours she still needed to qualify for entrance to Cochran's program — assuming she was accepted. As much as she loved flying, she couldn't justify the expense if there were no tangible goal to be realized. How would she explain her failure to her already doubting parents? To Shorty, who thought the whole idea was foolishness anyway. To Uncle Ike, who believed in her and had supported her.

Not everybody accepted into the women's pilot training program got to meet with Jacqueline Cochran personally. She had assistants with the power to accept or reject candidates. But Cochran, herself, was here at Lowry Field, waiting behind that door where the unsmiling sergeant now stood ramrod straight — waiting for her. Was it a good sign or was it a bad omen to meet the indomitable woman in the flesh?

Lacy stood, touched her hair caught smartly up in a French twist, and smoothed her skirt. Her high heels clicking on the tile floor telegraphed a coded plea to the gods of flight as she approached the sergeant on legs that didn't seem to belong to her. Then the door was closing behind her and Lacy saw a woman seated at a desk, her head bent over a file folder. Jacqueline Cochran looked up and Lacy felt the full impact of a pair of large brown eyes that pulled at her like twin magnets. They demanded her total attention and drew her deep inside a circle created by the aura of this powerful woman.

The signature honey blonde hair was drawn back in a neat chignon. Cochran wore a dark blue, tailored linen suit with a pair of silver wings pinned over her left breast. The total effect was one of authority, of command.

"Mrs. Stearns?"

"Yes, ma'am." Lacy fought the sudden urge to salute, not knowing the proper protocol in spite of having read everything she could find about the woman who now sat, so poised and so confident, in front of her. She knew that Cochran had pulled herself up out of Florida canebrake poverty, had trained as a beautician at age thirteen and had worked for Antoine's at Saks Fifth Avenue in New York. Lacy also knew that, while still in her twenties, Cochran had established the cosmetics company that bore her name, and that she had learned to fly in order to get around the country and call on her accounts. In 1938, Jacqueline Cochran had outraced the best men pilots to win the Bendix Transcontinental Air Race in a new military-style pursuit plane, the P-35. Recently, Lacy had even begun to use Jacqueline Cochran lipstick and face powder.

"Sit down, Mrs. Stearns." For less than a heart beat, Lacy was back in high school and Miss Fogarty, the algebra teacher, was ordering her to sit down and let someone better prepared answer the question on the blackboard. Fearsome Fogarty never smiled at a student, even if she got the correct answer. But Jacqueline Cochran did smile as she indicated a straight chair slightly to the right of center from the large olive drab steel desk at which she sat.

Lacy did as she was told.

"You just qualified for your private pilot's license, I see, and, in fact, have only been flying for a little over two months. That's a remarkable achievement. How did you do it?"

"I'm a teacher," Lacy said. "Once school was out for the summer, I was free to fly every day."

"Do you think you will return to teaching when the war is over?" The older woman's voice was pitched low and had a slight musical lilt to it, perhaps a vestige of her Southern roots.

Cochran's eyes never left her. They penetrated Lacy's outer core and seemed to see into her very soul. The woman appeared to be genuinely interested in her motivations and her answers.

"I don't know what I'll do when the war is over. I honestly haven't thought that far ahead. This awful war has taken from me the dearest person I'll ever know — my husband, John. We both planned careers as teachers. But with him gone, I haven't faced the fact that some day the world will be back to normal and I will have to live again. To be honest, I'm not sure I even know how. Or care. But right now, I want to fly airplanes for my country."

Cochran waited. Lacy took that to mean she should go on.

"I have to be busy. I have to work. Other than teaching, I'm not happy doing what's usually called 'woman's work.' Growing up on our ranch, I liked doing the outdoor chores and anything to do with horses. That's always made me different from the girls I grew up with who wanted only to get married and have babies." She paused, then added, "This war certainly is playing havoc with all our lives and our plans, isn't it?"

Immediately, Lacy wondered if she had said too much. Was that last remark too shallow? Did she appear to this woman, who held the key to her future, to be a thrill seeker or, worse, a woman who devalued the work of other women?

Cochran's eyes held hers, probing, searching. "Yes, Mrs. Stearns, some more than others, but all of us in one way or another." Cochran glanced down at the file in front of her, which Lacy could see contained the letter she had written a few weeks ago. "You, for instance, have already experienced an emotional trauma, a great personal loss."

Lacy groaned inwardly. Maybe Cochran thought she was too much of an emotional risk. Was this striking, self-assured woman about to tell her that she wasn't needed, wasn't wanted in the women's flying corps? Lacy held her breath and hoped if Cochran was about to turn her down, she could stem any rising tide of tears until she got out the door and past the granite-faced sergeant.

"I understand your desire to work and I applaud you for it. Women can offer so much to business and industry, and now to the war effort as well — if they will just let us," Cochran continued. "But, unfortunately, we must always contend with the good ol' boys club. Maybe someday. . ." a furrow creased the space between her eyes and her voice trailed off.

Lacy waited, barely able to breathe.

Then Cochran's face brightened, the furrow disappeared, and her smile came back. "But now we have a job to do. I like your spirit, Mrs. Stearns. Anyone who has the will to go out and do what you've done is welcome in this woman's army. Congratulations. You are a member of Class 43-W-9 of the organization that will soon be known as the Women Airforce Service Pilots, or WASPs. Please follow the instructions in the telegram we will send to you within the week and report to Avenger Field accordingly.

"Good day, Mrs. Stearns. And good luck."

Though she remained calm outwardly, Lacy's spirits soared to stratospheric heights.

Cochran rose and extended her hand across the desk. Lacy was shocked to see the statuesque woman who was now her commanding officer was a full four inches shorter than she. Behind the desk, Cochran had seemed so much taller, more imposing. But her carriage was erect, her bearing that of one who took command for granted. Lacy gratefully returned her warm, firm grip.

She was going to fly with the WASPs!

SEVEN

The pitted, two-lane, east-west highway stretched across the mesa to infinity. Tumbleweeds, carried on the incessant northwesterly wind, bounded across the road. That same hot wind blew through the open bus windows, whipped the girls' already travel-tossed hair, and added Texas grit to the grime of two or three days of train travel.

Avenger Field's rickety, all-purpose means of transportation, christened "the cattlewagon" by the trainees, had met Lacy and twenty-six other WASP hopefuls coming into Sweetwater on the morning and noon trains.

Lacy pulled her red bandanna from her purse and wiped the perspiration from her hairline and neck. Her father said Texas in July was like having the furnace in Hell going full blast and the last one in left the door open. The bandanna looked out of place with her traveling clothes, a trim dark blue skirt, matching weskit, white blouse and medium high heels. The outfit had been her most serviceable while teaching school the past two years.

"Do you think anyone will ever see or hear from us again?" laughed Andrea Sellers of Columbus, Ohio, when the city limits of Sweetwater were well behind them.

Lacy thought the girl looked to be barely out of high school, too young to be in the WASPs.

"Andy, you're just afraid all your boy friends won't be able to find you way out here in West Texas," the girl sitting next to her said.

"I gave all my friends, male and female, my address out here and made them promise to write. When they looked on the map of Texas and saw where I was going, they said I might as well be going to the moon," Andy said.

"It does look a little like the moon out here," another added.

The gate to Avenger Field was the tallest thing for miles out on the west Texas prairie and they could see it from a long way off. "That must be the insignia for the new name," Lacy said to Lucinda Stinson from Missoula, Montana, who had ridden the train down with her from Trinidad to Santa Fe where they changed to the east-west Texas & Pacific Railway line that took them into Sweetwater.

The Women's Flying Training Detachment was to be combined with the Women's Auxiliary Ferrying Squadron (WAFS), a more experienced women's flying group headquartered at Newcastle Army Air Base in Wilmington, Delaware. All the women pilots flying for the Army would now be known as WASPs. Walt Disney had designed their official insignia — a shapely, goggled, booted, winged female gremlin known as Fifenella.

A giant Fifenella now smiled down at them from the top of the gate. At Andy's request, the driver of the cattlewagon stopped just inside. The girl from Ohio had her Kodak Box Brownie with her and wanted a photo. The new trainees piled out and, after the dust settled, she took several pictures of them all standing under Fifenella.

Roaring out of the southwest, six low-wing, open-cockpit airplanes swooped down on them.

"PT-19s," said Josephine Bertelli of Bayonne, New Jersey.

Lacy shielded her eyes and looked up into the shimmering white-blue sky.

The aircraft flew directly over the cattlewagon and waggled their wings before soaring off toward a distant runway.

"I can hardly wait to fly one of those," Lacy said.

"Those?" Bertelli said, a touch of derision in her voice. She was a tall, busty, black-haired, black-eyed girl who, though trim now, with maturity, probably would fill out into a large, imposing woman, a woman to be reckoned with. "They're nothin'. Now the AT-6 — *that's* an airplane."

"But we have to learn how to fly the primary trainers first," Lacy said.

"Maybe *you* have to learn how to fly those podunky toy planes — I got my rating in those a year ago. I expect I'll be in and outta them and on to the BTs before you girls even get your panties on, let alone climb into the cockpit."

Bay assignments were by alphabet, so Lacy found herself living with Lucinda Stinson and Andrea Sellers as well as Trish Samples of Detroit, Arabella Sanders of St. Louis, and Caroline Simpson of Seattle. They were part of Flight Two. Lacy was glad that Josephine Bertelli was in Flight One and on the opposite schedule and side of the barracks.

Tall, slender, brown-eyed Lucinda wore her thick dark hair cut short and feathered like Amelia Earhart, and had been flying for three years. Cin, as she preferred to be called, claimed to be one-quarter Sioux and to have been on her own since she was eighteen.

Lacy also liked Andy who was fresh off the campus of Ohio State University, had just turned twenty-one and was the youngest cadet in the class. The petite blue-eyed blonde claimed to have eaten a half-dozen bananas and drunk a gallon of water before her final weigh-in in order to make the one hundred three pound limit for girls five feet three and a half inches.

"The doctor threw in the last three pounds for good measure, or I'd never have made it," Andy said. "I've been trying to gain weight for three months, but haven't had much success."

Later that afternoon, Lacy and Cin went looking for Andy and found her standing under the shower dressed in her army-issue zoot suit — baggy mechanic's coveralls in olive drab.

"I'm trying to shrink them," she wailed, as she stood dripping wet in the middle of the Spartan community shower room. "These are size forty! They promised me the first thirty-four that comes in from the laundry."

"Mine's not much better," Lacy said, pirouetting so Andy could see how her oversized coveralls looked. "They gave Cin and me forty-sixes because we're tall."

"Look where the crotch hits," Cin said, grabbing a handful of extra fabric that hung almost to her knees. "No cheap thrills with these."

Andy and Lacy looked at her and burst out laughing.

Later, over a dinner of steak, mashed potatoes, salad, ice cream and cake, all served on sectioned metal trays, the three got better acquainted. "They call the new class 'babies'," Andy said.

Cin nodded. "One arrogant little bitch, who's only been here since May herself, told me the whole base considers newcomers 'in the way' 'til we graduate to the basic trainers. According to her, half of us will be gone by then anyway."

"Well," Andy said, lifting her chin and setting her mouth in a firm line, "we'll just have to show them we're better pilots than they are."

"I'll bet you were a cheerleader in high school," Cin teased.

"College too," Andy said, the grave look dissolving into a grin.

"See," Cin said to Lacy, "we're rooming with a poster girl — a real live American Girl Next Door. Every GI's dream."

Jacqueline Cochran's chief establishment officer at Avenger, Leoti Deaton — called Dedie by the trainees — welcomed the new class after dinner.

"Miss Cochran organized the Class of 43-W-9 to meet the

increased demand not only for ferry pilots, but pilots to fly other missions as well. Your class marks the beginning of some changes in our training strategies, all of which are calculated to make you better pilots — better Army pilots."

Graduation, she told them, was expected to be the end of December.

Before returning to the bay that night, Lacy sent off a brief telegram to her parents:

> July 31, 1943
> Avenger Field, Sweetwater, Texas
> Arrived safely. Six others Avenger
> bound on same train. Airfield immense.
> Lots of airplanes. Two new friends.
> Love Lacy

Lying exhausted in her bunk, Lacy wanted to pinch herself to be sure it wasn't all a dream and she would be waking up the next morning back in her own bed. But when Reveille blared at six in the morning, Lacy knew she wasn't back in Colorado. A half an hour of calisthenics got her blood moving. After breakfast, dressed in their zoot suits, Flight Two lined up military style and marched in formation to the flight line and their first aircraft indoctrination.

EIGHT

"An AT-17's missing," Cin announced, breathless, as she banged the screen door shut and flopped on her bunk.

A few weeks into their training program, on a hot August afternoon, Lacy, Trish, Arabella and Caroline were relaxing in their six-bed bay waiting for Cin and Andy to show up before lining up to march to the mess hall for dinner.

"We heard somebody hadn't cleared the tower," Trish said. Not much bigger than Andy, dark-haired Trish had been a secretary for a Detroit tool and die shop before the war.

"That means it's 43-5s overdue," Arabella, the flame-haired dancer-nightclub hostess, said. "They're the only ones flying the AT-17s right now."

"My instructor told me this was a big day for 43-5. Nine teams, with instructors, went out right after lunch on cross country instrument flights," Caroline said. Plump, brown-haired Caroline was the daughter of a Boeing executive who had taught her to fly.

"Well, they're graduating in less than two weeks. The instructors are jamming in everything they can teach them now," Lacy said.

"I heard a 43-6 talked her way onto a night training flight with two 43-5s who were scheduled to solo in the AT-17," Cin said.

"Anybody know who it was?" Caroline asked.

"No one's talking. Hush hush. I guess she stowed away in the back seat where the instructor usually sits. Actually got to fly it while they were up. When they landed, the plane blew a tire. The stow-away jumped out the minute they stopped rolling and got away in the darkness just before the emergency vehicles arrived."

"Dumb! They'd have washed her out if they'd caught her," said Trish.

"She's lucky a rattlesnake didn't get her," Caroline said. "They crawl onto the runways at night because they like the left-over warmth from the sun."

"It's almost time for dinner. Cin, have you seen Andy?" Lacy said.

"I haven't seen her since this morning," Cin said.

41

"She was supposed to be in ground school with me this after noon," Caroline said. "We took down an engine for the first time and she'd been looking forward to that. But she never showed."

"At lunch, she told me she was going out to the AT-17 flight line to talk to one of the 43-5 squadron leaders about a graduation skit," Lacy said.

"You don't supposed Andy hitched a ride in an AT-17 today?" Arabella said.

"No way, not Andy. Too responsible," Lacy said. "Sounds more like something Jo Bertelli would do."

"Andy's been itching to get into something bigger and faster than the PT-19," Cin reminded them.

"I can't believe that Andy would risk being washed out just for a joy ride in the back of any airplane. She's too good a pilot. She knows she'll have a chance to fly all the fast planes she wants to later on," Lacy said.

Fifteen minutes later, Andy still had not appeared. Though the youngest member of the squadron, Andy had quickly earned the respect of the entire group and had been elected squadron leader. One of her duties was that of getting her group lined up and marched in formation to meals, classes and to the flight line. Lacy, chosen assistant squadron leader, now had to assume the duty in her absence.

"OK, squad," she called out to them. "Fall in. Looks like our Andy's a no show." She was more concerned than she let on.

Inside the mess hall, the tables were already filling up and the buzz level of conversation was at an unusually high pitch. The 43-5 squadron leader Andy had gone to talk to was consoling one of her classmates. Lacy could tell the girl was crying from her shaking shoulders and the handkerchief she held to her mouth — rather like Lacy remembered her mother doing.

Lacy made her way over to the two girls. "Any word yet on who's missing?"

"It's Helen Jo and Peggy," the squadron leader replied. "The other teams are all back. There's a search party out."

Lacy had met Peggy Seip once and knew she had taught instrument flying to Army Air Forces pilots before joining the WASPs. She had never met Peggy's best friend and flight buddy, Helen Jo Severson.

"Hope they find 'em soon. Say, you haven't seen Andy Sellers, have you?"

"Not since right after lunch."

"Was she out at the AT-17 flight line?"

"Yes. She came out to talk to me before we took off."

"But you don't know where she went after that?"

"No," the squadron leader replied.

No one had seen Andy in nearly four hours. Lacy sat down with Cin and their other baymates and reported what she had heard. Anxiety and uncertainty crackled like electricity through the mess hall that evening. Talk centered around the missing trainees and their instructor. Lacy had an eerie sense of impending disaster. Instead of smiles, frowns creased the brows of the nearly five hundred trainees as they finished dinner and exited the mess hall. The five baymates from 43-9 had even more reason for concern. Not only were two girls from 43-5 missing, their Andy was missing, too.

An hour before lights out, Lacy couldn't stand it any longer. She laid down her ground school manual. "I'm going to look for her."

"I'll tag along," Cin said. "It's too hot to stay in the bay and study."

Lacy remembered that Andy had complained of cramps at lunchtime. Flight Two had flown in the morning when it was slightly cooler, but afternoon meant lining up in the oppressive late summer heat and humidity and marching in formation to ground school classes held in stifling, airless classrooms. Maybe the combination of the cramps and the nearly one hundred-degree heat had gotten the better of her. Usually the nurse notified the squadron leader if one of her girls was in the infirmary, but, of course, Andy was the squadron leader and no one had said a word to Lacy as her assistant.

They found Andy sleeping soundly on a cot in the infirmary.

"She came in with a bad case of cramps about two this afternoon," Lieutenant Missy McCracken said, in her slow Southern drawl. "The duty nurse gave her something. She's been asleep since I came on at four. I didn't want to wake her. Didn't anyone tell you?"

Lacy and Cin shook their heads.

"With all the hubbub this afternoon, it slipped our minds. We'll keep her here the rest of the night. She'll be good as new in the mornin'."

Relief washed over Lacy, and she and Cin headed back for the barracks to report to the others.

When they walked in, Lacy thought they had walked into a funeral parlor.

"They found them," Arabella said.

"Dead, all three of them," Trish added. "Peggy, Helen Jo, and their instructor."

"Crashed in a farmer's field near Big Spring," Caroline said.

At breakfast, the morning after the crash, no one really knew what had happened and rumor was rampant. Who was at fault? Had someone gotten careless? Why didn't the instructor realize they were in trouble in time to land in a field somewhere?

"I've heard rumors about suspected sabotage at some of the bases where WASPs are already flying," Jo Bertelli said.

That sent shivers down Lacy's spine.

"Lots a' guys out there don't want us gals flying them airplanes," Jo added.

"But no one would resort to deliberate murder," Andy said, and put into words what Lacy had been afraid to consciously confront.

"You never know," Jo said, and thrust her chin out as if daring someone to question her wisdom. "There's a lot of stuff they don't tell us."

"When Cornelia Fort bought it, there was some scuttlebutt about a buzzing," Cin said. "When someone with her kind of experience goes down, it raises more than eyebrows."

"Who's Cornelia Fort?" Trish asked.

"She was one of the originals in the ferrying squadron in Delaware and a flight instructor before the war," Andy said. "God, she's a legend. She was flying with a student near Pearl Harbor when the Japs attacked on December 7th, and lived to tell about it."

Andy went on to explain that, the previous spring, Fort had been ferrying a BT-13 when another ferry pilot, a young man also flying a BT-13, flew too close. Some thought he buzzed her. Others said no, the group of several ferry pilots — all from Long Beach, California, delivering their aircraft to Dallas Love Field — were attempting to fly in formation, something Cornelia had agreed ahead of time to try.

Investigators, piecing the incident together later, concluded that the wheel of the young man's fixed-gear airplane came down on the wing of Fort's plane, dislodging part of it. Fort's plane spun out and crashed, killing her. Because Fort was a highly skilled pilot, the theory was that she was knocked unconscious and never knew what happened. It seemed to be the only explanation for the veteran pilot not recovering and pulling out in time to avoid the crash. By pure coincidence, the accident happened a few miles southeast of Avenger Field.

Jo snorted. "See what I mean? The guys resent us flying."

"She was the first woman pilot to die while on active service," Lacy said. "Now we've lost some trainees as well."

"She was one of the most experienced pilots in the women's ferrying squadron," Cin added, "which just goes to show it can happen to any of us."

By lunch time, Andy, as squadron leader, had found out through the grapevine that the undertaker in Sweetwater had placed the girls' remains in two rough pine boxes — paupers' coffins — and that Mrs. Deaton was very upset because the government allowed no funds to bury civilians. All the WASPs were civilians.

By late afternoon, Dedie had managed to find enough money in Avenger's administrative budget for two nice caskets and two train tickets. But she suggested that the trainees and staff chip in to buy two casket blankets of yellow flowers with WASP written in Texas Bluebonnets made of paper.

The following morning, after breakfast, Andy, Cin and Lacy stood together as the somber WASP corps watched two 43-W-5 classmates board the cattlewagon for the journey to Sweetwater and the train station. Dedie had asked a close friend and classmate of each of the dead girls to accompany the body home.

Lacy was dry-eyed. The control she had discovered deep within herself during John's memorial service six months earlier kept her as rigid inside as standing at attention in the morning sunshine did on the outside. I will not cry, she told herself.

"You gave us a real scare, Andy. That could be Lacy or me," Cin said, nodding after the two lone figures seated in the retreating cattlewagon.

"We sure were worried," Lacy added.

"I'd never pull a harebrained stunt like hitching a ride. You both should know that. But I appreciate your concern." Andy's eyes were misting. "You know, I talked to Peggy right before they went up. I still can't believe it."

"Whatever happens, we've got to stick together," Lacy said, as she wrapped one arm around Andy's waist and the other around Cin's. "Buddies."

"Agreed," Andy said.

"Right by me," Cin said.

Arm in arm, the three of them walked slowly toward the flight line.

NINE

By the time 43-W-9 was allowed a weekend off base, Andy had made friends with Karen Richardson who lived in the next bay and who had a car.

Auburn-haired, brown-eyed Karen had the tall, willowy figure of a model. Her father, a widower since Karen was fourteen, was a state senator in Arizona. Having made money in the Texas oil fields, he showered his daughter with affection and material goods — which included flying lessons. Her clothes were designer made, not off the rack, and her car was not just any car but a yellow Packard convertible.

The USO in Abilene was planning a dance for newly arrived second lieutenants stationed at the Army's Camp Barkeley and at the much smaller Abilene Army Air Forces base — both located near Abilene and about forty miles from Sweetwater. Karen's boyfriend, Bob Wilson, was a more senior officer stationed at Camp Barkeley and one of Andy's many boyfriends had just arrived to take P-47 pilot training at the air base. Both urged their girlfriends to bring a group of WASPs to the dance, so Cin and Lacy were invited to go along.

"I wondered how long it would be before the *real* boyfriend surfaced," Cin teased Andy who got several letters a day from her male friends, most of them stationed at Army or Army Air bases around the country and some overseas.

"Pink is not my boyfriend," Andy insisted. "We're just friends. He's from Columbus, too."

"I've heard that one before," Cin teased. "You talk about him all the time."

"He's got lots of friends who want to meet some girl flyers," Andy said, ignoring her. "So you both have to go to Abilene with me. I promised him."

"I really don't think I should go," Lacy said.

"You can't mourn forever, Lace," Cin said. "I bet your husband wouldn't want you to spend your life in a nun's habit."

"I'm not spending my life in a nun's habit," Lacy said, indignantly, "I just don't think it's right — yet."

"And when will it be right?" Cin pressed. "How long has he

been gone? Six months?"

"Seven."

"You need the break. You need to get out of here. We've all been working too hard."

"Just come along and have a good time," Andy threw in. "It's not a date. Everybody dances with everybody and you can have the pick of any of the guys you see — except Pink."

"Ah hah," Cin said. "I knew it. He *is* yours."

Andy threw her pillow at Cin and a free-for-all with Army-issue pillows ensued. The baymates from across the way joined in and soon feathers were flying.

The next day Lacy tried, again, to explain her misgivings to Cin. "I'm no prude, but I don't like parties where I don't know anybody."

"You know us."

"But I don't know any of those fellows. The thought of batting my eyelashes at some boy four years younger than me just to get him to dance with me is absolutely revolting."

"You won't have to bat your lashes, Lacy. They'll be lined up to dance with you. Just be yourself. We're just going to have some fun."

"That's what I'm telling you. Dancing with strangers is *not* my idea of fun. I don't feel at home with people I don't know."

"You certainly made friends with us easily enough."

"That's different."

Cin shook her head. "You've got a lot to learn about having fun, Lacy. Loosen up. Besides, I heard Jo Bertelli is going with another group. She's already bragging about how she's gonna 'give those poor suckers a thrill'. She thinks she's such hot stuff. Claims to have a boyfriend with the 101st Airborne. Says he can hardly wait to jump over Germany. We need someone like you, someone with class, to balance the scales."

Lacy repeated her concerns to Andy that evening.

"Come on, Lacy, we're just going for a good time. These guys that Pink knows are a lot of fun. They've been shut up for weeks just like we have. We all need to let off a little steam. It'll be fine. You'll feel so much better next week if you've danced off some of your flight nerves. You'll probably fly a lot better if you get away from here for awhile. Why do you think they're letting us go?"

"OK. I give in. I'll go."

That decision made, Lacy let Becky Rollins in the next bay cut her long brown hair. She was tired of fooling with braids or a twist. She wanted a carefree, aviatrix look like Cin's Amelia Earhart cut. She got it and decided it suited her — the new her.

The night before they left, Lacy lay in her bunk and thought about John and wondered what he would think about her going out dancing or maybe, eventually, dating again. Lacy had never really dated anyone else. She had run with the small crowd of boys and girls who made up the entire Baca County High School student body. Russell Wilson took her to the junior-senior prom, but they had been friends since first grade.

She met John at a freshman mixer at Colorado State Teachers College midway through the first quarter. Standing in line waiting to get a Coke, she was aware of someone behind her. She turned and looked up into a pair of earnest green eyes. "Hi," she said, "I'm Lacy Jernigan."

"John Stearns," he said, blushing, and she had a sense that it had cost him a lot to speak those words.

She stuck out her hand as she had been taught to do when making someone's acquaintance. Instinctively, she liked the tall, skinny young man standing there looking so shy, almost lost. Solemnly, he accepted her handshake and she liked the feel of his hand around hers. In spite of what seemed an innate shyness, his grip was quite firm and sure. His hands were large, but they weren't rancher's hands — not big and blunt like her father's and her brothers' hands. His fingers were long and slender, almost like an artist's.

They began to talk. When they got their drinks, they walked together through a warren of tables to an empty one. He touched her elbow, as if to guide her, and held the chair for her. His touch was gentle. They sat down together, still talking.

And, Lacy remembered now, they never stopped.

The four friends from 43-W-9 cleared post at 5 p.m. Friday after a full day of flying and ground school and headed east for Abilene singing their favorite WASP songs:

Zoot suits and parachutes and wings of silver, too,
He'll ferry planes like his Mama used to do!

and

We are Yankee Doodle pilots, Yankee Doodle do or die.
Real live nieces of our Uncle Sam, born with a yearning to fly!

A brightly lit king-sized Wurlitzer stood in one corner blasting out everyone's favorite tunes and the spacious dance floor was filled with a hundred or so couples jitterbugging to the Andrew Sisters' rendition of *Don't Sit Under the Apple Tree.* Around the perimeter, men in uniform and pretty girls in party dresses sat at rectangular tables.

When the four WASPs arrived, two men disconnected themselves from two separate table groupings and approached them. A stocky fellow with a blond crewcut and a scrubbed clean pink complexion grabbed Andy and lifted her off her feet swinging her around with great glee. A taller fellow with dark brown hair grabbed Karen and planted a long, languorous kiss on her lips while his buddies at the nearby table whistled and shouted, "Hubba, Hubba, Hubba!"

Pink led Andy, Cin and Lacy to his table and a group of men in khaki. Two men stood up and quickly grabbed chairs from other tables for them to sit on. Lacy was hardly seated when a tall, skinny fellow with a dark crewcut and glasses asked her to dance. He was obviously younger than she, probably all of nineteen. The Army liked its pursuit pilots young. Nevertheless, Lacy's heart was in her throat as he took her hand and led her to the dance floor. It was a slow dance and the fellow wrapped his long right arm around her waist, pulled her tight against him, and laid his cheek against hers. Gently, she brought her free left hand up to his chest and applied a small bit of pressure pushing herself away. He loosened his grip and looked down, surprised.

"I don't even know your name," she said.

"Carl," he said, and pulled her close to him again.

"Mine's Lacy," she said into his collar.

"Uh huh," he grunted.

When the dance was over, he led her back to the table and deposited her in her chair, leaned over and grabbed Cin's hand — she was, at that point, talking to two other second lieutenants and sipping on a Coke — and pulled her toward the dance floor.

Lacy leaned over to Andy and said "Such a gentleman," in such a sarcastic tone that Andy burst out laughing.

Pink asked what she was laughing at and Andy told him.

"Don't mind, Carl," Pink laughed, "he doesn't say much, but he loves to dance. He'll dance with every girl here tonight."

Lacy hoped that he did so only once. When Cin got back to the table, she shared similar sentiments. Then other men began to appear and ask for a dance. Most of them introduced themselves at least on

the way to the dance floor and Lacy began to relax and enjoy herself
— particularly the fast dances when she wasn't held uncomfortably
close by a stranger. The men were not particularly good dancers, but
then neither was she. Sometimes, during fast numbers, they stopped
to watch the more agile couples on the floor do the jitterbug.

One named Byron, closer to her age and a first lieutenant with
the 12th Armored Division at Barkeley, kept coming back and asking
her to dance, but each time, when the dance was over, he would
bring her back to the table and return to his own table and group
across the floor.

She asked Bob Wilson about him and learned that he was married.
His wife was in St. Louis expecting their first child.

"Ah," Lacy said, "he must be lonely." She decided to be nicer to
him.

The next time he asked her to dance, he whispered in her ear.
"Why don't we get out of here and go some place more comfortable."

"I beg your pardon?" Lacy said.

He repeated the suggestion.

Lacy looked at him and said, "And where would that be?"

"Anywhere we can relax and get to know each other better. Being
a widow, young as you are, you gotta be lookin' for more excitement
than what can be found on the dance floor with a bunch of teenagers."
He grinned broadly as he spoke, winked, and squeezed her hand.

Lacy dropped her left hand from his shoulder, extricated her
right hand from his, turned and walked off the dance floor, leaving
him standing there gaping after her.

"What was that all about?" Cin asked her when she got back to
the table.

"I just got propositioned," Lacy said, her teeth clenched.

Cin burst out laughing. "I wondered how long it would take."

Byron did not ask her to dance again, though he did ask Cin
one more time.

"My feelings are hurt," she told Lacy when she was deposited
back at the table. "He didn't make the same offer to me."

Lacy made a face at her.

"May I have this dance?" a deep voice from behind her said.
Lacy turned in her chair and looked up into a pair of startlingly deep
blue eyes. They focused on her for a long moment and then moved
across the table from her. "Hello, Lucinda."

TEN

Lacy looked at Cin and swore she saw her friend's eyes go soft for only a fraction of a second, then grow hard as she frowned. "Hello, Eric," Cin said in a voice Lacy didn't recognize. "What are you doing here?"

"I just flew in this afternoon from the West Coast."

"This is my friend, Lacy Stearns. Lacy, Eric Larsen."

"Hello," he said.

His eyes — the blue of the Norwegian fjords, Lacy thought, remembering the photographs in her fourth grade geography book — once again locked on hers. His hair was dark brown, not worn in the regulation crew cut sported by the cadets, but long enough to part and brush neatly to one side, except for a stray lock that fell forward onto his forehead. From where she was seated, she calculated he was over six feet. He wore the oak leaf cluster that said he held the rank of major and he was, perhaps, thirty.

"So where are you stationed now, Eric?" Lacy heard Cin ask, still with that neutral voice she didn't recognize.

"Long Beach. I'm with the Ferrying Division, Air Transport Command."

"You're a long way from home," Cin said. "What brings you to Texas and the wide open spaces?"

"I just ferried a P-47 into the Abilene Air Base next door. The cadets over there are learning how to fly them." He smiled, looked from one to the other and asked, "I'll turn that question back at you. What are you two lovely ladies doing here several hundred miles from nowhere?"

"We're in WASP training over at Avenger Field near Sweetwater. Been there since the end of July," Cin answered. "We were invited. Would you care to sit down?"

"I was invited too, by the the commandant of Barkeley. The colonel and I are old friends. And, actually, I came over to ask your friend here to dance," he said, staring down at Lacy again.

Lacy looked quickly at Cin, searching for affirmation that this man did, or did not, mean something special to her. She had never heard Cin mention an Eric Larsen. If Eric did, in fact, belong to Cin, why was he asking her, not Cin, to dance? But by now, Cin's eyes and expression were unreadable.

"Shall we?" he asked.

Lacy stood. To turn him down would look strange, if not downright impolite. Again she glanced at Cin, but got no answer to her questioning look. "Of course," she said and moved toward the dance floor with him, alarm bells going off in her head.

"So you're going to be a WASP," he said, as he slipped his arm easily around her waist, pulled her close, and began to slow dance to *Stardust*. His cheek grazed hers and she smelled Old Spice after shave. Lacy was surprised at how good it felt when he held her. He didn't crush her to him like Carl had, nor try to take possession of her as Byron had. Disturbingly close as they were, it seemed the most natural thing in the world — the two of them dancing.

"So how do you know Cin?" She tried to sound nonchalant, but her voice surprised her with an uncharacteristic breathiness.

He moved his cheek away from hers and looked at her, puzzled. "Sin? Oh, you mean Lu*cin*da." He laughed

"Yes, we all call her Cin."

"Well now," he said, seeming to digest that. "Lucinda and I have known each other since before the war."

"Obviously," Lacy said. "But how do you know her?"

"I taught her to fly — back in '41. I was a graduate student at Montana State in Missoula, teaching flying on the side for some extra money. One day she appeared at the field and told my boss she wanted to learn to fly. My boss didn't like women pilots, let alone having to teach one to fly, so he asked me if I was willing. I was. After all, her money was the same color as a man's."

Remembering Shorty's initial reaction to her, Lacy searched for an implied putdown in his comments, but found none. "Did you date her?" she heard herself ask and wondered where she got the nerve.

He hesitated for a heart beat. "Yes, I dated her."

When the dance came to an end, he continued to hold her, in suspended animation. Then when the next song began — *Smoke Gets In Your Eyes* — he gently moved her once again in time to the music. Lacy did not know what to make of this man. He was smooth, but she wasn't sure she liked his direct approach and she wanted, desperately, to know what his relationship to Cin was and what her feelings were for him. She thought she had caught vibes between them, but wasn't sure of what she had seen and felt. And he was far too noncommittal to her way of thinking.

"So you're a flyer," he murmured into her ear. "What made you decide to take up flying, or are you one of Amelia Earhart's girls who grew up yearning for the wild blue yonder?"

Lacy pulled her cheek from his and looked into his eyes. She was wearing high heels so their eyes were nearly level. "My husband died when his B-24 crash landed in England. I decided that the country needed me to fly in his place."

"So you're one of our valiant war widows trying to make the world safe for democracy."

Lacy fought the urge to slap his face, extricated herself from his grip, turned on her heel and, for the second time that night, left her partner stranded on the dance floor.

Eric recovered quickly and pursued her, elbowing his way through startled couples who turned to stare. He caught up with her just before she reached her table, which was empty since everyone else was dancing.

Lacy grabbed her purse and started for the Ladies Room. He caught her wrist.

"I'm sorry, I didn't mean that quite the way it sounded. Cool down a minute."

Lacy stopped and slowly turned to face him.

"As far as I'm concerned you insulted both my husband's memory and my ambition to do something for myself and for my country. Men don't have a lock on wartime sacrifice, you know."

With that, Cin and her dancing partner appeared at the table. She looked from Lacy to Eric and back to Lacy. "You headed for the Powder Room, Lace? I'll go with you." And they walked off together leaving Eric and the other soldier standing by the table.

"What on earth did he say to you?" Cin asked when they were inside the Ladies Room. She laughed. "He didn't proposition you, did he?"

"Something about being a valiant war widow trying to make the world safe for democracy." Lacy turned away and fished in her purse for her lipstick.

"That sounds like Eric. He doesn't know how to control that sarcastic nature of his. He really is an all-right guy underneath that bullshit."

Lacy whirled around, a stricken look on her face. "What does he mean to you, Cin? I saw the way you looked at him and he said you two used to date."

Cin hesitated. "You don't want to hear about Eric Larsen and me."

"Yes I do," Lacy snapped.

Cin looked quickly around the cramped powder room. They were alone.

"We planned to get married." Her voice was low.

Lacy stared at her friend. "What happened?"

Cin didn't answer.

"Cin?"

"I was pregnant." She spoke barely above a whisper.

"What. . .?" Lacy felt like someone had punched her in the stomach.

Cin began to talk, slowly and deliberately at first, and then, as the emotions tore loose inside her, her voice rasped like worn fabric parting when pulled taut.

"I thought the only reason he was marrying me was because I was carrying his child. Pearl Harbor came, inconveniently, in the midst of our discussion. He was in the Reserves, was called immediately to active duty and sent to California. He told me to wait, that we'd get married as soon as possible. But because of the national emergency, they wouldn't grant him any leave time. I broke it off. Told him I was going to have an abortion."

Anguish tinged Cin's voice. "He told me to wait, as if we had all the time in the world. I didn't know what I'd do when I started to show. I'd have been sacked from my job. I had nothing. A pregnant, unmarried woman with no one to turn to and nowhere to go. Do you have any idea how that feels?"

Lacy shook her head, her insides churning.

"I was terrified."

"So you went ahead with the abortion?"

"No, I was going to. But, you see, I met this couple. They wanted a baby so bad and couldn't have one. After talking to them I agreed to go through with the birth and let them take the child. I went away with them, where no one knew me and where Eric couldn't find me. I had the baby. I needed money and they paid me and they took care of me. They paid for everything and they adopted her."

Lacy shook her head, trying to fathom everything Cin was telling her.

"Her. You had a baby girl. Does Eric know he has a daughter?"

"No, he thinks I went ahead with the abortion. He came to my mother's house looking for me. She didn't know about the baby and, of course, he had to go and tell her. Later, I ended up lying to her as well. She thinks I had the abortion and. . .well, she disowned me — again. My actions never have fit in with her pious sense of religion. When I found out he had been to see her, I wrote to him and told him to get out of my life, stay out, and never come back."

"You still love him, don't you?"

"No, I don't love the sonofabitch. Too much has happened between us. I know him too well. And vice versa. But, damn it, I do still care what happens to him. After all, we made a child together. Maybe I haven't gotten him completely out of my system, but believe me, I'm trying and I'm winning the battle. I'd be happy if I never saw him again. Amen. . . end of story."

Cin turned her back to Lacy, yanked at the water faucet, leaned over and splashed water into her hands and onto her eyes. She tore off a piece of paper towel to blot them dry, then reached in her purse, pulled out her lipstick, compact and comb and fixed her face while Lacy stared at her. When Cin was done, she put all her things away, turned back to Lacy and said, "Let's go back out there and have a whale of a good time."

Emotionally drained, Lacy did not want to go back to the party, but she followed Cin out the door, chewing on her friend's revelation.

They were immediately snapped up by two second lieutenants and escorted to the dance floor. Lacy watched over her partner's shoulder as Eric cut in on Cin and the two of them glided around the floor — deep in conversation. Lacy answered the guy's questions in a bright "um hum," all the while watching her friend and the man who held her. Once, they glanced over at her, and Lacy quickly looked away and up into the eyes of the very young man with whom she was dancing. In fact, it was the first time she had looked closely at him at all. He was, maybe, twenty.

She laughed and began to talk to him, feeling the muscles in his arms as he held her close for the slow dance and then buffeted her around during the jitterbug that followed. Next dance, Eric cut in.

As he slipped his arm around her waist, she resisted being pulled close to him, but took his hand. "I pop off sometimes," he said. "I didn't mean anything by that patriotic crack. Actually, I rather admire your nerve. There aren't a lot of women who would do what you're doing. Lucinda tells me you gave up a teaching job to take flight training."

Lacy looked into those startling eyes, thought she read sincerity, relaxed, and let him guide her to the romantic strains of *I'll Get By*. Soon they were dancing closer than she had intended. They moved into the faster, throbbing *Begin the Beguine* and she felt as if she were floating. There it was, the once familiar and yet now foreign sensation of being held in a man's arms. John had not been a good dancer — not nearly as smooth as Eric — but she hadn't cared. When she and John danced together, it was another form of love making for them. Close, sensual, moving rhythmically together, being together, loving together.

Now that sensation was back and her conscious mind was doing its best to deny it. But her body was beginning to respond.

When someone else cut in on Eric — another senior officer, as no second lieutenant would have had the nerve to cut in on a major — she was actually disappointed, and then immediately angry at herself for dropping her guard for even an instant. She vowed not to let Eric hold her so close next time — in fact, to discourage any further movements by him in her direction. What she did not need right now was to end up between her new best friend and that friend's ex-lover. What she did not need now was anything that would distract her from her immediate goal — getting her WASP wings.

ELEVEN

"You solo today, Stearns," Wally, her flight instructor, said, as he shoved the pre-flight clipboard into her stomach. "Make sure you do it right the first time."

Lacy grabbed for the clipboard before it could fall with a clatter to the linoleum floor of the Ready Room. Her forced "OK" rang in her ears as she headed for the flight line, her parachute bumping against the back of her legs. How many times had she done this in the yellow Cub back at Shorty's? But this was the open-cockpit PT-19 with its big 175-horsepower Fairchild engine. And it was her first big hurdle on the way to her silver wings.

Since the party in Abilene the previous weekend, she had been distracted by thoughts of Eric and Cin, of Eric and his disturbing effect on her, and of John in light of that unsettling development. But right now, with the big trainer looming in front of her, Lacy shoved her personal troubles into a file drawer in her brain and slammed it shut, as she climbed up into the cockpit and began to run down the checklist. She eyeballed the gauges, tested the rudders, the ailerons, the elevators, the flaps. Everything checked out. She sat back and tried to breathe evenly.

Her surroundings were stark. Metal everything. All semblance of softness and comfort was left on the ground — more accurately, back in civilian life. In the Cub, Lacy had gotten used to being tightly enclosed, as if form-fitted to the inside of the airplane. But the PT-19, with its open cockpit, made her feel like she was out in the air with the birds. That, plus the leather flying helmet and goggles she wore because of the open cockpit, made her feel closer to the pioneer women flyers like Ruth Nichols, Louise Thaden, Amelia Earhart.

She gazed out at the landscape beyond the runway. West Texas vegetation was sparse, buffalo grass, mesquite trees and a few greasewood. Landmarks were at a premium in the flat expanse atop the mesa and tumbleweeds tumbled at will. Avenger Field was seventy miles north of San Angelo, forty miles west of Abilene, seventy miles east-northeast of Big Spring and 2,385 feet above sea level. And it was hot! Oh lordy, was it hot! Lacy could already feel the perspiration forming under her leather helmet and parachute straps.

It was barely ten a.m. and already the thermometer was inching toward ninety. The northerly wind was blowing in at its usual brisk twenty-five miles per hour, whipping clouds of red dust that threatened to obliterate visibility at crucial points during takeoff and landing. Lacy was next in line for takeoff, engine purring.

When the signal came, she shoved the throttle in, felt the roar reverberate around the cockpit. She began to roll. . .faster. . .faster. . . faster. All that horsepower and it was at her fingertips. God, what a feeling!

The wind plastered the goggles tight against her face. She felt the tail come up and then the wings begin to lift. She eased back on the stick and was airborne. Lacy headed for the practice area to complete the drill demanded during one's first solo flight in the Fairchild.

Everything went as it was supposed to. Uneventful, she thought, pleased with herself. The mark of a good pilot is execution: *do it right and you won't have problems.* How often had both Wally and Shorty told her that?

She came out of her final maneuver and settled back into her straight and level and was preparing to turn for home when another airplane appeared on the horizon, directly in front of her and heading straight for her. Her heart leaped into her throat as it approached, seemingly unaware that they were on a collision course. It was bearing down on her, coming closer. . .closer. She heard her pulse hammering in her ears.

Get outta here, she thought, and she pulled the stick right, hit the right rudder, and put the PT into a steep banking turn.

"Damn!" she breathed as the other aircraft shot past her on the left, missing her by only a few feet. It was a BT-13, another trainer, but the BTs from Avenger flew miles away from here. That wasn't one of ours, she thought. Some cowboy from one of the other bases. Lost!

Her hands shook. Her ears rang. In an effort to calm her shattered nerves, she gulped the clean cold air present at that altitude. For the first time in more than two months of flying, the bile rose in her throat. "I will not be sick," she shouted defiantly into the wind, which tore the words from her lips and threw them over her shoulder and out into blue space behind her. "I-will-*not*-be-sick." She swallowed hard, clenched her teeth, clamped her mouth shut, and willed her breathing to return to normal.

It did. The training, the discipline worked. Moments later, she let her breath out in a long sigh as she felt her tightly coiled muscles relax. Her heart rate slowed and her breathing returned to normal as she headed back to the airstrip. When she came parallel to the middle of the runway on her downwind leg, she pulled back on the carburetor heat, then back on the power. Across from the end of the runway, she put the flaps down ten degrees, made her left turn to base leg and flew at right angles to the runway.

One more ninety-degree turn to the left. On final approach, into a thirteen-knot crosswind, she adjusted the airspeed, put the left aileron into the wind and applied opposite rudder in order to compensate for the wind and keep the airplane gliding straight toward the runway. Fifteen to twenty feet from the ground, she eased the stick back and did her flare out for a three point landing. The wheels touched the runway and she felt the rush of exhileration — her first solo landing in the PT-19.

When Lacy had rolled the airplane into position and parked it, she climbed out to be greeted by a crush of her classmates, cheering. She had done it. She had soloed.

She checked in with Wally and told him about the airplane that nearly caused a mid-air collision. He blanched. "I'll check it out," he growled. "There's no BTs flyin' on this side of the field, at least not our BTs."

Fifteen minutes later, after Lacy had gotten her official sign off from him, the entire Flight hopped the cattlewagon back to camp. There, she and two other first solo classmates were lifted up and dunked into the Wishing Well, zoot suits and all, though someone thoughtfully removed their shoes. As the cold water slopped into their eyes, noses, ears and mouths, the three young women sat in the water laughing, splashing, the elixir of accomplishment racing through their veins.

"Pick out your lucky coin," someone yelled.

The other two found theirs quickly and climbed out, but Lacy lingered, savoring the moment. The first coin she brought up turned out to be a nickel. "I can do better than that," she said, tossed it back in and continued her search until her fingers closed over what was unmistakably a silver half dollar.

Some trainee must have wished a very big wish and put her money on it to toss in a half dollar, Lacy thought. But, then, she herself had just had an equally big wish come true — to say nothing of her close call. A fifty center if ever there was one. It was all she could do to contain her joy. She made a silent vow to carry her lucky coin with her on every subsequent flight she took as a WASP.

Dunking was an Avenger tradition. Every WASP trainee before her who had successfully soloed had received the same treatment and all those to come after her would receive it as well. Lacy took pleasure in the fact that Andy, not Jo Bertelli, was the first to solo the PT. Word was, Miss Hot Shot Bertelli knew how to fly a PT-19 all right, but not "the army way." And at Avenger Field, the trainees, no matter how well they flew coming in, had to fly the way the army wanted them to fly or they weren't going to fly at all. Bertelli, by all appearances, was a good pilot, a natural — almost as good as Andy, some said. But she was going to have to learn to conform if she was going to stay in the WASPs.

Lacy took perverse pleasure in this knowledge.

The next morning, Cin soloed. When she crawled out of the Wishing Well, clutching her lucky coin, Andy and Lacy were waiting for her. Each put an arm around her waist and, ignoring her dripping coveralls, walked her back to the bay so she could get into some dry clothes before lunch.

"OK, we're over that hurdle," Cin said, grinning. "What's next?"

TWELVE

One night, with the Texas heat and humidity making the airless bays too hot to sleep in, the three friends took their cots outside and joined several other classmates sleeping under the stars, in spite of warnings of rattlesnakes who liked to crawl in bed with sleeping humans. The row on row of barracks were built so close together, the women could only get two cots end to end in the space between the buildings. Still, it was decidedly cooler out in the open air than inside.

They pushed Andy's cot against the side of the barracks and sat, side by side, leaning back propped on their pillows, looking at the stars, talking.

"You serious about Pink?" Cin asked Andy, as their talk turned — as it most often did — to men. She took a drag off her cigarette.

"What do you mean by serious?" Andy parried.

"Are you gonna marry him?"

Silence hung in the humid air. "I don't know," she finally responded in a voice so low Cin and Lacy could hardly hear her.

"Do you love him?" Cin pursued the subject at hand.

"I don't know. I think so."

Again silence.

"I know I'm happy when I'm with him. But I'm happy up there in the air, too. When he holds me and kisses me I feel all gooey inside. But when I come out of a barrel roll I get the same sensation in the pit of my stomach."

Lacy and Cin laughed. Everyone knew Andy was the top aerobatics flyer in 43-W-9, possibly in the entire camp. She had a knack for it. In fact, she delighted in telling them that when she took her initial flight training, she taught all the men in her class to do the barrel roll. In return for the instruction, they paid for her time in the airplane.

"Lacy, you've been married," Andy continued. "How do you know when you're really in love with someone? That you're ready to spend your whole life with *that* guy?"

Lacy took her time responding. "When John and I first started going together, I wanted to be with him all the time. I thought I couldn't possibly love him any more than I did then. After we got married, I was shocked at how shallow my feelings were before because at that point I knew him so much better and all the good in him. When we found out he was going overseas, I wanted to hold on to him and never let him go. For awhile, I almost wanted us both to die right then so we'd be together forever, but . . ."

And though it had been almost a year — a lifetime ago — she remembered that last night with him like it was yesterday.

She had awakened, startled, from a sound sleep, sat up in bed and looked around. What was it? A noise? Nothing stirred outside the open window or in the sparsely furnished hotel room. Lacy looked over at John sleeping peacefully beside her. Whatever it was that jarred her awake had not bothered him.

A replay of their long night of lovemaking washed over her. Just the thought made her warm all over. The tenderness — the slow, steady arousal, the pleasure each of them took in the other and the other's pleasure. The passion — the growing intensity, the heat that followed and culminated in a climax that shook them both and left them spent and satisfied, though secretly wanting more.

More, though, would soon be a thing of the past. It was already three in the morning and John and his crew, along with the entire wing, were scheduled to leave for England at six. She would not see him again — would not hold him again — until . . .

The clouds parted long enough to let a few moonbeams fall to earth. One found its way in the window and John's face was illuminated by the light. Could he, she wondered, possibly comprehend how much she loved him? Of course he could, she told herself. And she was as sure of his love as she was of anything in her life. She reached out her hand and touched his cheek. He stirred. As she leaned over and brushed her lips across his forehead, he stirred again and his arm went around her, pulling her to him.

"Lacy," he whispered sleepily in her ear. "I love you, Lacy."

He smiled and though his eyes weren't open, she knew he was awake. She stretched her naked body out alongside his and caressed his warm skin, marveling in the hardness beneath. He groaned with pleasure. Then she eased her body atop his. As she moved on him, he made a low growling sound. She gave in to that now familiar aching, the overwhelming desire to blend irrevocably with him.

For the last time. . .

* * *

She had paused in mid-sentence. Cin and Andy were looking at her, waiting. Tears began to roll down her cheeks. When she resumed talking, her voice sank so low only a hoarse whisper came out.

"When he left that morning for England, I went dead inside. I was sure I would never feel again until he came home. When he died, I wanted to kill myself. I still don't know why I didn't. But I feel like half of my soul, half of my self is in that grave in Cambridge with him."

The end of Cin's cigarette glowed as she took another drag. "Has time healed the hurt, even a little?" she asked.

Lacy looked up at her through tears. "It will never be the same again, but yes, I guess the hurt has eased a little, if for no other reason than I'm getting used to it."

"I've found time to be a great healer," Cin said, her voice husky.

Andy had been staring at the ground, listening to them. Now her head came up with a jerk. In the moonlight, Lacy could just make out a frown on the younger girl's face — a creasing between her eyebrows. She looked from Cin to Lacy. Lacy saw this and sensed that Andy was puzzled by Cin's response.

Cin talked disparagingly of men. She regaled the baymates with tales of her many boyfriends — "none of 'em worth the powder to blow off a rattlesnake's head." Only Lacy knew that one had penetrated her carefully constructed veneer and that she had loved him — probably still did — though she professed no longer to care.

Lacy shook her head almost imperceptibly, hoping Andy would see it, understand and back off. Andy looked at her for a long moment then cocked her head to one side.

"I'm afraid to let myself care too much about Pink because I know where he's going and what he will be doing when he goes overseas. I can't help but think that what happened to Lacy and John is what will happen to Pink and me if I let myself get too serious."

"Love's about risks," Cin said, suddenly. "It's about being willing to take risks. Taking them is scary, but sometimes it turns out that if you don't take them, everything turns to shit anyway." She tossed her cigarette down, stood up and ground it out with her heel. "I need to stretch my legs. . ." And with that she stalked off.

"What's the matter with her?" Andy said, astonished at Cin's sudden departure.

"She's got some issues she's dealing with," Lacy answered.

"What issues?"

"I think it would be better if she told you herself."

"It's that Eric guy, isn't it? The one at the dance the other night. The one who kept dancing with you. They knew each other before, didn't they?"

"Yeah. He taught her to fly."

"My guess is there was a whole lot more to it than him teaching her to fly. I saw how she looked at him. So did you."

"Yup, I saw how she looked at him," Lacy sighed. "But she says it's all in the past. Over. Done with."

"And you believe her?"

Lacy stopped and collected her thoughts. "I don't know if I believe her or not."

"He was making a play for you."

"I think he was just on the make, period. Any convenient female. I want nothing to do with him. He's bad news. Besides, I'm not interested in men now. I've got enough on my plate without having that kind of entanglement get in the way. I've got all I can handle here."

"You sure there's not more to it than that — with Cin, I mean?"

"No, I can't be sure, but I have to take her at her word. She told me it — whatever *it* was — was over."

"You know, Cin seems to take most men with a grain of salt," Andy said, shaking her head. "But not that one. I'd swear she was in love with him from the way she acted. And he sure seemed interested in you."

Lacy thought about telling Andy what she knew, then held her tongue. It was Cin's place to tell their friend if she wanted her to know. "Ask her," Lacy said, standing up. "I'm going to bed." She got up, helped Andy turn her cot in the same direction as the others so she might catch some breeze, then crawled onto her own cot, plumping her pillow hard under her head.

But she could not get to sleep and lay awake for a long time watching the stars.

After awhile, she saw Cin's silent form move past her and crawl onto her own cot. Once after that she thought she heard a snuffle, like Cin was crying. But that was ridiculous. She had never seen Cin cry and doubted that any of them ever would.

THIRTEEN

Lacy grasped the metal frame behind her head and pulled the black cotton hood forward on the track until it completely blocked out the world beyond the airplane's laminated glass and plastic canopy. The humped back of Cin's seat blocked any forward view. Her universe was reduced to the instrument panel in the back cockpit of the BT-13.

Shut away like that, Lacy began to think her eyes were playing tricks on her. The cotton walls seemed to move in on her, then retreat. She passed her bare arm over her brow, wiping away the sweat before it could drip into her eyes. She kept the long sleeves of the coveralls rolled above her elbows in an effort to get cooling air to her skin and to keep the loose fabric out of her way.

The incessant west Texas wind was blowing out of the north, twenty-five miles per hour and whipping up a storm of red dust. The outside temperature was a fall-like seventy-five degrees, but inside the airplane, with light and air shut out, Lacy would have sworn it was a hundred degrees with humidity to match.

The members of the class of 43-W-9 were now past the mid-way point of their training. Sixty-four of the original one hundred and two remained. PT-19 checkrides and BT-13 cleckrides were all behind them. The basic trainer phase had proven too much for their baymate Trish Samples. She had washed out when she failed to pass her checkride on the second try. When the rest of them returned from the flight line for lunch, her mattress was rolled up and her gear gone. Just like that. She didn't even say goodbye.

That she might wash out was always in the back of Lacy's mind, but Shorty had done right by her, working always at her confidence level as well as on her flying skills. She knew he had taught her well. And now that she had notched the PT-19 and the BT-13 in her belt, she dared to imagine victory — the sought-after, much-cherished awarding of her silver wings.

Most recently, her class had completed the first two phases of instrument training. First there were the seemingly endless sessions in the ground-based Link trainer, where if you made a mistake you crashed, but you opened the door, climbed out and walked away. Then came the flights under the hood in a BT-13, with the instructor in the front seat talking, explaining, guiding, watching out for other aircraft and making sure the trainee, flying blind beneath the hood in the back seat, kept the trainer flying straight and level.

Now, she and Cin and Andy had graduated into the "buddy" phase. Trainees paired up and acted as observers for each other. Since your very life depended on the woman you chose to sit in front of you on these flights, pilots tended to be very careful who they selected to be their buddy.

Cin and Lacy opted for each other. Andy paired up with Karen Richardson.

"OK," Cin's voice came through the earphones. "We're next in line."

Lacy's mind came back to the present. It was time for their first buddy flight. Lacy under the hood. Cin, the lookout — the safety pilot — in the front seat.

Rain had put them behind. In an effort to keep the training program on schedule, several Flight Two trainees who were ready for their first "buddy ride" were assigned a late afternoon flight while there was still sufficient daylight.

Lacy rubbed her sweaty palms on the legs of her zoot suit then patted her breast pocket where her lucky coin was stored.

It wasn't there!

She dug her hand down inside to be sure. Empty. Then she remembered taking the half dollar out of her other coveralls the night before and putting it in her small jewelry box. At least she hadn't sent it to the laundry with her other pair.

"We're next," Cin's voice, more insistent this time, came through her earphone.

"Damn!" Lacy said under her breath.

"What the matter?"

"I forgot my lucky coin."

"Too late now," Cin said. "We gotta go."

Fear niggled at the recesses of Lacy's brain, but she pushed it back. She wished she could get out of the airplane, run back and get the coin. Of course, that was impossible. She and Cin were in line to take off. To abort now would mean losing today's flight. You just didn't do things like that. It would be a mark against them. Some of the instructors were dead set on washing out any and every female trainee they could on the flimsiest of excuses. Don't give them any ammo, she thought.

"Lacy?" Cin's voice came through the earphone again.

"I'm ready."

"Roger." The BT-13 began to roll forward.

"We're cleared for take off," Cin said a few minutes later, keeping Lacy, encased in her black fabric cage, posted on their progress. "You still there?"

"I'm still here. Where else would I be?"

The two-seat, tandem cockpit BT-13 had dual controls. Both student and instructor could fully control the airplane. Lacy could see when Cin activated the rudders and when and where she moved the stick. As the thrum of the engine swelled, Lacy knew Cin had pushed the throttle forward. She felt the plane move as the rpm's climbed — they were rolling.

Eyes riveted on the instruments that constituted her world now, Lacy felt her confidence oozing away with the sweat that continued to form on her forehead and run into her eyebrows. *It won't get off the ground. We're going too slow. I should never have left that coin.*

Rolling. . . rolling. . .

The sounds were there, but not the sensation of movement as she couldn't see the ground flashing by. She heard her heart pounding over the roar and felt her own intake of breath. And then the wind caught under the wings and the airplane lifted. Lacy felt it — miraculously she felt the plane lift and begin to climb out just as Cin's voice came over the earphones. "We're away." Lacy realized she was holding her breath and let out the pent up air in a long, slow sigh.

She watched the stick between her legs move back. Then she checked the altimeter, set, as required, for sea level, and now registering several hundred feet higher than the 2385-foot altitude of Avenger Field. The needle swung through 3000, then 3500 feet.

Lacy and Cin were off on their first "buddy ride."

"Keep your eyes on your instruments." The words, spoken so often by her instructor, came back to Lacy as the single engine trainer climbed. "Trust them. Believe them. If they say you are banking left, you are, even if your body tells you differently. It's so easy to get vertigo."

When the altimeter read 4500 feet, Cin called out, "Ready to turn south, one eight zero. We are clear. You ready to take over?"

"Roger," Lacy said, employing the familiar military response. Eyes on the instruments, she placed her feet evenly on the rudder pedals and her right hand on the stick. Gently, she shook the controls and called out, "I have it."

Lacy, on a zero-one-zero heading, applied gentle pressure to the right rudder and eased the stick to the right to establish a bank, putting the aircraft into a right turn. She kept her eyes on the bank and turn indicator and compass and, before the one-eight-zero heading came up, she began to back off the rudder and ease the stick back to neutral as the plane swung into the correct heading. She was now traveling due south, headed for the training ground a few miles ahead. Once there, and with Cin's assurances that she was clear of all traffic, Lacy began to put the trainer through the routine she needed to complete her practice flight.

They were almost at the end of the checklist, nearly ready to turn back to base, when she heard a small but distinct noise — one she had never heard before while in flight — a muffled metallic ripping sound. The airplane still flew, but Lacy knew something was wrong.

"What was that?"

"I don't know," Cin answered. "I'm checking everything."

It took all Lacy's will power not to pull both the hood and the canopy loose, look out, breathe the fresh, cool air. Now she understood the terror of the claustrophobic.

The engine gave off a series of guttural coughs.

"Get that hood back, quick!" Cin yelled. "I've got the controls."

"What's wrong?" Lacy let go the stick and removed her feet from the rudder pedals then scanned the dials again. The cylinder head temp gauge was rising.

"Oil line's busted," Cin shouted.

Lacy pulled the hood release ring on the left side of the cockpit. It wouldn't budge.

"Damn!"

"What's wrong?" Cin's voice was tense.

"Hood won't release."

"Rip the goddamn thing off if you have to. We're going down. I'm shutting everything off. We've got to bail out, now."

Lacy glanced at the altimeter. It was dropping. *Forty-two hundred feet.* She strained and put all her strength into freeing the balky ring. The movement was awkward because the small ring was attached to the side wall of the cockpit near her left elbow. Still it wouldn't budge. She shifted her weight to get better leverage and tugged again, her heart racing. *Forty-one hundred feet.* Her whole body was bathed in sweat. What could she use to cut the fabric loose? Another frantic pull.

Finally, the hood release gave and she raked the bar and the black cotton shroud back over her head.

Cin had her canopy open and was standing on her seat facing Lacy, one leg over the side of the airplane. Lacy slid her canopy forward. That was when she saw it. Black viscous oil smeared the front of the windshield and streaks of the stuff, whipped by the wind, were feathering out to the sides where globs of the hot, thick fluid were being torn loose and flung back at them.

"Cin," Lacy screamed into her microphone.

Lacy watched as Cin slid down the left wing, holding onto the handle set in the side of the fuselage between the two pilot stations, hesitated for a split second, and slipped off the wing into space.

Likewise, Lacy pulled herself up, placed her left foot on her seat and climbed over the side of the cockpit. Just before she crouched down on the back side of the wing to get ready to jump, she looked back and saw another spurt of oil coat the front of the canopy, felt hot windborne droplets spatter on her face. Fear gave her all the adrenaline she needed to fall head first off the backside of the wing — to avoid decapitation by the tail section — and out into the empty air.

She counted three, as they had been instructed to do, then pulled the rip cord. Moments later she felt the wrenching jerk when her parachute opened and yanked her back skyward. In the distance, she saw Cin gently swinging at the end of her white mushroom-shaped chute. Then Lacy turned her head and watched the U.S. government-issue flight trainer fly itself into a freshly plowed neighboring field and burst into flames while the two of them floated safely to the ground.

The strong winds aloft carried her downwind, away from the crash site. The slow descent gave her time for reflection, time to think about what had happened, what they might have done wrong.

She knew she would never forget the feeling in the pit of her stomach as the two-seater buried its nose in the west Texas soil. Despair at having failed in her mission. Despair at failing to bring the airplane safely back to base. Despair, in spite of the thankful realization that she was alive, that Cin was alive, and they would walk away from this. Despair at the sense of helplessness that overcame her as her feet hit the ground.

Avenger trainees were instructed in the proper procedure should they need to jump from a stricken airplane, but they never had an opportunity to practice. The first time was always for real. Lacy remembered to bend her knees to cushion her landing and roll with the movement of the wind in the chute. She wrestled with the buckles and belts and got herself out of the harness, then she hauled in her chute, turned westward into the setting sun and began to trudge through the Texas twilight back toward Cin, who was now walking towards her.

When they met, they stared for a moment at each other. Lacy saw that Cin was trembling. She put out her arms and Cin fell into them. Lacy felt her friend's tears on her cheek and registered surprise. Cin was crying. Then Cin pulled back, looked at Lacy and began to laugh. In a heartbeat Lacy was laughing too. They sat down abruptly as the strength in their legs seemed to desert them at the same time. And soon they were rolling in the red dust and the mesquite brush, laughing and crying.

Finally, exhausted, they sat up and looked at each other again.

"I knew I should have gone back to get my lucky coin," Lacy said, shaking her head.

"I'm just glad you remembered your parachute," Cin answered back. And when they both realized the enormity of what she had just said, they collapsed in laughter again.

"I saw a road over that way as I was coming down," Cin said when she finally got control of herself a second time. They stood, collected their chutes, and turned toward the road — toward the airfield and an official inquiry.

It wasn't long before a rancher came along in his pickup truck. He had seen the plane go down and noted the two white mushrooms blossoming in the sky over his land. He seemed moderately surprised at finding that the figures who rode the two parachutes down were female. He took them in to town to the local sheriff's office where they put through a call to Avenger and received a promise that a crash team would be on its way in minutes, along with someone to pick them up and drive them back to the base that evening.

They were to talk to no one about the crash, save any debriefing until the crash investigation team could get there. One of the sheriff's deputies took pity on them, called his wife to set two more places at their sparse, ration-book regulated table, and took the two bedraggled and now very tired flyers home for dinner.

When they stumbled into the bay after midnight, Andy was awake and waiting for them.

"I couldn't sleep, I was so worried," she whispered.

FOURTEEN

Cin and Lacy were grounded until the results of the crash investigation could be completed. It took three days to collect enough evidence from the crash site to begin the inquiry, three days during which the two sweated over their futures with the WASPs and attended double sessions of ground school. Then Jacqueline Cochran flew in the fourth day on a surprise visit and rattled sufficient chains to get things moving.

She questioned Cin first, while Lacy sat outside the office designated for the Director of Women Pilots and waited. The wooden bench was hard and unyielding against her back. She wore her tan slacks and a white blouse — the non-flying uniform of a WASP in training at Avenger. Her Amelia Earhart haircut was freshly washed, toweled dry, brushed and feathered so that it looked casually windblown but was, in fact, carefully composed. She consciously had to resist the urge to run her fingers nervously through her hair and ruin the effect. She was convinced that she had to look absolutely composed, confident, and competent for her debriefing with Cochran. Instead of raking at her hair, a nervous habit she had picked up since cutting off her braids, she twisted a handkerchief in her hands and used it to wipe her perspiring palms. She recalled having done the same thing four months earlier while waiting for her initial interview with Cochran in Denver. Everything turned out all right then, she told herself. Surely it would be OK now.

The door opened and Cin emerged. "She said for you to come in."

Cin held the door open and beyond her lanky, white and khaki-clad frame, Lacy could see Cochran's blonde head bent over papers on a desk. Cin looked like she wanted to say something, but apparently changed her mind. Her eyes held Lacy's for an instant, but Lacy couldn't read them. She had no sense of what had transpired between her best friend and their commanding officer.

"Thanks," Lacy said, and tried to smile at Cin, but didn't succeed. She was too scared, and as she walked through the door, she felt as if her life was about to fall apart again.

"Sit down, Mrs. Stearns." The smile was there, but it was not the broad, welcoming one that had been in place on their previous encounter. Lacy sat on a hard folding chair that she swore was the same one she had sat on in Denver.

"Please tell me, in your own words, what happened to you and Miss Stinson during your instrument training flight of October 18." Her voice was flat, impossible to read.

Lacy told her the story of the flight from before takeoff, when she ran the checklist, to watching the BT-13 bury its nose in the field. The only thing she omitted was forgetting her lucky coin. Somehow, she thought, that was not relevant to Jacqueline Cochran's official inquiry.

When she had finished, Cochran nodded, her brown eyes telegraphing a gravity that unnerved Lacy.

"Mrs. Stearns, first I want you to know how thankful I am that you and Miss Stinson were not hurt. Second, thank you for being so candid with me. You and Miss Stinson, both, have excellent records so far here at Avenger and I, personally, had no reason to doubt your competence. However, your lives were endangered and we lost a valuable airplane.

"There's another concern. Some of the instructors continue to raise doubts as to the ability of the women to fly these planes. They are quick to report any transgression or weakness. Though I don't so much agree with their motives, I cannot fault their over zealousness if it saves lives. We want no more occurrences like the deaths of Miss Seip and Miss Severson a few weeks ago."

Lacy nodded.

"You had no warning whatsoever that there was a problem with the airplane?"

Lacy shook her head. "Only that strange metallic ripping sound we reported. Then the temperature in the cylinder head began to rise. I took my eyes off the instrument panel to try to pop the hood, but the release ring stuck. It took me several tries to get it loose. Several seconds. Maybe a half minute — I don't know for sure. While I was doing that, I heard the engine quit. Then Cin — Miss Stinson — yelled to me that we were going down. When I finally got the hood released and pushed it out of the way, I saw the oil on the windshield and Miss Stinson getting ready to jump."

Cochran's eyes bore into her. "Had you had problems releasing the hood before?"

"No. I don't ever remember a hood release ring sticking before."

A deep frown creased Cochran's forehead. "I don't like it," she said.

"I beg your pardon," Lacy said, mystified.

"I don't like some of the things that are happening. Accidents will happen, true, but there are just too many little things. Some of the equipment we are flying on active duty is old and tired, and in the interest of keeping the vital parts working, sometimes the little, seemingly unimportant things are overlooked. But you girls here at Avenger are flying new, top-of-the-line equipment. Still, little problems have a way of getting bigger.

"For instance, if you hadn't gotten that hood loose, you could have gone down with that airplane. We've had cases of canopy latches that won't open. On the surface, that doesn't sound serious. But one young woman died when her plane caught fire after she crash landed. She wasn't injured in the crash, but she couldn't get the canopy open to escape." Cochran hesitated, then added, "Too many coincidences."

Lacy remained quiet. She sensed that Cochran had almost forgotten she was there and was thinking out loud — probably voicing things Lacy shouldn't be hearing. Then Cochran shook her head and seemed to come out of her reverie. "Mrs. Stearns, can I trust you to keep to yourself what you just heard?"

"Why, yes," she stammered.

"As for the broken oil line on your plane, the maintenance people tell me that metal fatigue is most likely the culprit. A tiny crack in one of the lines wouldn't have been obvious, even to the most methodical mechanic."

As simple as that, Lacy thought. Still, what she also had heard was that the Director of Women Pilots was concerned about sabotage at other fields. If so, none of them were safe in the air. And that opened up a whole new set of concerns — life threatening ones.

Cochran was speaking again. "I'm absolving you and Miss Stinson of any blame. Pilot error did not cause this crash. Ideally, if you two had been more experienced pilots, you might have been able to land in a field. But that's strictly conjecture. Many other things could have gone wrong as well. Try not to let this affect your desire to fly. Things happen to all of us aloft and we must learn to live with them. Makes better pilots of us in the long run. That will be all, Mrs. Stearns. Keep up the good work."

Lacy stood up to leave, but Cochran spoke again. "Oh, Mrs.

Stearns. I spoke with your various instructors this morning. A Mr. Wallace Moore tells me that you had a near miss with an unknown aircraft a few weeks ago and that he has narrowed the possibilities to a BT-13 being ferried from California to Dallas. In fact, he believes he has the pilot's name. Apparently the young man didn't report the incident until much later, after a similar incident cost the life of a member of his own squadron. At that point, he realized the seriousness of what he, himself, had done.

"I assured Mr. Moore that I would see that the pilot flying that airplane was severely reprimanded and that his entire flight record be looked at again before he receives further assignment."

The final verdict on their ill-fated flight was a blown oil line. Lacy and Cin were, in fact, lucky to be alive. The word sabotage wasn't even hinted at in any of the reports Lacy saw then or later, but in the back of her mind was Cochran's obvious concern as well as Jo Bertelli's warning when Helen Jo and Peggy went down that there existed the possibility of sinister mischief directed at the WASPs themselves.

With Cin and Lacy reinstated, and with their second weekend pass coming up, the three friends plus Karen were planning to attend another USO party in Abilene. Andy and Karen had not seen their boyfriends for nearly two months.

"Stearns, phone call, office on the double," the word was passed to the bay.

Startled, Lacy immediately suspected the worst. Was something wrong with her mother, her father? Had her brother Kenny, fighting in Sicily, been killed? Or her brother Jared, who was serving with the Marines in the Pacific? She knew it was something bad. She reached the office on a dead run and, panting, gasping for breath, grabbed the phone lying threateningly on the sergeant's desk.

"Yes," she breathed hoarsely into the receiver. "What's wrong?"

Male laughter greeted her. "Nothing, that I know of."

A chill that was part relief and part anger went through her. "Who is this?" she asked. She already knew who the voice at the other end of the line belonged to, but didn't want to give him that satisfaction.

"Eric Larsen. Who did you think it was?"

"I thought it was someone calling from home with bad news."

"Well, you can relax. It's only me and I've got good news. I'm going to be down that way tomorrow and I'd like to see you. Take you out for dinner if you can get out of Cochran's Convent for the evening."

Lacy was speechless.

He kept talking. "I hear you had some trouble, you and Lucinda. You're OK though, right? Both of you?"

"Yes. How did you hear?"

"Rumor mill is flying. What about dinner tomorrow night? You can tell me all about it."

"I'm going to Abilene with Cin and Andy and Karen."

"OK, then I'll pick you up there."

"What about Cin?"

'What about Cin?" he repeated her question.

Lacy was silent.

"Lacy?" she heard his voice say tentatively from wherever it was he was calling. "Lucinda and I have no demands on each other's time. I thought she told you that. I'd like to have dinner with you. Would you like to have dinner with me?"

Lacy's mind raced. Part of her wanted very much to see this man again. Part of her was totally repelled by the fact that she was even remotely interested and would consider it. And what would John think? But John was dead and couldn't think and she would never see him again and hadn't she said she wanted to get on with her life?

"You still there?" Eric's voice intruded on her thoughts.

"Yes, I'm here and, yes, I'll have dinner with you tomorrow night. We'll be at the Hilton Hotel."

"Seven o'clock. I'll pick you up. Gotta go." And he hung up.

Lacy stood there with the phone in her hand, staring into space. What had she done?

FIFTEEN

Fresh from a bath that washed off the grit accumulated from riding in Karen's convertible, Lacy stood in front of the bathroom mirror and stared at her image.

Arriving at the hotel in Abilene at six, Andy, Karen and Cin had hurried to freshen up, change out of their slacks and into their party dresses and high heels. Knowing she had at least an hour before Eric arrived, Lacy stayed out of their way and watched their preparations, a bit wistfully. There was safety in their company and they were leaving her.

Why are you putting yourself through this agony? she asked the serious young woman whose gray eyes stared back at her. You don't like him. You're a little afraid of him. But why? What's there to be afraid of? That he's a pilot? That he could die tomorrow just like John? You could be dead now. So could Cin. That's the risk pilots take. And you don't have to fly to die. Ginny fell off a horse and died. Just living is risky. Might as well fly or ride horses if that's what you like. You're going to die someday anyway.

Is it that Eric once belonged to Cin? Even though she says he means nothing to her now. You told Andy he was no good. For you or just in general?

Lacy turned away from the mirror. *Damn it, John, why did you have to die and put me in a predicament like this?*

She dressed slowly and deliberately, knowing that her best dress, a royal blue shirtwaist, emphasized her broad shoulders, narrow waist and gently rounded hips. Her black patent leather pumps and matching purse, and a white cardigan sweater for the cool West Texas autumn night, completed the outfit.

She returned to the mirror and applied the little bit of makeup she always wore — some powder, a touch of rouge, and her bright red Jacqueline Cochran lipstick. She ran her brush through her hair then feathered it with her fingers. Just as she finished primping, the phone rang. Eric was downstairs.

"Well, you look just as good in daylight as you do in a USO hall," he informed her as he opened the hotel door for her. "But dinner tonight is going to be by candlelight." He ceremoniously opened the door to the dark green English roadster that sat at the curb.

"Where did you get this?" she asked. "Didn't you fly in?"

"Belongs to my friend, the colonel. The CO at Camp Barkeley. He loaned it to me for the evening when I told him I was taking out the prettiest WASP trainee at Avenger Field. He's the one who recommended the restaurant." Eric climbed in behind the wheel and started up the car. Moments later they were out of town heading down the highway into the sunset.

"Where is this restaurant?" she asked. She had to shout to be heard over the wind which had now destroyed any attempt she had made to tame her hair.

"The Officers' Club," he shouted back.

Further conversation was impossible, but Eric did reach over and take her hand. When she pulled it away, he turned and looked at her, then smiled. But he did not try to take her hand again — at least not until after drinks and dinner with wine and the surface, non-threatening conversation of getting acquainted had evolved into a more relaxed repartee. He didn't try to take her hand again until they sat across from each other enjoying after-dinner coffee and a cognac.

"You don't like me, do you?" he asked after, once again, she withdrew her hand.

Lacy wasn't sure how to answer. "It's not that I don't like you."

"Then what is it? And why did you come out with me?"

She thought for a minute, daring to look past that smile and into his eyes. "You move too fast. I came to dinner with you because it's been more than a year since I had the company of a man to myself and I wanted to find out what it felt like again — whether I could still act normal."

"And can you?"

"Not yet." She looked down, unable to hold his eyes in hers.

He said nothing.

Finally, she looked up at him again. The laugh had faded from his eyes and a more serious expression had come to dwell in those deep blue pools. "Tell me about your husband."

Momentarily, Lacy was at a loss for words. Then, slowly, she began to tell one of her favorite memories of John — one she knew Eric would understand.

* * *

John Stearns was meant to fly. He got his chance while attending Colorado Teachers College. In 1939, as the possibility of a war loomed ever greater for the United States, Army Air Corps General Hap Arnold ordered a government-sponsored Civilian Pilot Training program to begin training potential pilots should America enter the war. The civilian airport in Greeley offered school-sponsored flying lessons, so John jumped at the chance. One day, not long after he got his private pilot's license, he took Lacy up with him.

It was that morning she would never forget.

"Severe clear, Lace," he said. "That's what they call it."

The sky was cobalt blue, no clouds were showing over the mountains forty miles away — though Lacy knew the towering thunderheads would appear sometime after noon, just as they always did as the heat built up and moisture rose when it came in contact with the backs of the Front Range of the Rockies.

The plane was a yellow J-3 Cub.

"I don't know, John," Lacy said, looking at the little plane. "It doesn't look safe. It's so small."

The idea of not having her feet on solid Colorado soil, of being suspended in air two thousand feet above the ground with nothing but a little metal, fabric and wood between her and sudden death, was unsettling. But the flight had taken on all the attributes of a dare. Normally Lacy didn't duck a dare. Now, John's green eyes challenging her to partake of this thing that he loved so intensely, Lacy knew deep inside that she really did not want to fly. But the thought of telling him she was afraid was more unpalatable than strapping herself into that yellow cardboard crate with wings. At least if it went down, they would go together.

"OK," she said, and climbed into the front seat.

The canopy rose in front of her and she could look up and out at one of the propeller blades and the blue sky beyond. Another pilot came over at John's request and gave the prop a mighty pull down. The little plane roared to life and sat vibrating noisily on the ground.

"Check your seatbelt, be sure it's fastened," John yelled. "Keep your hands off the stick. Don't touch the rudders with your feet. Otherwise, enjoy the ride."

Lacy shut her eyes when the plane started its dash down the runway, gathering speed as it went. But when the wind caught the little plane under the wings and lifted it up and away from the airfield, her eyes flew open and she felt a thrill stab deep in the pit of her stomach and her breath caught for just a moment, then released.

The view was magnificent. The mountains were coming closer as John was angling west to give her a better view. Then he banked the airplane to the left and did a gentle, 360-degree climbing turn, careful not to stall out in the process, then brought the nose back to level and continued on his path to the edge of the rugged gray-brown foothills. Closer in they began to show the iridescent green of the budding cottonwoods and the deeper green of the pines that covered the ridges.

Flying back to the east, out over the high plains, John practiced his turns and then a stall, gently easing the plane into a climb. Up. Up. Lacy couldn't see the ground, only blue sky above her. And then the shudder. She knew she would never forget that first shudder and the slight kick as the plane righted itself. John told her later that all he did was take his hands off the stick and the plane came back to level flying.

But Lacy found her stomach was in her throat after that maneuver. Admittedly, she liked the thrill at takeoff and the view was stupendous. But she did *not* like the sensation created by the stalls John continued to practice — with too much relish, she thought — nor the fact that he landed the plane on one wheel, the right wing nearly scraping the runway before he could get the left wheel down properly.

No sooner were her feet on the ground than Lacy knew she was going to be sick. She ran to the far side of the airplane and threw up.

When she had recovered, she made a quick exit to the ladies room to put a cold towel on her neck and rinse her mouth out with water. Then, chewing a piece of gum to rid her mouth and breath of the taste of vomit, she rejoined John and his buddies beside the airplane.

"Want to go up again, Lace?" His eyes glowed with excitement. She knew he had loved sharing this daring mistress of his with her, but she knew deep down that she really did not want to go flying again anytime soon.

So she lied. "I'll think about it. But not right now," she said.

When John got his instructor's permit several months later, he tried to get her to let him teach her to fly, but Lacy refused. She told him she was light-headed enough around him as it was without taking her feelings up in the air with her. He grinned and kissed her hard on the mouth.

* * *

That he would never kiss her like that again brought her abruptly to the end of her recitation. She blinked and waited for Eric to say something.

"I began flying in much the same way, though not through the CPT," he said after a somewhat awkward silence. "I learned to fly back in '37, the summer before I went to graduate school. But it was something I had always wanted to do — ever since I saw my first airplane at the age of seven. After Lindy flew the Atlantic, I was convinced that there was nothing in the world I wanted to do more. But my father prevailed. Depression or no, he sent me to Princeton. He did, however, promise flying lessons as a graduation present.

"So then I came west to Montana State — I won that battle with Dad — got my masters and discovered I was a good teacher. I decided that was what I wanted to do with my life. While I worked on my doctorate, I taught mathematics in college during the week and flying on weekends. And I gave private lessons as well."

"That's how you met Cin?"

He nodded. "That's how I met Lucinda."

Over a second cognac, Lacy felt a warm glow beginning in her belly. She had never drunk the golden liquid fire before and wasn't sure she liked it. But she began to imitate his movements, holding the snifter the way he did and swirling the liquid round and round, warming it with her hand. A combo began to play in the lounge next to the dining room. He reached for her hand again — this time to lead her to the dance floor. It took some effort on her part to negotiate the steps because of the strange buzzing in her head, but Eric guided her now holding her arm firmly at the elbow. When they stepped on the dance floor, he gently spun her into his arms.

I'm dizzy. I'm drunk. What am I going to do now?

But Eric held her tight and close and she began to regain her equilibrium. Lacy felt herself melt into his body as they moved as one around the dance floor. She was now powerless to do anything but what he directed her to do through the pressure of his right arm around her waist or his left hand holding her right one. His cheek rested against her hair. But he said nothing. They danced until the combo stopped to take a break. Again, Eric propelled her through the lounge back to the dining room and held out her chair for her.

"I think I need to excuse myself for a minute," she said and, using every ounce of self control she had, carefully guided herself to the ladies room where she doused her face with cold water until she could think straight again. She repaired her makeup — marveled at her soft wide eyes in the mirror. She thought she resembled a deer caught in the headlights of a Mack truck just before annihilation.

When she returned to the table, Eric stood, held out her chair and they both sat silently looking at each other. Then they both spoke at once.

"I wonder. . . " she said.

"Have you. . . " he said.

And they burst out laughing.

"Ladies first," he said.

"No, please, what did you start to ask me?"

"Have you flown since the crash?"

"No. We were grounded and that was just lifted today. We go back up Monday. Cin and I will re-take our solo buddy ride Tuesday and, if all goes well, get our instrument checkrides later in the week." She paused. "I'm scared to death. I've never really been frightened by a checkride before, but this one has me worried. I'm afraid that I've lost my confidence and I'll wash out."

"You won't wash out," he said. "Let me give you a couple of tips." Eric pumped her full of as much instrument expertise as he could in the space of a half an hour. When he led her back to the dance floor for one last dance, she had the same exquisite feeling of melting into his body as they began to move to the rhythm of the beat. Somewhere, in the back of her mind, Lacy knew she didn't want the feeling to end, but her conscious thoughts tried to keep that knowledge and what it meant at bay.

On the way back to Abilene, Lacy planned how she was going to repel the advances she was convinced Eric would make once the car stopped in front of the hotel. The electric current that flowed between them on the dance floor could not be ignored. There was only one answer for that: she could not see him again. And in order to bring that off, she would have to begin right now. So she steeled herself.

But when the car stopped, Eric slid out from behind the wheel and came around to open the door for her. At the entrance to the hotel, he took her hand. Here it comes, Lacy thought, expecting him to try to pull her into his arms and kiss her. But he raised the palm of her hand to his lips in an almost European gesture. "Good night Lacy and thank you for having dinner with me." And then he was gone.

SIXTEEN

The second Friday in November, the day after 43-7's graduation, what was left of 43-9's Flight Two waited in the ready room for their turns to go up. Lacy, Cin and Andy had all soloed the AT-6, their first airplane with a retractable gear, and now they were building time and awaiting their checkrides.

"I heard via the grapevine that the instructors have been told to wash out half of us before graduation," Cin said.

"*Half* of those remaining?" Andy said. "Our Flight's already down to twenty-eight from fifty-one."

"I heard it from one of the 43-7s after graduation yesterday," Cin said. "She meant half of those of us still here."

"I thought they were desperate for pilots," Lacy said.

The door to the Ready Room opened and the colonel strode in followed by a lieutenant colonel none of them had ever seen before.

"Fall in, ladies."

The twenty-eight trainees quickly lined up at attention.

"This is Lt. Col. Brax Thompson. He's here to take some of you up for checkrides tomorrow morning. You've selected eight, right?" he asked the visiting officer, who nodded yes.

From where Lacy stood, Brax Thompson looked to be at least six feet three, broad shouldered and broad chested. His massive square jaw seemed to have preceded him into the room. But in spite of the brusque, purposeful air, his blue eyes telegraphed a twinkle of mischief that he seemed only half heartedly able to hide.

"O eight hundred tomorrow, ladies." Thompson smiled. "Here's the list."

Lacy's was the first name he read.

She reported to the flight line Saturday morning at eight only to find that fog had grounded all the flights. The eight of them, like lambs awaiting slaughter, sat in the Ready Room and stared out at the eerie ghost planes that stood nearest to the hangar. Beyond the second row, the aircraft disappeared into the wet gray blanket that wrapped its way around every object, animate and inanimate, that came in its path.

Finally, around nine thirty, the fog dissipated, leaving a damp residue clinging to all those exposed metal surfaces. The trainees went outside and performed pre-flight inspections on the planes assigned to them for the morning.

Lacy held her breath when Thompson strode into the hangar at five minutes after ten and the eight women stood and again lined up at attention as if awaiting inspection which, in reality, they were. Lacy stared straight ahead, aware of his footsteps as he walked down the line checking out each girl's nametag. She was at the far end of the line. When he stopped in front of her, she forced her eyes to look up into his.

"Stearns," he barked.

She clenched her jaw and barely was able to keep from jumping. "Yes SIR!"

"What say you take me up in your favorite AT-6."

"Yes SIR!" she said, turned on her heel and headed for TAC 991, the airplane that she remembered to be the most responsive. She did one more quick walk-around inspection of the aircraft and moments later she and the colonel were buckled in. She pressed the starter. The engine caught on the third try, vibrated, and they moved off down the taxiway.

While they waited to take off, Lacy re-ran the checklist. This was not the time to have something go wrong because of carelessness.

"Eric Larsen told me to look you up, Stearns. Seemed pretty stuck on you, if you ask me. You two got something going?"

Lacy, who had just checked the mags and was finally confident that she had forgotten nothing and the airplane was, indeed, ready for flight, felt her face go hot. She looked up from the clipboard strapped to her right knee, turned around in her seat and found he was smiling broadly at her.

Quickly she turned back and faced the instrument panel, hoping to hide the flush that had rushed to her cheeks. "Major Larsen and I barely know each other, SIR."

"OK, OK, don't get in a huff. He just told me to tell you hello."

Now Lacy was sure that, in one unguarded moment, she had thrown away her chance to fly for the WASPs. He'd wash her out for sure now. But she didn't have time to beat herself up too much because, at that moment, the tower called, "Tango Alpha Charlie Niner Niner One, you are cleared for takeoff."

"Roger," Lacy responded, recognizing her aircraft's call letters.

She let off the brakes, pushed the throttle forward, and they were rolling down the runway, gaining momentum. She gritted her teeth and put everything she had into a flawless takeoff. When she had executed the required turn out to the left upon achieving the proper altitude, Lt. Col. Thompson began firing orders at her as quickly as she could complete the previous maneuver he requested of her.

Five spot landings, four forced landings, two power turns, four stalls — two with power on and two with power off — and several chandelles later, she completed her final landing. She knew that it wasn't a pretty ride because she had reacted too quickly to each barked command, making the flight a bit jerky at times. But she knew that, technically, it was right on the money.

Back on the ground, he gave her the wind and airspeed and told her to plot a course to Oklahoma City and give him the ETA. She got out her maps and E6-B computer. The instructor nicknamed "Square Root" had showed her how to use the Army-issue flight computer and, for that, she was eternally grateful to the young man with buck teeth and freckles and a mind worthy of MIT. That he had a crush on her hadn't hurt.

She worked out the whole problem and, a few minutes later, had ground speed, course, and ETA. Thompson returned, put down the two Cokes he was carrying, and took the sheet from her. "I'll check it with my computer."

But before he could pull his from his flight bag, she said, "Here, use mine," erased the wind vector and handed it to him.

"You use a computer?" he asked.

"Yes SIR," Lacy answered. "Do you expect me to work all this stuff out on paper?"

"You're OK, Stearns," he said, a look of frank approval crossing his broad face. He cocked his head at the two Cokes. "One's for you."

From that point on, Lacy sensed she had it made. The upcoming twin-engine AT-17 training and solo, the cross country exercises, the final Army checkride all would be tough going, but her confidence had just risen several notches.

Thanksgiving found the fifty-five remaining members of the Class of 43-W-9 a long way from home — many for the first time — and afflicted with varying degrees of homesickness. Turkey Day brought an unprecedented holiday mail call. The mailbags, scheduled for delivery on Wednesday, were delayed by fog and brought in the following morning, even though it was a holiday.

"It says Eric Larsen on the envelope." Andy handed Lacy her letter and watched her tear it open. "What's he say?"

"Don't you have mail of your own?" Lacy asked, looking at the stack of letters in Andy's hand. The girl must have half of Columbus, Ohio, writing to her, Lacy thought.

"Yes, but I'm interested in yours," Andy grinned, impishly.

"Obviously, I haven't had time to read it yet."

Andy sat down on Cin's bunk across from Lacy and waited. "Well, go on, read it."

Lacy scowled at Andy. "It's really hard to read a letter when you haven't any privacy."

"Seems to me you never have any trouble reading letters from your parents and your aunt and uncle with company around. Have you fallen for that guy, Lacy?"

"No, of course not! It's just that, well, I don't know how Cin would feel about him writing to me. Who knows, the letter may even be about her. Maybe he wants me to be a go-between and help them patch things up," Lacy said, hoping that was not the case and feeling yet another twinge of guilt.

"Yeah, right," Andy said. "You're the one who went out with him a few weeks ago. Come on, read it. Don't mind me. You can fill me in on the good parts," Andy teased and stretched out full length on the bunk, grinning, elbow bent, head resting on her hand.

Two pages of flowing script, the lines cramped together, were written on the crinkly, thin V-mail paper. He apologized for not having written sooner following their evening together. He had been ferrying planes to the Pacific theater and when he was Stateside, he had been too busy planning the next trip to think about letter writing. But he had a couple of hours before taking off for Honolulu and had been thinking of her.

He had enjoyed their dinner together and hoped they could do it again if and when he ever got back to Texas. He gave her his address and asked her to write to him. It was the last paragraph that, once again, set off the warning bells in her head.

> I understand that you are still mourning your
> husband. All I can say is, when you have come to terms
> with his death and want to get on with your life, I'd like

to see you again. I felt something when we danced. I thought you felt it too. Write to me if you have time between flights in the ATs and advanced mathematics. My spies tell me you're doing very well.

    Fondly, Eric

Spies — he must mean Brax Thompson, she thought, as she folded up the letter, stuffed it back in its envelope. Thompson had just about had time to get back and tell Eric about her checkride. That's probably what prompted him to write the letter.

"Looks to me like he said a whole lot more than you're telling me, but suit yourself," Andy said with a grin. "Come on, let's find Cin and go play some Ping Pong until dinner. I can hardly wait to see turkey, stuffing, cranberries, and pumpkin pie served on an army-issue metal tray."

The three friends left the mess hall and started back toward the barracks, discussing how to spend the rest of the afternoon. "I don't know about you two, but I need to study. I'm behind in navigation and avionics," Lacy said.

"Sleep," said Cin, "or go down to the flight line and see if there's any action."

"Write letters," was Andy's almost predictable reply.

While they were inside, the ever-present, 25-miles-per-hour wind they lived with and flew in daily had kicked up to nearly 40. The sun peeked capriciously beneath dark, building cumulus clouds in the southwest, but the muted mid-afternoon light surrounding Avenger wore an ominous cloak of dusty red. Remembering what she had learned in ground school, Lacy recognized it to be a convective storm — caused by a thunderstorm somewhere. The atmosphere wasn't oppressive, but that was some wind.

She checked the western horizon, scanning the 180 degrees from Trent Mesa to the south all the way around to due north. Now it was visible. The massive, roiling, reddish-brown cloud coming toward them out of the northwest stretched ten miles across and a mile into the sky. It hit and the gusts sent grit into their eyes, ears, noses, mouths, and hair. Lacy felt instantly dirty in spite of a shower that morning. The temperature already had dropped dramatically from an Indian summer 82 degrees at noon to 60.

"My god." Andy, standing next to Lacy, staggered from the force, turned her back, and hunched her shoulders up to her ears. Her white long-sleeved shirt billowed around her slight figure and she looked like she might blow away. "What is it?"

"Dust storm," said Lacy. "Nobody flies this afternoon. Come on!" and she led the way to their quarters at a sprint.

But at the entrance, Lacy stopped, let the others file in while she waited on the steps, then turned, curious, to face the onslaught of the sinister cloud that now enveloped Avenger Field, its buildings and grounds, its airplanes, its inhabitants. Somewhere an open door banged repeatedly in the gale. Lacy shielded her eyes with her hand and stared into the yawning visage of West Texas' fabled weather phenomenon. She shuddered. The winds of change were blowing as well. She could feel it as surely as she could feel this terrible wind.

At first Lacy found the final and most advanced of the trainers, the AT-17 and its twin engines, an absolute bewilderment. She wrote to Shorty that it lumbered down the runway and took all day to climb.

> They weren't going to let us train in them, but
> changed their minds. We are, however, the last class
> that will get twin engine transitioning before going on
> active duty. Ours is not to reason why, but we are called
> the guinea pig class. I know the twin engine time is an
> advantage, so I'll try and like it.

It was petite Andy who ran into problems with the AT-17. Her feet didn't reach the rudders. Where she had learned to compensate for her small stature in the primary and basic trainers by using pillows and her parachute to sit further forward, that ploy didn't work in the AT-17. No matter how many cushions she piled behind her, she still was a couple of inches away from making contact.

After their first day up in the advanced trainers, Lacy noticed Andy talking at length to Buddy, an instructor who had a crush on her. The next day, he had fashioned blocks for her to use on the rudder pedals of the AT-17. Sure enough — the next time Andy flew the AT-17, she had the problem licked.

Drawing on her new-found confidence forged during her checkride with Brax Thompson, Lacy waltzed through the AT-17 segment of their training. Three days after Christmas, she passed her final Army check ride in the twin-engine airplane.

Because their class had been assigned two weeks of additional instrument training after they were settled at Avenger, graduation, which should have been held before the end of the year, was rescheduled for January 11, 1944.

On January 2, the trainees of 43-9 learned that, like the two previous classes, most of them would be stationed with the Flying Training command rather than with one of the Ferrying Squadrons in the Air Transport Command. That opened a whole new set of bases to which they might be sent and some additional jobs to which they might be assigned, including further multi-engine training and target towing.

Lacy stood for several minutes in front of the posting on the bulletin board. She scanned the list for Palm Springs first as she had been hoping for a chance to attend Pursuit School and learn to fly the hot single engine, single-seater fighter planes like the P-47 and P-51. Disappointment stabbed at her stomach. No one from their class was going to pursuit training.

Instead, Lacy, Cin, Andy, Karen, even Jo, had been assigned to Mather Air Field near Sacramento where they would learn to fly the twin engine B-25 — the same airplane General Jimmy Doolittle had flown in the April 1942 bombing raid on Tokyo.

Second choice isn't so bad, Lacy thought as she headed into the mess hall.

SEVENTEEN

January 11, dawned cold and clear. As the ten a.m. ceremony approached, the winds once again mounted an assault on Avenger that whipped the flags to a frenzy and turned the fine red dust into millions of razor-like cutting edges that threatened to serrate human skin and take the paint off the cars and airplanes parked near the parade grounds.

Tradition had it that the entire WASP Corps marched down the runway in front of the parked line of AT-6s and in front of an outdoor reviewing stand to the music of a military marching band. But the West Texas weather, capricious as always, decreed the winter ceremony protocol be followed that day. Lacy and her classmates had watched every graduation since the 43-5 WASPs marched off to serve their country September 11, 1943. But like 43-8, the graduating class before them, they would have to settle for the indoor ceremonies.

Folding chairs were set up on the gymnasium floor. The class of 43-9 would have center stage, flanked by the classes that would graduate in the months ahead. At nine thirty in the morning, fifty-eight graduates — those who remained out of the one hundred three who had reported more than six months earlier — lined up at the front of the column and prepared to march in.

The Abilene High School band performed Sousa's *Indiana State Band* with gusto — forty young musicians playing horns, woodwinds and drums as the khaki and white clad lines of women pilots marched four abreast to their seats.

Jacqueline Cochran flew in the night before and delivered the commencement speech herself. Then, aided by Mrs. Deaton, she pinned silver wings on all fifty-eight. Shorty and Clara had flown down for the occasion and Lacy's mother and father, Uncle Ike and Aunt Virginia had ridden the train. Andy's mother came all the way from Ohio and Karen's father flew in from Arizona. Since no one came to see Cin graduate, Lacy's family and friends widened their circle to include her best friend when they gathered for the reception afterward.

But Lacy groaned inwardly when her mother, tall, angular, and forbidding in the black suit she usually reserved for church and funerals, asked Lucinda why her mother had not come down from Missoula. Lacy's back was turned to the two of them when she overheard the question and she immediately excused herself from Shorty and Clara and moved to Cin's side in case her mother pressed for too many personal details.

"My mother's not well, Mrs. Jernigan," Cin said. "She felt the trip would be too much for her. Missoula's a long way from here."

Her mother, much to Lacy's surprise, let it drop at that. Other than Cin's revealing outburst that night when she told Lacy about her ill-fated relationship with Eric and her mother's reaction, Lacy hadn't heard Cin mention her mother. She knew that her friend's relationship with her mother was, at best, strained. She didn't want her mother prying.

Lacy's mother, who had previously been so critical of Jacqueline Cochran and "her scheming and dreaming," appeared to be absolutely taken with the glamorous Director of Women Pilots in person and wasted no time telling Miss Cochran that, from the beginning, she had supported Lacy's decision to join the WASPs.

Since the four friends had eleven days combined leave and Permanent Change of Station time to make their way from Texas to central California, they planned to take off in Karen's yellow convertible, head west at their leisure, and do some exploring. But Lacy's mother invited all four to come home to the ranch in Two Buttes and spend a few days.

"Mother, they don't want to drive that far out of the way just to see a ranch."

"Oh, I'd love to see it," Andy said. "It will be my first look at the real west, other than Sweetwater anyway."

"It's nothing special. Looks a lot like what you've seen here in west Texas."

"That's not what you've been telling us all this time," Cin chimed in. "You told us Colorado is God's country. We want to see for ourselves."

The following day, the four of them wedged what suitcases they could into the small trunk of the Packard and shipped the remainder of their belongings to Mather Field via Railway Express. Following a tearful farewell to Dedie and the other staff and instructors they had grown close to, they headed for the little town of Two Buttes in the southeastern corner of Colorado, three hundred fifty miles away.

* * *

Lacy had to admit, her mother made her guests feel at home. Cin and Karen got Jared and Kenny's room and Andy, the small guest room off the kitchen. When the girls arrived, windblown and dirty from their journey over the pot-hole strewn, wartime roads of the Texas and Oklahoma panhandles, she had a home-cooked dinner waiting. Ration books or no, Janice put on a spread that included steaks from a prize steer they had slaughtered, hash brown potatoes from the cellar, home canned green beans, fresh baked biscuits, and her famous peach marmalade. Dinner was topped off with chocolate cake that Lacy figured had to have taken the family's sugar ration for the month of January.

Norman fell all over himself trying to impress his sister's friends, and even though Andy was three years his senior, and by now unofficially engaged to Pink, he was smitten and followed her around the entire time they were in residence.

After dinner, sitting in the living room warmed by the pot-bellied stove, Janice set the tone of the conversation. "My daughter suddenly came up with this notion to fly — right out of the blue. What about you girls? Andrea, your mother says you're practically engaged to a young pilot, but that you two have decided to wait until the war is over to get married. What makes flying so attractive to a young girl like you that you want to put off marriage?"

Lacy stiffened at the question, tried not to show her irritation at her mother. But Andy took the question in stride. "When I'm flying, I feel like I've really found myself. We have a swing in our yard back in Columbus. It must be twenty feet high. I used to climb in that swing and pump and pump and pump until I was flying as high as it would let me go. I'd put my head back, hold tight to the ropes, lean back against the pull in my arms and let my feet lead me even higher and then I'd close my eyes and soar. I knew that's what it must feel like to be in an airplane.

"I used to look out the window at school and watch the birds land on the telephone wires. I wanted to fly like those birds. But, as you probably know, there weren't many opportunities for anybody to fly back in the '30s, particularly for a teenage girl who was barely over five feet tall and looked like a Charles Atlas ninety-pound weakling."

Andy paused, looked around at her audience. Lacy watched

her intently and when Andy's eyes met hers, she smiled and gave her the imperceptible nod of approval she sensed her friend needed.

"By summer of '41, most of the boys I knew had already gone to war. For two years I listened to my father tell my older brothers 'there's going to be a war and it will be won in the sky, not in the trenches'. So when my older brother went out to learn how to fly, that did it. I told my father that if he was going to let Al take flying lessons, he could darn well let me take them as well. The CPT had stopped taking women by then, but I still persisted and my father agreed to pay the two hundred fifty dollars for me to take the course.

"I knew my first hour in the air that this was where I belonged. I could feel the wind."

"She was the aerobatics champ of our class," Cin added.

"Karen, what about you?" Janice probed.

In Lacy's opinion, Karen, used to wealth and privilege, took her affluence in stride. Other than exhibiting an expensive spendthrift tendency, which she could afford, she was quite matter of fact about it. Not the least bit snobbish, at least with her friends. Still, Lacy feared her mother had been unnecessarily impressed by the aura of Senator Richardson's power when she met him at graduation. The senator had flown into Avenger in his own plane.

"When I was a little girl, I wanted to be a ballerina in the worst way," Karen began, smiling at Mrs. Jernigan. "My mother started me taking lessons before she died. I loved it and didn't understand my dance teacher's hesitation to encourage me. I thought I wasn't good enough. My father is six feet three. My mother was five nine. I was already five feet six by the time I was ten, and, as you can see, big boned. It was obvious to everyone but me that I was going to be too tall — and probably too heavy — to be a ballerina. My teacher and my father discouraged me as gently as they could. So I turned to riding horses.

"Then, when I was a senior at the university back in the fall of '40, I needed one more Phys Ed credit to graduate. Now I could have taken modern dance. But for obvious reasons, I didn't want to. The school was offering flying lessons through the CPT and that sounded a lot more interesting than swimming and tennis. I'd been doing both all my life at the club. So I signed up and learned to fly.

"The first time I went up, I didn't want to land. I kept flying after graduation. I was about to buy my own airplane when I read about this program in a magazine. I knew I *had* to try. And here I am.

After the war's over, I'm going to be my father's personal pilot."

"And Lucinda," Janice turned to the girl who sat quietly on the sofa between Karen and Lacy. "Why do you want to fly, my dear?"

Lacy held her breath. Cin answered few direct questions about herself. Lacy knew only that she had left home upon graduation from high school and had made her own way ever since.

"Nothing nearly as romantic as these two," Cin began in a voice that told Lacy everything was OK. Lacy relaxed.

"I was working at the local five and dime during the days and waitressing at night and I was bored stiff. A guy I knew decided to learn to fly. He wanted a job as a crop duster.

"I let him talk me into taking lessons too. But I turned out to be a better pilot and he thought I was trying to show him up. He took off after some little sweetie who sold tickets at the downtown movie theater in Missoula. By then, I liked flying a whole lot better than I liked him. So I quit the five and dime and went to work, days, as a payroll/scheduling clerk-receptionist for the Missoula airfield FBO. — Sorry, Mrs. Jernigan, that means Flight Base Operator — I kept the night waitressing job."

That she fell in love with her instructor in the process was not part of her narrative, Lacy noted.

Janice leaned forward and fixed Cin with her most sincere look. "But if you were of age and had flying experience when the war started, how come you weren't in one of Miss Cochran's earlier classes?"

Lacy, who had wondered as much herself but had been afraid to ask, was surprised that her mother knew enough about the WASP program to realize that the more experienced women pilots had made up those earlier classes. Cin's baby, she now knew, was born in June 1942, three months before the original Women's Auxiliary Flying Squadron had been formed by Nancy Harkness Love, and five months before Jacqueline Cochran's 43-W-1 recruits had reported to the first women's training site in Houston. Cin could easily have been in the first or second class — or maybe even been one of the WAFS — if she had wanted to.

"I had a pretty good job in one of the war plants by then," Cin answered. "I was Rosie the Riveter for Boeing up in Seattle before I decided, on a lark, to see if Cochran would take me on. I still wonder why I did it. I was making good money manufacturing war planes and I knew I wouldn't get rich flying for Blondie the cosmetics queen.

But it seemed the right thing to do. Besides, it was the only chance I was going to have to fly those god-d. . . , sorry, hot ol' army airplanes."

Cin paused, smiled at her companions. "So, after being on my own for nearly ten years, I ended up in this girl scout camp at Avenger Field in Texas. We nicknamed it Cochran's Convent because they treated us like delinquent adolescents and locked us up at night. Even my family life wasn't that confining and my mother is the champion when it comes to imagining the worst in her daughter's behavior. And my father, when he was alive, took a belt to me first and asked questions later."

Lacy held her breath, but Janice made no comment. Cin continued.

"These three are all a good bit younger than I am and haven't seen near so much of the world. We had nothing in common, but somehow, being thrown together, we found more than bunkmates. We found friends."

Lacy smiled, relieved. Cin's story might not be what her mother expected or wanted to hear, but it was told with such forthright honesty — no apology or embellishment, just "this is who I am" — that Lacy was sure Cin rose a notch or two in her mother's estimation.

She stole a glance at her mother's face, somewhat hidden by the shadows cast by the fire in the old iron stove, and noted that she was looking at Cin if not with approval, at least acceptance. It was good, Lacy thought, for her mother to see that they were not the only mother and daughter living with some degree of discord.

EIGHTEEN

Lacy, who had spent her life in the saddle up until the last few months, wondered what it would feel like to have a live horse under her again. The morning after they arrived at the ranch, she headed out to the corral to see Dusty and get reacquainted.

The little sorrel nickered and tossed her head as Lacy approached the fence, cut up pieces of apple in her hand. Dusty snuffled her hand and took the proffered pieces of apple one by one. Then Lacy hugged the mare's neck, buried her face in the thick red gold mane and stroked her soft, velvety muzzle.

"Hi, old friend. Did you miss me? Has Norman been giving you enough exercise?"

Breath from the mare's nostrils hung suspended for an instant in the frosty air, as did Lacy's. She was glad she had slipped on her old fleece-lined jacket and earmuffs from the hooks beside the back door that led out to the barn and corral. It would be a cold day for riding. The winter wind was blowing in from the northwest and the threat of snow hung in the air. Better start soon, Lacy thought, or the snow might catch up with them before they finished their ride.

It was pushing noon, the pale winter sun — low to the south — had long since disappeared behind an ominous white-rimmed cloud and the first of the snowflakes had just begun to drift down from the slate gray sky. The twin buttes stood silent sentinels in the distance. Only the plodding of the horses' hooves broke the silence. No meadowlarks like there were in springtime to trill joyfully of another magical day. No dove to coo softly to its mate. Just winter silence in stubbled, buff and brown fields.

Karen fell in beside Lacy as they started back up the road that led to the barn and house two miles away. "Cin seems to know her way around a horse pretty well."

"Growing up in western Montana would explain that . . ."

"How about a little race? You, me and Cin."

"Daddy doesn't want us running the horses. Besides, what about Andy? She's never ridden before. Her horse would probably take off after us and she wouldn't be able to stop it."

"I don't know, she seems to be taking to horseback as readily as she takes to barrel rolls in the air."

"We can't take that kind of chance. She could get hurt," Lacy said, and realized her voice had a short edge to it when she spoke. Racing was the last thing the three of them needed to be doing.

"Just a thought. Have some fun."

"Um, hmmm," Lacy said, and watched Karen rein up her horse, turn and trot back to where Cin and Andy were riding. Moments later, Cin and Karen came trotting back up even with Lacy.

"You're on," said Cin, grinning.

"I didn't agree to a race."

"But it sounds like fun. We can't race our airplanes because they're government issue, but we can have a little horse race," Cin said.

"Daddy won't like it."

"He'll never know, Lace," Cin said. "Just a short one on the road here. What's the harm? No rattlesnake holes. I looked for them when we rode out."

"And we'll cool the horses down properly when we're done," Karen added. "Come on, Lace, just a little quarter mile race."

The memory of the Fourth of July 1936 came back to her. That summer, she and Dusty beat Evan Strong and his gelding, Jester, in the eighteen-and-under race at the Baca County fairgrounds.

"First one to pass that gate down there," Karen said, pointing at what was about a quarter of a mile away.

"You three gonna race?" Andy asked as she joined them.

"These two want to," Lacy said. "I'm not too keen on it."

"If it's me you're worried about, why don't I ride down to the finish line, dismount and hold old Trinket here so she won't take off. Then I can declare the winner."

"I don't know . . ." Lacy started.

"Oh, pooh, don't tell me you're gonna turn into a panty-waist on us," Cin scoffed. "Andy says she'll be all right. I say let's do it."

"Can you dismount OK, Andy?" Lacy asked.

"Sure," the younger girl said. "Just give me time to get in position." Andy kicked Trinket into a trot and took off down the road. Since she had not yet learned to sit a trot in a western saddle, Andy did what she had seen the riders back east do. She posted up and down in rhythm to the mare's movement.

Lacy laughed. "I guess we'll have to teach her how to sit a proper trot, right ladies?"

"Right," said Karen.

When Andy had reached the designated end of the race course, she dismounted, a little unsteadily it appeared from where the three sat, but she made it to the ground all right, grabbed the reins tight under Trinket's chin and moved the horse back away from the road. Then she looked at them and waved.

"All set?" Karen said.

"I guess," Lacy said.

"Ready, set, GO!" Cin yelled, and the three of them kicked their horses to a gallop and took off down the dirt road. Cin broke in front, Karen right behind her. Lacy realized she was a slow third. As she felt the surging muscles of the sorrel cow pony between her knees, the lust for victory she remembered from that Fourth of July race returned. She leaned forward in the saddle, low over the mare's neck. Sand and dirt flew in her face from the hooves of the two horses in front of her, but she clamped her lips shut and squinted to keep the flying debris out of her eyes.

"Come on, Dusty," she urged the game little mare through clenched teeth. Lacy knew Dusty still had a good run in her as she began to close the gap. The mare seemed to stretch out and shift into high gear and suddenly her nose was at Cin's stirrup. Then they were neck and neck until Dusty broke free carrying Lacy in front of the other two horses just as they flashed by Andy and Trinket standing at the gate. Lacy knew she had won.

She heard a shout and began reining in her gallant little steed, talking to her, praising her, patting her heaving flank. Lacy turned and stared, horrified. Karen's horse was trying to rise from the dusty road. Andy had dropped Trinket's reins and was running toward her. The stricken horse was up now, but limping badly, favoring its right foreleg. Karen was sprawled face up, dust swirling round her still form. Her hat was knocked forward, covering her face. The memory of another still form lying on the ground passed before Lacy's eyes.

Lacy dismounted in a flash and ran to her, but Andy got there first, Cin right behind her. Cin dropped beside Karen and pushed the hat back off their friend's face. In a sharp voice she said, "Karen! Karen, are you all right?"

Karen didn't move. Lacy held her breath and knelt beside Cin. "Is she breathing?"

"She got the wind knocked out of her." Cin slapped Karen's cheek. "Wake up! Wake up, Karen."

"Cin, don't," Lacy said, alarmed. She caught Cin's wrist before she could slap her again. "She may be hurt."

Karen's eyes flickered and she gasped for breath.

"Can you sit up?" Cin asked her.

"She shouldn't try moving until we're sure nothing's broken," Lacy cautioned, but Karen was already trying to rise. With great effort she lifted her shoulders and then her upper back off the ground, but then sank back in slow motion like a flower wilting in a sudden frost.

The snow was swirling around them now and beginning to stick on the road.

"Can't . . . get up." Karen shivered. "I'm cold."

Lacy wiggled out of her fleece-lined jacket, laid it over Karen's arms and chest and tucked it around her.

"Can you move your fingers and your toes?" Lacy asked. Moments that seemed like eons later, the fingers of Karen's right hand appeared over the jacket collar.

"Fingers . . . OK," she said. "Can't tell about the toes. It feels like they're moving inside my boots. My head hurts though and so does my back when I try to move."

"You may have a concussion and you've done something to your back," Lacy said. "You need a doctor. I don't think you should try to move any more." She looked up at the grave faces of the other two. "You stay here with her and keep her warm. Don't let her try to get up and don't let her go to sleep. I'm going to ride to the ranch house and call Doc Barrows."

She said nothing about how long it might take her to reach him by phone, depending on if he was out and where, and also how long it might take him to get here.

"What about the snow?" Andy asked. "It looks like it's coming down pretty hard."

"One of you sit on either side of her. Here, I've got some cover for you." Lacy went to Dusty, standing with her head down, reins dragging the dirt. She untied a slicker that was always kept rolled up and tied to the back of her saddle, a precautionary measure she learned early because weather had a way of coming up fast out on the high plains. "Make a tent out of this over your heads. Between that and your jackets, you should stay warm until I can get back with the truck. Whatever you do — Cin, you know this and Andy, you need to know — don't wander off for any reason. That's the fastest way to get lost in a snowstorm. You're on the road. That's the next best place to be if you can't be inside. Daddy and the doc and I will be back on this same road."

"You don't have a jacket," Andy called out to her.

"But I'm going to be moving, and fast. I'll be back before you know it."

Lacy climbed up on Dusty and took off down the road at a gallop. Two of the horses tried to follow — Pal, Karen's stricken mount, and Cin's horse, Pardner. Pal, after two halting steps, stopped and whinnied mournfully after them. Pardner stopped as well and returned to stand by Pal. Trinket stood her ground.

Lacy made a mental note to herself to bring a rifle back with her. She was sure Pal's leg was broken.

The snow swirled harder, stinging her face and making her shiver with only a sweatshirt over her denim work shirt. She leaned low over the mare to break as much of the wind as possible, pulled her hat down low over her eyes, and squinted as she rode down the road as fast as she dared let Dusty run.

She may have appeared outwardly calm to her friends waiting back there on the deserted road, but they had no way of knowing the inner turmoil that was tearing at her. The past had come galloping back to haunt her on the sure, steady hoof beats of chance, and she tried to shake the eerie feeling of disaster as she rode.

The years and the seasons fell away and she was fourteen, not twenty-three, and she and Ginny had gone for a ride. It was late summer, that golden time right before school was due to start, and the two cousins wanted to get in one more full day's ride together before returning to a stuffy, cooped up classroom. It was before Dusty. Lacy was riding Lochinvar, the bay gelding that had been hers since she was old enough to feed, water and groom him. Ginny was riding Silk, the young mare Ike had bought for her last birthday.

They were coming back just before dinner. The shadows were getting longer, but there was still plenty of light. They decided to have one more good gallop before walking the horses dry. Ginny removed her hat and took off with a whoop, her long blonde hair flying loose. She often told Lacy she loved the feel of the wind in her hair. Lacy and Lochinvar raced after her.

Without warning, Silk reared and lost her footing, crashing sideways to the ground. Unseated, Ginny landed on her head and shoulders. It had been nine long years ago but Lacy had never erased that frozen tableau from her mind nor forgotten the sequence leading up. It played over and over in her mind, in slow motion, right up to the point of impact when time stopped.

Ginny didn't move. Silk scrambled to her feet, loped off, then stopped. Lacy was off Lochinvar in a flash and ran toward her cousin. Twenty feet away, she saw the cause of the horse's erratic behavior. A large rattlesnake was coiled and poised, ready to strike. Lacy was afraid to get any closer to her very still cousin with the agitated rattler that near by. Slowly, she backed away until she stood by the trembling Lochinvar.

In a scabbard slung on the saddle was a Winchester bolt action 22 rifle that her father had given her for her twelfth birthday. He had taught her how to shoot and, an apt pupil, she was now a crack shot. He called her his little Annie Oakley. In the depths of the Great Depression in 1934, her dad had trusted her to bring home an occasional rabbit for the family larder. Plus, it was always good to have a gun along because of rattlesnakes.

Carefully, she withdrew the rifle from the leather. As always, it was loaded with a five-shot clip. She slid the bolt open and then closed it, seating the first round in the chamber.

"Easy, Lochinvar, easy boy," she spoke softly to the horse who knew the snake was there. "Don't leave me, boy," she said, as, making no sudden movements, she led the horse several yards away. Then, with the rifle held ready in her hands, she walked slowly and deliberately back to within a few feet of her cousin.

Still no sign of life. Maybe that was good. If Ginny had stirred she might have further agitated the snake.

Methodically, Lacy raised the rifle, pushed the butt securely against the meat of her right shoulder and laid her right cheek along the sleek polished wood of the stock. She closed her left eye and, with her right, sighted down the gun barrel, her single eye meeting the snake's glinting eyes in the cross hairs. Then ever so gently, so as not to move the weapon off its target, she squeezed off the first shot and blew away the rattler's head.

Three more times she opened and closed the bolt in smooth, swift movements and fired, only now, for each well aimed shot, she lowered the barrel a fraction in order to aim at the bulk of the serpent's coiled body. It was over in a matter of seconds.

The reptile bucked and jerked as the bullets found their mark, but it did not strike out and the rattle died away as surely as did the four gunshots that echoed in the emptiness of the landscape around them.

Lacy took her cheek away from the stock and surveyed the damage she had done. Surely the snake was dead. It didn't move. But, just in case, she walked as close as she dared and put the final bullet from the clip into the snake's thick neck.

When she looked up, Silk was running hell bent for leather back to the barn. Good, Lacy thought. That plus the gun shots will bring them running.

Steady Lochinvar had not moved from where she left him. Now she called to him and he trotted toward her. She stored the spent rifle back in its scabbard and then went to her cousin, whose head, she now noted, lay at a very strange angle.

"Ginny?"

There was no answer.

Lacy sank down in the dust beside her cousin's still form to wait for help to come. She hoped wherever Ginny was, she could feel the wind in her hair.

The sight of the ranch house through the swirling snow brought Lacy back out of her reverie. She shook her head to brush away the cobwebs and was once again in 1944, the present.

She slowed Dusty to a trot as she turned into the yard. Her father was already out the back door and striding toward her. She knew he had seen her coming alone, riding hard, and sensed something was wrong — just as he had that day when Ginny's riderless horse galloped into the yard.

That time, when the horse appeared, he was already saddling his own horse to ride out and investigate the series of five gun shots that had brought him out of the barn. This time, Lacy thought, seeing his daughter riding alone through a snow storm, without her fleece-lined jacket, must have moved him to action once again.

As Lacy dismounted, she realized her cheeks were cold and wet. She brushed the tears and snow away with her hand and turned to tell him what had happened.

NINETEEN

Doc Barrows probed and prodded Karen's body and, having asked her to test all her moving parts, determined that nothing vital was broken. He was sure she had sprained her back, and he advised them that she would need to be watched for signs of concussion.

"You're not going to be flying airplanes for a while," he told her after learning where she and her three friends were bound.

Lacy winced when she heard that. In three days, they planned to head west. Their orders were to report to Mather Field outside Sacramento by fourteen hundred hours on January 22. Karen was not going to make that deadline.

Using a makeshift stretcher, Doc Barrows, with the help of Jared, Norman, Lacy, Cin and Andy, loaded Karen into the back of his pickup truck. She was wrapped in layers of blankets and quilts.

Lacy's father drove, with Andy and Cin riding up front with him, while Lacy and Doc Barrows stayed in the back with Karen, trying to keep her as warm and comfortable as possible. Norman, riding Trinket, led Pardner home. Just as Lacy had suspected, they had to put Pal down. His right foreleg was broken.

The snow, now several inches deep and falling even faster, made for rough going. They drove barely more than five miles per hour the two miles back to the ranch house.

After consultation by phone with the nearest hospital in La Junta, more than one hundred miles away, Doc Barrows decided to keep Karen bedded down at the Jernigan's until the following morning when the storm would have blown off east and an ambulance, or at least a more suitable vehicle than an open pickup truck, could be brought in to transport her to the hospital. Then a phone call was put through to Karen's father in Arizona. He vetoed La Junta and said that he would charter an airplane and fly into Shorty's airfield in Lamar — as soon as the weather cleared and he could land — and airlift his daughter back to the hospital in Phoenix.

Either way, Karen — who was in considerable pain — was going to have to spend the night at the Jernigan's. Doc Barrows gave Janice instructions to wake her every hour during the night and to call him if a problem arose. He'd check up on her in the morning.

Lacy's mother immediately became the nurse in charge and shooed everyone else out of the bedroom while she tended to her patient.

"I think the girl will have first rate care right here with Janice until her father can come get her," Doc Barrows told Jared and Lacy before heading back out into the storm.

In an effort to keep her quiet, Janice had planned on only allowing one of the girls at a time to visit with Karen, but Lacy prevailed upon her mother to give them some time to revamp their plans. After all, Karen owned the transportation the four of them planned to use to get to California. Mrs. Jernigan relented after dinner and let them all go in — but only for ten minutes.

"Looks like my flying B-25s is going to be delayed a bit," Karen said. "But I want you three to take the car and head for Sacramento. Keep it there for me until I get better and can come join you."

She remained adamant through their protests. "Since Daddy's coming to get me in an airplane, you girls might as well use it and enjoy it. Besides, how else are you going to get to California at this late date? Don't worry, I'll be back to pick it up. Maybe they'll let me learn to fly B-25s with the next class."

Lacy felt keen disappointment for Karen. She wondered what Cochran would do about a disabled pilot. Would Karen be allowed to pick up where she left off, or was her training destined to be in vain? Would she be assigned somewhere when her back was healed?

The next day, Senator Richardson, his aide, and an ambulance arrived over the freshly cleared roads. They were greeted by the classic Colorado sunshine and clear blue sky that follows storms off the mountains. The melt had already begun.

That night, after he and Karen had gone, the three friends sat around the pot bellied stove with Lacy's family and contemplated what had happened.

Lacy thought the upheaval of the two days, plus the emotional wrench of having to shoot one of his favorite horses, had left her father looking unusually tired. He was showing his age.

Janice lost no time expressing her displeasure with her daughter and her friends. "You're all grown women. Responsible women, supposedly. Miss Cochran and the Army let you fly their airplanes. You'd think you'd have better sense!"

Cin cleared her throat. "Mrs. Jernigan, it wasn't Lacy's fault.

She tried to talk us out of it. It was Karen's idea to race and I joined in. Lacy told us her father didn't want us racing his horses. Karen and I pushed her. Karen wants to pay Mr. Jernigan for the horse. Right, Mr. Jernigan?"

Jared nodded, but said, "Pal was old. He was only of use as an occasional saddle horse. It's no great loss to the ranch." And he added, with just a glimmer of a twinkle in his eye, "I understand that Dusty and my daughter came away with the win. There was a time Pal could've held his own. He was fast as the dickens in his younger days." And with that, he rose, stretched, and said, "It's been a long day. I'm turning in. Janny, you 'bout ready?"

Lacy realized she had never heard her father say anything like that to her mother. He was trying to get Lacy's mother out of the room so the three girls could regroup.

They stayed up late that night, talking and staring into the orange glow of the fire in the stove, visible because they left the door open for the extra warmth on a very cold night. Lacy still was plagued by an uneasy feeling of impending disaster, which made no sense in lieu of what had just happened. The three concurred that they would leave in two days, giving them five days to drive to California.

Alone in her room that night, Lacy opened a letter from Eric that had been forwarded from Avenger and had come in the morning mail. By this time she had received several letters from him — none of which came near the intimacy that he had implied in the first one, to her relief, but still, preferring to read it in private, she had tucked it away for later. It was dated January 9.

> In a couple of days you will have your wings. I know how proud you are and I, more than most, appreciate the effort that went into it. Please accept my congratulations and pass the same on, in turn, to Andy, Karen, Lucinda, and the rest of your class. I have occasion to meet up with several of the women ferry pilots now stationed here in Long Beach. They are a dedicated, hard-working crew of truly excellent pilots.
>
> Scuttlebutt out here is that a bill will be put before Congress soon to militarize the WASPs. Are you and the other girls aware of this? Sounds like this is something Cochran may have been angling for all along. How do you feel about actually being part of

the armed forces rather than a civilian volunteer?

I hear you are assigned to Mather. I have to be up there next month and look forward to seeing you. I'd like to take you out to dinner again. I'll call ahead when I know I'm coming.

The rest of the letter went on to describe his travels, what airplanes he had ferried and where. Once again, he closed with "Fondly, Eric."

The next afternoon, Lacy was in the kitchen with her mother helping prepare the evening meal when she heard a car start down the driveway from the main road. Cars visiting the ranch this time of year were a particular rarity. She went to the front window to look out and her heart stopped. It was a military car and, in an instant, she was thrown back an entire year to the January day when the officer had brought her the telegram about John.

"No," was all she could say. "No!"

Her mother appeared by her side, took one look, screamed, wrapped her arms tight around her lank body and began to rock back and forth, gasping, as sobs tried to escape from her heaving chest. Andy and Cin came running from their rooms where they were packing.

"What's wrong?" they said in unison.

"Mom, don't," Lacy said, and put her hand to her mother's shoulder. "We don't know what he wants. He may only be lost, looking for another ranch."

But Janice wrenched away and continued to rock and sob.

Lacy opened the door and watched the uniformed man get out of his car and approach the door.

"Is this the Jared Jernigan residence?" he asked.

Lacy nodded, her hand at her mouth. She realized suddenly that she was biting the meaty part of her index finger. Consciously she lowered her hand.

"I'm from the War Department . . ." he began.

She held up her hand, palm out, as if to stop him. "I know. Which one of them is it?"

He looked puzzled. "I beg your pardon?"

"I have two brothers at war, one in Europe, one in the Pacific. Which one is it?"

The officer, a captain by his insignia, looked down at the telegram in his hand. "You are First Lt. Kenneth Jernigan's sister?"

"Yesssss," Lacy said, her breath escaping in a hiss. "Is he dead or has he been wounded?"

"Are you alone, ma'am?" the man asked.

At that moment, Janice flung the door fully open and screamed. "I'm his mother. Give me that telegram." And she snatched it from the captain's hand, clutched it to her flat bosom, turned, and stumbled to her rocking chair.

"Come in, please," Lacy said.

"Thank you, ma'am." He stamped his feet on the mat outside the door and stepped over the threshold.

"My husband was killed . . .flying. . . in England. I received a telegram a year ago right about now. We knew what kind of news you were bringing."

"I saw the gold star in the window. I'm very sorry for your loss — losses — ma'am."

Lacy turned and saw that Andy was trying to comfort her mother. Cin was standing very still, staring at the telegram in Janice's hand.

"I must go find my father. Will you excuse me, please? Cin, will you get the captain a cup of coffee to warm him up. It's very cold outside." Suddenly very cold herself, in spite of the warmth of the house, she turned, headed for the back hallway and her fleece-lined jacket and boots, and then outside to her father's domain, the barn and corral.

It was a replay of January 1943. Family and friends, each carrying a covered dish, began to arrive after the early winter darkness fell. Word spread rapidly. As friends and neighbors got home from work or in from the range, they began to gather at the Jernigan house to pay their respects to a fallen hero and comfort his mother and father.

The roles were reversed from just a year ago. This time, Lacy was in charge and her mother was the one prostrate with grief, but Lacy remembered her own numbing pain, the ache in her soul. She remembered, as if it was yesterday, her mother's voice through her closed bedroom door. "Lacy, Ike and Virginia are here. Even in time of sorrow, we must do what's right. Come out for awhile and see them."

Her mother's voice had been soft, but there was steel in it. The message beneath the words was "your family cares about you and they want to share your grief. This will be a long war and there will be others like John. Let us help you now while we can."

And it had been a long war and there had been others, and now it was her brother, Kenny, closest to her in age, only thirteen months older. Her best friend in their early childhood. The one who dared her to jump from the hay mow the day she was six when she realized that she could do anything her brothers could do. The one who sat up with her and held her hand and listened to her cry and talked to her until dawn the night after Ginny died.

Now, once again, Ike and Virginia were in the doorway and Lacy hugged them tightly as they exchanged condolences.

"There's been too much death in this family," Virginia said, her tear-reddened eyes rimming with a fresh flow. "Dear Kenny. Such a sweet boy. How's Janice taking it?"

"She's calmer now," Lacy said. "Doc Barrows gave her a sedative. She was lying down until a few minutes ago, but she's up now. You know Mother. She felt it was only proper she should see people."

"I'll go to her," Virginia said, and moved toward the rocker where Janice was seated, holding court among several women including Andy. Lacy was pleased with how attentive her friend had been to her mother ever since the telegram came. Young, seemingly inexperienced Andy, Lacy was discovering, appeared to have a knack for comforting people.

"How are you holding up, darlin'?" Uncle Ike asked her, peering into her face.

"About as well as could be expected. I keep getting these flashbacks in my mind to a year ago. Like it's happening all over again. And I guess, in a sense, it is. Just that this time it's my brother, not my husband."

"Well, you're not the same young woman you were a year ago," Ike said. "You were so fragile after the news came about John. I worried about you. Yes, Jared and Janice worried, and so did Virginia, but I sensed some deeper despair in you. For a long time, I was afraid you weren't going to come out of it. That you were going to be one of those ghost-like widows, wrecks left in the wake of wars. It happens to some women, you know. But the day you told me you wanted to fly and why, I knew you had turned the corner."

Lacy hugged her uncle. Her father's brother could always see through her. Even when she was a little girl.

"You know, I broke down once in the classroom," she said. "A couple of months after John's death. The children didn't know what to do with me. They were very kind, very sweet. They kept saying,

'Mrs. Stearns, is there something we can do?' Finally, I got control of myself and finished the story I was reading to them. Funny, it was about a girl and her horse, not about men and war and death. But it made me think of Ginny, and I was overcome with such a sense of sadness, I started to weep and just couldn't stop. . ."

Lacy shook her head. "That was when I knew I had to do something."

"And you did. You're strong, Lacy. And because of that, you're going to take some more hard knocks from life. But I know now that you'll come out OK in the end and be a better person for it. Remember that," her uncle said, and left her to go comfort his brother and his nephew, Norman.

Norman was taking his brother's death almost as hard as his mother. Due to a mastoid during infancy, he was partially deaf in one ear. He'd been turned down by the Army when he went to register for the draft on his eighteenth birthday. He was more than ready to go to war, but now he was forced to remain home and help his father on the ranch. He had talked briefly about joining a medic unit or taking some other non-combatant role, but his father and Uncle Ike had talked hard and fast to him about the economic necessity of staying on the ranch. Without him, his father might be forced to sell the land the family had owned since 1913. So Norman was fighting his own battle right now.

One by one their relatives, neighbors and friends arrived. Lacy continued to greet everybody. Because of the war, many of the men were gone, so it was the women and the older men who came. Some of the women held her hand and implored her to be strong — again. Others hugged her quickly and then moved away and kept their distance, as if getting too close or touching for too long might render what ailed her and her family catching.

"We know how much you loved him," her mother's sister, Aunt Allie, said. "You two were so close growing up."

"We saw the car go by out on the highway," Susanna Parker, from the next ranch over, said. "Frank was out mending the fence on the south pasture and I was helping him. We knew it was bad news. Just didn't know whose."

"I tried to call the War Department to find out more," Lacy heard her father telling Ike, "but because of the time difference between here and Washington, and it being Saturday, it was too late. The officer who delivered the news was able to tell us that several Allied units attacked the Gustav Line between Naples and Rome a few nights ago. Kenny's unit was one of them. But that's all they know so far."

It was after eleven when Lacy turned out the light. She and Cin and Andy planned to leave as early as possible the next morning, but Lacy lay awake for a long time after that. She dreaded the scene she knew was coming with her mother when she announced that she was, in fact, going.

"You can't leave! Your brother's dead. You can't walk out and leave me now." Janice was up early making breakfast biscuits when Lacy and her two friends, followed by Norman and her father, began to wander into the kitchen in search of a cup of wake-up coffee.

"Mother, you have Daddy, you have Norman, you have Uncle Ike and Aunt Virginia and you have Aunt Allie. There's nothing I can do here that they can't do."

"A daughter's place is by her mother's side in her time of need," Janice said, anguish creeping into the last few words.

"But I have an obligation to fulfill. The Army has just spent six months training me to do a job. I can't back out now."

"You're not part of the military," her mother snorted. "You don't have a commission, even though you've certainly been all high and mighty about the possibility of getting one. I read what you signed. I talked to Miss Cochran. You're a civilian volunteer. You're free to resign whenever you want to."

"That's not the point, Mother. I'm honor bound to do the job I was trained for, for as long as they need me. It's my duty."

"This job is more important than your family, than your mother, than her grief?"

Lacy took a deep breath. Her father was looking at the floor. Norman was looking at her, his mouth open. Cin and Andy had slowly risen from their chairs at the breakfast table and were making their way, quietly, out of the room.

"Mother, it doesn't mean I love you less, or, God forbid, that I love Kenny any less. But I'm fighting the same war he died fighting in. I gave my word. I'm needed — thank God, I'm needed because I don't know what I would have done with myself all this time if I wasn't. I have an obligation to go. I want to go."

"You're needed here." Janice was grim faced, her ever-present handkerchief pressed to her lips.

"Not really, Mother. For a day or two, maybe. Until you get

over the shock and begin to feel better, physically if not mentally. But that will happen whether I'm here or not. Believe me, I know. You remember how it was with John. It was a couple of months before we had the memorial service. I'll come back for Kenny's. The Army will give me leave. But if I don't report for duty now, I won't have a job. They'll give my slot to someone else and I will have lost my chance to do something to help win this war that has taken both John and Kenny from us."

"Jared, talk some sense into her," Janice cried.

Lacy saw her father's face when he looked up. She was shocked to realize he was an old man. He had just lost his middle son and he was devastated, but all the attention had been focused on his wife, the boy's mother. Lacy's heart went out to him.

"Daddy?" she appealed to him, feeling and sounding very much like the little girl she was a long time ago, pleading with her father to be allowed to do something her mother had forbidden her to do — had once again failed to understand the importance of. But Lacy always won. Her father always backed her.

He sighed, but would not look up. "Your mother says she needs you. You should honor her wishes. Stay home, girl."

Lacy couldn't believe her ears. She searched her father's face, and when he finally looked up at her and met her gaze, he wore a mask she had never seen before.

Janice sobbed, more softly now. She had won.

The big man rose slowly, as if it hurt him to do so, Lacy thought, moved to his wife's side and put his arm around her heaving shoulders.

"No," Lacy heard herself saying. "No, I can't do that. My honor and integrity are at stake. You brought me up to be true to my word. I believe, when you think about it later — when things are clearer — you will understand that I have to do this."

As she stored her bag in the trunk of Karen's automobile and climbed into the front seat, Lacy wanted very badly to talk to Uncle Ike. She needed his blessing, or at least to make him understand. But there wasn't time. It was time to go. What was it he had said to her the night before? Something about taking knocks because she was strong. Well, she had been strong and she had taken one helluva knock, and now there was no one on the porch to wave goodbye to her.

As Cin started the car, Lacy looked back one more time. She caught a glimpse of Norman standing in the barn door. Slowly, he raised his right arm and broke off a perfect salute.

"Stop the car, Cin," she said. Cin braked.

Lacy leaped out and ran to her brother. He met her with open arms and she hugged him fiercely, fighting to keep the tears back.

"Oh, Norman." She looked at the tall, lanky eighteen-year-old boy who had now become a man. From the looks of his red-rimmed blue eyes — so like their mother's — he, too, had been fighting back tears. His hat covered all but one lock of dark brown hair. Lacy recognized, for the first time, that as Norman had matured, he had turned into the image of their mother.

"Fly those airplanes, Sis, and help give Jerry and ol' Tojo hell. You can do it. You and Jared do it for Kenny. And for John. And do it for me, too." His voice caught and Lacy saw his Adam's apple bob as he swallowed hard.

"I love you, Norman. Take care of Mother and Daddy."

"I will."

Lacy turned and ran back to the car, got in, and this time did not look back.

Just after nine, Sunday morning, January 16, 1944, Lacy and her two friends began the rest of their journey to B-25 school and their real entry into the fight to win World War II.

TWENTY

"I can't wait to get my hands on the controls of one of those big airplanes," Lacy said at breakfast their first morning at Mather.

"Piece of cake," Jo Bertelli said. "My boyfriend says the difference between the trainers we've been flying and the B-25 is only in the wingspan and the distance you have to climb up through a small trap door to get to the cockpit. You don't notice it once you're inside and at the controls."

"Which boyfriend is that, Bertelli?" Cin asked. "The one who flunked out of flight training or the one who went AWOL and ended up in the stockade?"

"The one who's flying B-25s overseas right now. At least I've got men interested in me. I haven't seen you going out on a lot of dates, Stinson. If it wasn't for Andy, here, you'd be a total wall flower. You and Stearns both."

"Ease up on Lacy," Cin growled. "She's still in mourning."

"Cin, don't . . ." Lacy started, but Jo interrupted.

"The guy's been gone a year now, Stearns. What are you waiting for, an invitation to the nunnery?"

"Who's ready to go fly airplanes?" Andy said, pushing back her chair and standing up. "By my watch, it's o-seven-hundred and we're due on the flight line in half an hour."

The WASPS considered Mather Field almost palatial after the rigors of living at Avenger Field. Each girl had a room of her own. Lacy's room was on the first floor of the BOQ, midway down the hall from the lounge. It was big enough for a cot and a desk with a lamp on it and even an extra chair. The windows had no curtains, but there was a quick flurry of purchases from the PX and now material had been fashioned into window coverings of a sort.

They had only been at Mather two weeks when Lacy heard from Eric. He was flying in the following day and wanted to take her to dinner in town. She chose not to tell anyone who she was going out with. "A friend from home — actually a friend of my brother's," she lied. "He's only in town tonight."

Dinner was in a steak house a block off the main drag. Red and white checkered tablecloths made the place look more like an Italian restaurant than a Kansas City-style steak house in downtown Sacramento. One red globe wrapped in fish netting with a white candle inside graced each table. A bottle of Cabernet Sauvignon from Beringer's winery in nearby Napa Valley stood on the table between them.

"How's the B-25 instruction going?" Eric had set the tone for the evening early by discussing his various ferrying assignments. If she hadn't re-read his Thanksgiving letter a dozen times, Lacy would have thought she had made the whole thing up in her mind. He made no mention of the feelings he had practically come right out and admitted on paper.

Then, after the waiter had cleared their plates, served them coffee and disappeared, Eric reached across the table and took her right hand in both of his. "Lacy, I've got something to say and I want to say it without you interrupting me. OK?"

She nodded. She was sure she couldn't have said anything if he had asked her to.

He began slowly and picked his way, carefully, like a rifle squad traversing a mine field. "When I first saw you with Cin at that party in Abilene five months ago — seems like a lifetime ago — I wanted you." He dropped his head, embarrassed. "No, that's not what I mean. Well, yes it is, but what I mean is, I knew instantly that I wanted to know you. Everything about you. I was almost jealous when I saw you dancing with those oafs there."

"Eric . . ."

"No, please, you promised to hear me out." He grinned. "I had to figure out a way to meet you. I was going to cut in but then you walked off the dance floor leaving that guy staring after you. By the way, what did he say to you?"

Lacy gave a tight little laugh. "He suggested that two old married folks — one widowed and the other several hundred miles from his wife — should go somewhere and . . . help ease each other's loneliness."

"Oh shit. Pardon me, that slipped out. What a rat."

"Yes, that's what I thought. So I left him standing on the dance floor." Lacy reached for her nearly empty wine glass and drank the last of the dark red liquid.

"Well, there you were with Cin. I didn't want to come up and rub her nose in it, but I had to meet you. From the look on your face when you walked off the dance floor, I was afraid you were going to leave the party. That's when I came over to your table."

He stopped short, embarrassed.

Lacy, still holding her wine glass, looked at him wide-eyed.

"Ah, damn it, Lacy, I'm to the point now that when I know what I want, I'm inclined to go after it."

Lacy felt breathless suddenly, her mind dancing between doubt and want and uncertainty and caution. Carefully, she put her wine glass down as Eric plunged on.

"I'm in love with you." He shook his head as if he couldn't quite believe it. "God, here we are, in the middle of a war, with all its crazy uncertainty — I thought I had steeled myself against that happening." He paused. "Did Lucinda tell you that we once planned to get married?"

"Yes. She also told me she was pregnant."

A look of pain swept across his face. "Cin and I were friends, Lacy. Good friends. But that was all."

"All! Eric, what kind of fool do you take me for?"

"No, listen to me. I taught her how to fly and we had a good time together. We liked each other. But it wasn't *that* kind of relationship until one night when we'd both had too much to drink and we slipped. We made each other feel good. After that, we became lovers for a short time, but it wasn't love we felt. It was lust or need or maybe just plain old loneliness. She'd had a hard home life and I had pretty much told my father to get lost. We both needed someone. We were good for each other at that point in our lives. But we never, neither one of us, intended for it to go as far as it did."

"She was pregnant!" Lacy cried, louder than she intended. Then she repeated it again, only more softly but with great intensity. "She was pregnant, Eric! With your child."

"Yes, and after she told me, we decided to get married. You know Lucinda. She's impulsive. If she thinks something will work, she's game to try it and she doesn't stop and think through all the possible consequences. That's one of the things that drew me to her, and probably drew you to her, too. I certainly was willing. But before we could do it, Pearl Harbor came. I was called up and sent away — for all practical purposes under lock and key.

"I telephoned her. Promised we'd get married just as soon as I could get a three-day pass. She didn't believe me. She thought I was making up the quarantine just to get out of marrying her. I have to admit that, in spite of everything, we both knew it wasn't love that

121

drew us together. But I was willing to try to make a go of it — and she was carrying my baby."

"Eric . . ." Lacy started to speak, but he held up his hand.

"No, please, let me finish." He took a deep breath. "I can't tell you what the thought of being a father did for me. Suddenly, it made all the stupid things my father did, and that I resented so much, not seem so stupid anymore. I never expected to feel that way. The thought changed my whole outlook on life. In a matter of days I went from relishing this war like a holy warrior to resenting the hell out of it for interfering with my getting on with my life as I now saw it.

"Then Lucinda called and told me she was going to have an abortion. I begged her not to. To wait. It was only going to be a couple of weeks. I wonder what I might have done or said that would have changed her mind. But she got tired of waiting, told me to get lost, that she never wanted to see me again and, before it was too late — her words — opted for the abortion. She left, ran away, without saying goodbye."

Lacy reached across the table and laid her hand on his forearm. "You don't have to tell me this, Eric. Cin's already told me."

"I want you to hear *my* side. It really rocked me. I went on a three-day drunk. Couldn't fly for a week. They wouldn't let me. Nearly got myself permanently grounded and kicked out of the Ferry Command. Fortunately for me, they needed experienced pilots to train the new guys coming in — needed me so desperately they bent the rules and kept me. But they sent me to Hawaii where I couldn't get out overnight and go see — as my CO so graphically put it — 'that bitch who had caused me all my problems'.

"I came out of that week of hell with my armor on again, ready to go out and do battle or whatever the hell the Army Air Corps had planned for me. And that's what I've been doing ever since. I went back to Missoula looking for her several months later — August of '42, after I was reassigned Stateside. I went to see her witch of a mother. She didn't know where Lucinda was either. I didn't see her again until I walked into the party in Abilene a year later."

"Eric, I think she did love you. I think she still does."

He shook his head. "No. But because you think that, you want nothing to do with me. Loyalty is a good thing, Lacy, but in this case it's only going to ruin one more life than Lucinda and I have already ruined."

"You are so full of it I could scream," Lacy hissed from between clenched teeth. "You're so full of what *you* want and *you* need. You think you can make everything right just by waving your hand. I'll bet what you're telling me you feel for me now is exactly what you felt for her when you climbed into bed with her for the first time."

"Lacy." His voice had gone very quiet. "I never thought I could feel toward anyone the way I feel about you. I hardly know you, though I feel like I've known you my whole life. I came at you the wrong way from the beginning and, in the process, I may have spoiled any chance we have. But, if you can, try to understand. I mean it when I say I'm in love with you."

Her heart was thudding so loudly in her chest she thought surely he could hear it. "Let me tell you about love, Eric." And she told him about the last day she and John spent before he left for England a year and a half earlier. She thought she would enjoy the pain in his eyes as she described how much they had meant to each other, what they did and what they said, and how they felt, and was disappointed when no enjoyment, only more pain, came instead.

She and John had taken a picnic lunch and gone for a hike in a beautiful forest in New Hampshire the day before he and his squadron left for England. They held hands and walked a couple of miles on a carpet of thick pine needles. It was cold for a summer day and misty, so they both wore jackets and tied slickers around their waists in case it began to rain hard. Every few hundred yards they stopped and kissed and clung to each other. Then John spread their slickers out on the pine needles behind a rock encircled hideaway and they made love with the rain falling softly on them.

Now Lacy pulled herself together and told Eric of the conversation she and John had in that piney cathedral.

"While we were sitting there — afterward — eating the lunches we brought along, John said something that has forever changed my life, though I didn't know it at the time. 'If anything should happen to me, Lace, I hope you'll think about doing something for the war effort in my place.'

"'What do you mean?' I said. 'I'm going back home to teach. What could be more important than that?' By then I had lined up a teaching job in the school in my home town in Colorado. I asked him if he wanted me to go work in one of the war plants. I laughed when I said it.

"'The military needs smart civilians doing the backup work that's needed to produce this war-winning machine,' he said. 'If I couldn't fly airplanes, I swear I would've done my best to land a berth in Washington. I'm not one of these guys who needs to come home and brag about how many Germans he's killed in hand-to-hand combat. I'm interested in the mechanics and logistics of what it will take to get this war won. I'd be happy to stay behind and work on this side of the Atlantic, if that's what it takes.'"

Lacy looked at Eric, his eyes intent on hers.

"My heart sank. Here, all along, I thought he really wanted to go abroad and fight. Turns out, he would have been satisfied doing what you're doing. What I'm doing. What all the people stateside are doing.

"'Why did you wait 'til now to tell me that?' I asked him. It's like he knew he wasn't coming back. And, the next morning, he got into the cockpit of that B-24 and flew away from me forever. He was so good, too good to die, but he died anyway."

"Lacy. . ." Eric tried to speak, but she waved him to silence.

"I thought about it. I thought about it a long time while I cried and when I quit crying I did something about it. I did what he asked, and what difference has it made? I miss him terribly. I'm twenty- four years old and I don't know if I can ever love like that again."

"I'll take you back to base now," he said quietly.

The sentries passed him through the gate with one glance at the sticker on the car he had borrowed from the base CO. In front of the BOQ, Lacy started to get out but he reached over and took her hand. "Wait." And she did. "I can't compete with a dead man, Lacy, because I'm still making mistakes and will go on making more of them. He can't make any now. He's set in your mind forever. And I understand your love for him. I can deal with that. But you're alive. He's been gone a year now and you have a life in front of you. If you've mentally climbed into that coffin with him, then you might as well climb in physically as well and be done with it. But that would be a real loss.

"I love you and I am alive — a real flesh and blood man. Give me a chance to prove that love, Lacy. Let me in. You won't be disloyal, you'll be human."

Lacy felt the pressure of his hand, the warmth of his whole body seemed to fill up the car. She knew she wanted him.

"I'll try," she said simply, then leaned toward him and kissed him lightly on the lips. "Give me time, but give me another chance."

As he tried to draw her closer and deepen the kiss, she pulled away, got out of the car and ran inside, shutting the door behind her.

TWENTY-ONE

"Eric was here last night. You went out with him."

Lacy was washing her hands at a sink in the latrine when Cin came in from the morning's flying and confronted her. Lacy looked up, startled, and her gray eyes met Cin's blazing brown ones in the small mirror. "Yes."

"Why didn't you tell me instead of making up that story about a friend of your brother's?"

"Who told you? Who found out?"

"Bertelli. She was coming home from the canteen just before ten o'clock and she saw you sitting in the staff car with him out front. She said you two were kissing and then you jumped out of the car like a snake had bit you. She was pretty sure you didn't see her."

A little piece of Lacy's soul wilted under her friend's accusing glare. "No, I didn't see her. And I had enough on my mind without having to contend with her." She paused and took a breath. "It wasn't you I was keeping it from so much as the others. After all the snide remarks Bertelli's been making, I didn't want the whole place buzzing with 'Lacy's going out with that Larsen guy. Takin' pity on the old widow woman.' You know how they all are. And, well, yes, I admit it, I was uncomfortable with telling you because . . ." she halted.

"Because of my past relationship with him."

"Yes. And I tried to tell him that, too."

"What did he say?"

"He told me the same thing you did, that it was over between you two a long time ago." Lacy paused. "I told him I knew about your pregnancy."

"You didn't tell him about Ashleigh, did you?" A mix of fear and anger flashed in Cin's eyes and was present in her voice.

"No, of course not! Just that I knew you had been pregnant. Then I let him tell me his side of it."

"You mean how the precious army know-it-alls wouldn't even let him have a weekend pass so that we could get married."

"He says he asked you to wait, but that you refused and ran

125

away without even saying goodbye."

"So now you know the whole story, both sides of it."

"I guess so, unless there's more you want to tell me."

Cin shook her head. "Are you going to see him again?"

Lacy looked at her friend for several seconds. "Yes, I'm going to see him again."

"When?"

"I don't know. He didn't say when he'd be back. I don't think he knows from day to day where he'll be."

"He's wearing you down, isn't he?"

"What do you mean by that?"

"At first, you wanted nothing to do with him. Now you've gone out with him twice — at least twice that I know about. Have there been other times, Lacy?"

"You know where I've been every minute of the day and night for the last seven months. What do you think?"

"But you are going to see him again?"

"Yes, I'm going to see him again — *if* he calls after the way I treated him." Lacy sighed. "Cin, I loved a man with all my heart and lost him. He filled up my life and I'm just beginning to get used to the fact that he's never coming back. I've held everything inside for so long. I've drowned myself in my work — first teaching, then learning to fly, then getting my wings, and now learning to fly these bloody bombers that are dropping even more death all over Europe and the Pacific."

Lacy took a deep breath. "I'm tired. Eric is attractive, articulate, intelligent. Pretty rare combination in a man, I've discovered. He's interested in me — enough that he keeps coming back even though I've done nothing to encourage him. Nothing! Just the opposite in fact."

"Sure!" Cin snorted.

Lacy ignored that and continued. "Last night he told me that he couldn't compete with a dead man. He accused me of climbing into the coffin with John. But that's not really true. Half of me still feels like it died with John, but I've begun to realize that the other half of me is all too alive, too human — too physical. I never thought I'd look at another man other than John. But he's gone."

She paused. Took a deep breath. "Yes, I am terribly attracted to Eric — physically and personally — and that frightens me. Up until now it frightened me enough to want to stay clear of him."

"But you said you'd see him again."

"That's right. Guess I'm not nunnery material — contrary to Bertelli's opinion. Recently, I've begun to allow myself to think about what it might be like *not* to spend the rest of my life alone. After John died, I figured that would be my fate. I couldn't see beyond it, until now. Eric has opened my eyes to that."

She stopped. Cin was staring at her. "What are you saying?"

"Cin, you told me at the beginning that Eric meant nothing to you anymore. Have you changed your mind? You must tell me now. Do you want me to break it off with him before it goes any further? Do you want him back? Because if you do, now's the time to tell me while I can still walk away from him. If I see him one more time, I may not be capable of doing that. But I must know now."

"Jo says you were all over each other last night."

"That's not true. I kissed him, yes. Once. It was a spur of the moment thing. Just before I got out of the car." Lacy didn't like reliving the previous night with Cin. It was none of her business. But the guilt of not being totally up front with her best friend about going out with Eric hung over her like a pall.

"But you liked it." It was a statement, not a question.

"It didn't last long enough for me to think about it," Lacy lied.

"He wouldn't come back to me even if I did want him." The bitterness in Cin's voice was obvious. "I lost him when I told him I was going to have the abortion."

"No, I think you lost him when you walked out on him and left him no alternative. He thought you didn't care." Lacy almost blurted out what Eric had said about fatherhood, but she thought better of it. It could only hurt Cin more.

Cin turned on her heel and ran out of bathroom. Lacy didn't follow but stood looking in the tiny shaving mirror over the sink — a mute reminder that these had been quarters for men and would, someday, be quarters for men again and that they, the women of the WASP who were living here now, were merely transients, interlopers, aliens in a male culture they didn't understand, never would understand — and maybe didn't want to.

She stared at her image, not sure who was staring back at her.

That night at dinner, Cin sat at a different table. Instead of joining Lacy and Andy and their regular group, she sat down with Jo and a group of 43-8s and struck up a conversation.

After dinner, Colonel Wilkins stood, cleared his throat and made an announcement that would affect the lives of all thirty-two WASPs currently stationed at Sacramento. The eighteen women from 43-8 would complete their training the following week and the training of the 43-9s was being shortened on orders from Washington. They would be finished in three weeks rather than five and be sent on to postings where they were sorely needed. New assignments for 43-8 would be posted tomorrow and for 43-9 by the end of next week.

"Congratulations, good luck and God speed wherever you go from here," he said.

That raised the buzz level of conversation several notches and the thirty-two began to speculate on where they might be going next.

Lacy and Cin avoided each other the remainder of the week. Andy, obviously worried, talked to Lacy about it and Lacy did her best to explain.

"So you did go out with Eric that night. I wondered. I thought a friend of your brother's was a bit farfetched. But you should have just told her. I know Cin. She's probably more hurt by your not confiding in her."

Lacy looked at Andy. That thought had not occurred to her.

"I don't know, Andy, I asked her whether she wanted me not to see Eric again and she never answered me. I don't know what I'm going to do if he calls."

"I think you are going to have to make up your own mind about that. What Cin thinks is not the issue. She already told you she had no claims on him."

"I don't want to lose her friendship."

"What kind of friendship is built on a lie — on your giving up a guy who's interested in you and who's not interested in her? Provided you really are interested in him. You know, he's had his chances to get her back. He saw her the same night he saw you in Abilene. He could have pursued her instead of you."

"Andy, there's something you don't know about Cin and Eric." And Lacy told her the whole story — except about Cin giving birth to a daughter and letting her be adopted by another couple. That was privileged information that even Eric didn't know.

"I wondered if it wasn't something like that," Andy said when Lacy had finished.

"Anyway, she hasn't spoken to me in three days and I haven't tried to make up with her. Maybe I should be the peacemaker and try. I don't want to lose her friendship."

"Give it a couple of days," Andy said. "Maybe she'll come

around. If she doesn't, then consider your options. Who knows, we may all be sent to different bases and never see each other again."

That, Lacy thought, was an alternative she hadn't even considered, and it was one she didn't want to consider now. Her friendship with Andy and Cin had become more important to her than she realized.

Eric called that night. What were the chances of her getting a weekend pass to go to San Francisco? Lacy froze. Suddenly, their innocent dinners for two appeared to be turning into something else. A mixture of flattery, embarrassment, and anger galloped through her blood stream as she fought the implications she heard and sought to give him an answer.

"Colonel Brax Thompson — you met him — is getting married, Sunday. He's reserved rooms at a small hotel on Nob Hill for everything — the rehearsal dinner, the ceremony, the reception. He's taken enough rooms to accommodate any guests who come. You'd have a hotel room and private bath all to yourself, Lacy. I'll bet you've forgotten what that's like."

"My own room?" she stuttered, and quickly added, as her face flushed, "my own bath?"

"All to yourself." Then, as if he sensed her original dilemma. "No strings. Surely you didn't think. . .ah, well, of course you probably did. No, I'm not suggesting that the two of us — well, you know."

He was embarrassed too. Lacy could sense it and it surprised her. He was so cool, so sure of himself. Could it be he had a sensitive side? Something professional pilots, particularly military ones, seldom had, or at least didn't show.

"I'll fly in and pick you up," he added.

"You've sold me," she said, lightly. "When should I be ready?"

"Pick you up Saturday at fifteen hundred at the airstrip. I'm flying up in a two-seater I think you'll enjoy taking a spin in."

"I'll be ready. Do I have room for a bag, though?"

"One. Your B-4, but bring something pretty to wear Saturday night for the rehearsal dinner and Sunday afternoon for the wedding and reception. I'll have you back by Sunday night."

Lacy hung up the phone, which was in the hallway just inside the door. She turned to head back to her room and saw Jo standing there looking at her.

"So the chaste and saintly widow has decided to throw off the veil and take up with the opposite sex again. Will wonders never cease?"

"And were you eavesdropping on purpose, or just by accident, like you spied on me the other night?"

"Don't flatter yourself, Stearns. You're not worth spying on. That kiss you gave that flyboy didn't rate a one on the scale of one to ten. At least you didn't get his blood moving enough to make his ride home a painful one."

"You're disgusting, Bertelli, you know that?"

"Not nearly so disgusting as a woman who would lie to her friends and try to cover up the fact that she had a real live date — with her best friend's ex-boyfriend. At least I call a spade a spade."

"Talk about lying! You told Cin we were petting up a storm in that car and if you saw anything at all, you know damn well we weren't. It was all in your nasty little imagination."

"It was such a surprise to see you in a compromising position, Stearns. Miss Holier Than Thou. I just wanted to have some fun. How was I to know you were stepping out behind your best friend's back with some guy she used to go with instead of entertaining your brother's friend like you told us you were. All I said to her was, I was surprised when I saw Miss Prim and Proper Widow Lady playing kissy face with her brother's friend who just happened to be driving the CO's staff car. Stinson is the one who came up with who it was. She was on it like a fly on flypaper.

"'No chance Lacy's brother's friend was driving the CO's car,' she said. 'Only one man could swing that.' Those were her exact words. Some flyboy she used to know, she tells me. She sure put two and two together quick enough. Guess this isn't the first time you've been out with this guy, Stearns. But she was really pissed. That's when I figured out she and handsome used to be an item."

"You've got a real mouth on you, Bertelli. Did she happen to tell you that 'used to be' are the operative words. She introduced me to him. And, though it's none of your business, she told me that they called it quits a long time ago."

"Yeah, she told me that too, Stearns. And you know what? I didn't believe her any more than you do."

TWENTY-TWO

The hotel was, as promised, atop Nob Hill, a fashionable address, old, elegant and immensely comfortable. Lacy took one look at her room and decided she was dreaming. A canopied double bed out of a Victorian novel dominated the interior. Luxurious tapestry draperies extended across an entire wall of windows and, when they were drawn back, revealed a view of the Golden Gate Bridge and Marin Headlands beyond. Since Lacy had never been to San Francisco before, she drank in the fabled view with all the enthusiasm of a novice tourist.

Her private bath, the size of the area used by twelve WASP trainees back at Avenger, was of gleaming white tile with gold fixtures and stocked with oversized, thick terry towels. Best of all, it was all hers for twenty-four hours.

The first thing she did was take a long, hot bubble bath. The girls back at Mather would be jealous. Then she dressed carefully in the best dress she had — a soft black wool that clung nicely to her body — and added the tiny diamond pendant John had given her.

Lacy looked at her hands. They had always been working hands — a rancher's daughter's hands, a teacher's hands covered with chalk, a mechanic's hands while she was in training at Avenger — never pretty and never soft. Strong hands with short blunt nails. Her third finger left hand no longer bore the shiny indentation rubbed by the plain gold band she had worn from August 14, 1940, when John put it on her finger, until she began flight training with Shorty in May, 1943.

Rings are not a good thing to wear in the cockpit of an airplane, Shorty told her. They might catch on something. But she had kept it with her, buried in a ring box deep inside her trunk at Avenger and now in her quarters at Mather Field.

Promptly at 6:30 p.m. she took the elevator down to the lobby where Eric, in full dress uniform of the Army Air Forces, was waiting to take her to the rehearsal dinner. "You look stunning," he said as he took her hands, held her at arm's length while he looked at her, then drew her close.

Lacy thought he was going to kiss her right there, but instead,

131

he folded her arm in the crook of his elbow and, still holding her hand, led her into the salon where the party was getting started.

Brax Thompson greeted her like a long lost friend. "Mrs. Stearns — or more appropriately, WASP Lacy Stearns. Maureen, friends, this is one of the stellar graduates of Dragon Lady Cochran's flight training program. I checked her out myself — this lady can fly!"

Lacy blushed and wondered if the bridegroom wasn't already in his cups this early in the evening. But those merry blue eyes were clear. The man, obviously, was enjoying himself. He was far from the pale, nervous bridegrooms she had known about all her life. But then Brax Thompson was probably close to forty years old, far older than any of the young men Lacy had seen married in the First Methodist Church of Two Buttes.

"I'm so glad Eric invited you to come," said Maureen, a slender redhead of medium height with warm brown eyes. Lacy figured her to be in her late twenties. "He talks about you all the time."

Lacy shook her extended hand and found the woman's sure grip warm and comforting. Soon, in the course of conversation, she discovered that Maureen, too, was a war widow with a four-year-old daughter who was to be the flower girl. Now Lacy began to understand even better why Eric had invited her to the wedding.

Dinner was as elegant as the Nob Hill address promised it would be and Brax had ordered wine from the best California vintner to top it off. After a series of toasts and mildly off-color jokes and allusions, the party adjourned to the hotel lounge for dancing to a trio that alternated current dance tunes with the cool jazz that was rapidly gaining popularity among the American troops stationed on the West Coast.

Hours after the festivities began, floating pleasantly on the excitement of the evening and the atmosphere of one of America's most romantic cities, Eric and Lacy finished up two cognacs in the dim cocktail lounge before strolling hand in hand back to her sixth floor room. At her door he said, "Give me your key, I'll open it for you."

Lacy handed him the room key without hesitation and he unlocked the door. When he turned and looked at her and took both of her hands in his, Eric's eyes conveyed a level of emotion that caught her breath. But his voice suddenly went formal.

"Thank you, Lacy, for coming with me. I wanted to see you again and this was the only off time I could manage. Thompson wanted me as one of his groomsmen so he had to give me a pass in order to get me here."

"I've had a wonderful time, Eric. Thank you."

"Do you think we might do this again — not on so grand a scale, of course, but spend another evening together away from Mather Field?"

Lacy laughed, and hardly recognized the throaty chuckle that came out. "I'd like that. The problem is, after the next two weeks, I don't know where I'll be. We're up for reassignment, but they haven't told us where yet."

"Any chance it might be Long Beach?"

"Well, I've asked for a chance to take Pursuit training in Palm Springs."

"So you want to fly the hot ones. Why am I not surprised?" He seemed to relax again and leaned against the doorframe. Planes were safe territory, apparently.

"Cin and Andy have asked for Pursuits as well. Right now we're just hoping to stay together, though Cin and I had a fight after you and I went to dinner the other night."

"About me?"

"About you."

"Well, you were willing to come with me this weekend, that must say something."

"Andy told me the decision was mine to make, not Cin's, whether I wanted to see you again. I thought about it, and decided she was right."

"You wanted to see me again?" He was looking intently at her.

"Yes, I wanted to see you again." She looked down.

He put his hand out and touched the side of her face, tracing his index finger down the line of her jaw until it rested under her chin. Gently he tilted her head back and Lacy found herself looking directly into those deep blue eyes.

"Lacy, I want to kiss you."

"I was hoping you would."

Eric straightened and took her in his arms. Their lips met in a surprisingly sweet, lingering kiss that telegraphed only a hint of the hunger she sensed in the rest of his body. After a moment Lacy was aware that a soft moan caught in the back of her throat and then escaped and that he heard it. With a shudder, her lips parted, ever so slightly at first, in answer to his.

Eric hesitated. Drew away. "Lacy?"

She nodded, smiled, pushed open the door, drew him inside with her. They stood in the dark behind the closed door. This time their kiss was slow but erotically deep as they let what they had avoided for so long engulf them.

Lacy was spinning, spiraling out of control like the primary trainers she had deliberately spun in order to learn how to pull out before crashing to earth. But this time she didn't pull out. She allowed herself to circle down, down until she was consumed by the fire in the physical presence that was Eric Larsen. The sensation was familiar, achingly familiar, but it had been John, always John. Until now.

Now John was melting into the distance and her whole being was filled to overflowing with Eric. She understood with perfect clarity what was happening to her — sensations she thought were dead, sensations she had successfully buried, were reawakening and over-taking her whole body, carrying her further inside herself and taking Eric in with her. So familiar. So familiar. Her heart was thundering in her ears. The wetness was there between her legs — legs she thought were going to desert her.

Now she sensed, no, felt the hunger and it was her own — a gnawing emptiness that had settled in her innermost core the morning John left for England. Here in the darkness, she knew that Eric promised to fill up her wanting.

He released her and she felt him move away. For an irrational moment, she thought he had changed his mind. Then she heard him fumbling with the lamp on the bedside table. Its muted pool of light caused shadows to climb the walls and creep around the bed covers. Then his arms encircled her once more, his fingers finding the zipper of her dress. She felt the fabric loosen and fall away as, gently, he slid if from her shoulders. His jacket, shirt and trousers joined her dress on the floor.

The sheets were cool against her back when Eric gently lowered her onto them. She reveled in the long forgotten sensations — the psychic joining, the physical coupling and the incredible fullness of becoming one — sensations she thought she would never experience again after John died. Now, they all came rolling back over a sea of longing. She let herself be carried on wave after wave after wave until they both climbed the final crest and descended the other side together.

Lacy got her first view of the Pacific Ocean the next afternoon when — after the wedding and the reception were over — she and

Eric took off in the twin engine AT-11. He flew out over the water, banked and came back over the Golden Gate bridge, giving her a birds-eye view of the Bay before taking a nine zero heading for Sacramento.

That morning, still lying in bed, they had watched the fog roll past the Marin Headlands and back out to sea. Now the fog had dissipated and the Pacific was gray in the mid-afternoon light of winter, the sun laying a slender westerly ribbon of silver across the water.

When he had the airplane trimmed, Eric reached over, took her hand and raised it to his lips. In the tight quarters of the cockpit, they could hardly have sat much closer. Lacy leaned against him, the warmth of total security washing over her.

"Now do you believe what I've been trying to tell you all these months?" he asked. "I love you, Lacy."

Lacy thought about that and the turmoil her feelings had gone through since she met Eric back in August. And she thought of Cin and how she was going to tell her.

"You're here for two more weeks," Eric was saying, still holding her hand.

"That's right."

"Well, I'll just have to find an excuse to fly up before you move on to your next duty station. Then I'll put your new posting on my preferred stops list." He paused. "I don't know how long I'll be in Long Beach, though. There's something in the wind."

That statement took Lacy's breath away momentarily. She changed the subject in order not to dwell on it and before long they had the runway at Mather Field in their sights.

Rumors were flying. All over Mather Field, and from anyone who flew in from elsewhere, something, very definitely, was in the wind. The tide of the war had turned a corner while they weren't looking. The pessimism of 1943 had turned to hard-won optimism in 1944.

A week before their B-25 training was due to be completed, the postings for 43-9 went up outside the officers' mess. Andy and Jo were being sent to Palm Springs for pursuit training. Lacy and Cin were going to Biggs Field in El Paso where they would tow targets for gunnery practice. The triumvirate was being broken up.

Eric flew in the next weekend. He didn't mention the "something in the wind" again and Lacy decided it must have been a false alarm.

Because he only had a couple of hours, they had dinner at the Officers' Club at Mather. They sat together on one side of the far booth of the dining room, their backs to the rest of the diners. There they huddled, talking in low tones, oblivious to anyone else in the place.

When Lacy got up to go to the powder room, she bumped into Cin and three newly arrived WASPs from 44-1 at a table in the bar. Cin followed Lacy into the ladies room. Lacy steeled herself for what was to come, but Cin surprised her.

"I was a real pill the other day, Lacy. I'm sorry. I won't ask you if you had a good time in San Francisco. Andy told me. Besides, it's written all over your face."

Lacy frowned. "Cin, are you sure you're all right with this — with Eric and me?" Not that there was much she could do about it now, she thought as she searched her friend's face.

Someone in one of the stalls flushed at that moment. Cin pulled Lacy out into the ante room where a big wall mirror invited the women to check their makeup and the seams in their stockings.

"I was out of line. I told you at the beginning that Eric and I were through. I was hurt when you felt you couldn't confide in me, that's all. And I let it get to me. Bertelli made it worse. She was so damn cocky. And I made the mistake of letting my feelings show. You'll be good for him, Lace. You'll be good for each other."

She followed Lacy back to the table, gave Eric a congratulatory hug, then returned to her friends in the bar.

TWENTY-THREE

It was spring in southwest Texas when Lacy, Cin and eight fellow WASPs arrived at Biggs Field.

Their job was to tow canvas target sleeves five hundred feet behind the aircraft they flew while the men on the ground fired away at them. This flying feat was performed at heart-stopping low altitude, which kept the pilot constantly on alert because at low altitude there is little room for error.

It wasn't pursuit flying like Andy and Jo were learning, but Cin and Lacy found it to be exacting work.

Lacy flew the afternoon flight from noon until dark and had to contend with the late afternoon thermals that came off the desert floor as it warmed under the spring sun.

"Damn, but they make it hard to control the airplane, especially at that low altitude," she told Cin. "Sometimes I think one of those swirls is going to come up and get me and slam me into the ground."

Cin was assigned to the night flight from dark to midnight and proved to be quite good at it because she had superior night vision.

As promised, Eric flew in at the end of the second week but could only stay overnight.

After he left Sunday afternoon, Lacy retreated to her room to get some rest. She was lounging on her cot when Cin knocked and popped her head in the door.

"You sleeping?" she asked.

"Nope, just lying here studying the cracks in the ceiling."

"Considering the amount of time you didn't spend in your own bunk last night, you ought to be sleeping."

Lacy laughed. She sat up, plumped her pillow back against the wall and leaned against it. "What's up?"

Cin sat in the one chair provided in the austere rooms, tipped it back, and propped her feet on Lacy's bunk.

Lacy looked closely at her friend, trying to gauge her mood.

"I got something in the mail yesterday I thought you might like to see."

Cin let the chair legs down to the floor, reached into her shirt pocket and pulled out a photograph. Without even looking at it she handed it over to Lacy.

It was a color tinted picture of a little girl with dark curly hair. Lacy thought her to be about two. A pair of deep blue eyes stared out at her — familiar eyes. Lacy looked more closely. Eric's eyes. She gasped. Her head jerked up and she looked at Cin. "Is this . . .?"

"That's Ashleigh, my daughter." Her voice was soft. "Eric's daughter."

"But . . ." Lacy began, then stopped.

"I know. She belongs to someone else now, but they promised to send me pictures now and then. No one knows about her but you. I had to show her off. I hope you don't mind."

"Mind! Good heavens, Cin, of course I don't mind. You have every reason to be proud, to want to show her off. Believe me, I understand. It's just that you . . ." she paused, searching for the right words. "You don't seem like the motherly type, that's all. It means looking at you in a whole new light. Takes a little getting used to." Lacy broke off, embarrassed. "She's beautiful, Cin."

"I know." Cin said it so quietly Lacy almost didn't hear her. But she did hear the catch in Cin's voice when she added, "That's what makes it so hard."

"Oh, Cin." Lacy pushed herself off her cot, knelt in front of her friend, and put her hand, tentatively, on Cin's arm. "Talk about her all you want to — to me. I won't tell anyone."

Cin shook her head, her eyes closed. "Oh, Lacy, it's all so complicated."

"Complicated because of Eric and me? Or because of Eric and you? Or because of you and your mother? Complicated how?"

"All of the above," Cin said, letting out a sigh. "No, not you and Eric now. I told you, he and I could never have survived marriage. I'm not in love with him. Don't know that I ever was. We were such good friends, it just seemed the next step. But we aren't suited. You are. You and Eric are meant to be together."

"Then what . . .?"

"I told you, I couldn't look after a child alone and my mother would never have acknowledged a grandchild born on the wrong side of the blanket. There is no love lost between me and my mother. She disowned me long ago."

"Why, Cin, or don't you want to tell me?"

"I think I'd like to tell you, Lacy, if you want to hear it."

"You already know the answer to that."

Cin nodded, took a deep breath, and began. "Spring of my senior year, I went to a dance in the next town with this boy. We had been going together, but it was nothing real serious. Hand holding, a quick kiss at the front door when he brought me home from a date. No necking. No heavy petting in the backseat of his father's Chevy. I really wasn't into that and neither was he. Anyway, we had car trouble on the way home, spent the night in the car, and got a ride into town with a farmer the next morning.

"My mother and father were very religious, even though he came home drunk many a night. She didn't believe me when I told her that nothing happened." Cin looked directly into Lacy's eyes. "Nothing did. We talked and slept in each other's arms to keep warm, but that's all." She squared her shoulders and got a defiant look in her eye.

"She called me a slut and trash."

"Oh, Cin!"

"That wasn't so bad. My dad broke my jaw."

Lacy could think of nothing to say that wasn't a useless platitude.

"I walked out. She wouldn't even let me take my clothes. I went to stay at a friend's house. A friend whose mother understood and took me in. I borrowed my friend's clothes to wear to school. But I finished the year. I graduated. They didn't show up for the ceremony.

"I also went out with Billy the next weekend and, this time, we did it. I talked him into it. Figured if I was gonna get blamed for it, I might as well get some enjoyment out of it. Neither one of us knew what we were doing. He was scared to death. So was I. Of course, there was no enjoyment — at least on my part. Just pain and shame and disappointment. But I decided that I was going to learn how to do it right, so I practiced every chance I got until I learned how to get more than I gave."

Lacy felt tears welling in her eyes as she listened to the pain in her friend's voice.

"My mother thought I was a whore. Call it a self-fulfilling prophecy. So, you see, even now, ten years later, my mother would look upon this beautiful child as a curse from an unforgiving God."

Lacy reached out again and this time took her friend in her arms and held her while she sobbed, shoulders shaking, tears staining the front of Lacy's blouse.

They stayed that way, clinging to each other until Lacy thought the worst of the spasms had subsided. Then she reached for the box of Kleenex on her desk, pulled several out and handed them to Cin who took them, wiped her eyes and blew her nose. Then she looked at Lacy with red rimmed eyes that had a haunted look to them.

"I haven't slept with a man since Ashleigh was born. Since Eric. I don't know that I ever will again."

Lacy now knew what it felt like to have a leaden heart because that was how hers felt at that very moment. Ashleigh's picture still lay on her pillow where she had placed it when Cin began her story. Carefully, she picked it up and handed it back to Cin with a strange mixture of pity and envy that she couldn't explain.

Eric flew back in two weeks later. Before he left, he told them he needed a ferry pilot to bring a replacement BT-13 from Long Beach to Biggs. The BT was one of the planes used for towing the smaller target sleeves. And, of course, the two seater had room for a passenger, so they both could come if they could get passes and bring the plane back for him. Were they interested?

It was a chance for them to see Andy. Eric already had convinced her to secure a pass to Long Beach from her pursuit training in Palm Springs that weekend on the chance he could swing it.

"I really miss you guys," she wrote to them. "Bertelli's no substitute as a friend, but she is fun and I have to admit, she's a damn fine pilot." Pink, she told them, had finished his training and had been sent overseas so she was both lonely and depressed. "If there's any chance you can get a hop up here for a weekend, do it! Please, for your old buddy Andy."

So when Eric made his offer, Lacy and Cin jumped at the chance and Eric put everything in motion once they had secured the necessary permission from their commanding officer in El Paso. On Friday, March 30, they caught a hop from El Paso to Long Beach.

The four of them had dinner together that night at a little seafood restaurant Eric had discovered down on the wharf. Then he escorted Andy and Cin back to the quarters occupied by the women of the WASP squadron that was part of the 6th Ferrying Group stationed in Long Beach. Lacy, he spirited away with him to a hotel room that he had booked for Friday night and, once again, they made love in comfortable if not Nob Hill luxurious surroundings.

At lunch the next day, Andy regaled them with tales of pursuit flying. By then she had transitioned in four of the famed pursuits: P-39 Bell Airacobras, the Curtiss P-40, the massive P-47 Thunderbolt built by Republic, and North American Aviation Corporation's P-51 Mustang.

"First, I had to prove to them that I could fly the AT-6 — from the backseat no less. Can you imagine? Since me and that ol' AT-Texan were such good friends at Avenger, I could hardly wait for a chance to get at it again. And did I fly it!" Andy's eyes sparkled as she related her first flights in the AT-6 at Palm Springs as she showed the pursuit instructors what she could do.

"I'll tell you, though, flying it from the backseat was an experience not to be believed. All I could see was the instructor's back — and most of those dudes are BIG! — and beyond him, that clear desert air and blue sky. There is nothin' bluer than the desert sky!

"Then, after they had talked us to death tellin' us everything they could about the pursuits, they let us start flying them for real. And, of course, the first flight is a solo cause, as you well know, they're single seaters."

Lacy felt a twinge of jealousy. She didn't begrudge Andy what she was doing. She just wanted to be there with her doing it, too.

"Well, the first time I took one of those babies up," Andy said breathlessly, "the instructor knelt out there on the wing and told me, 'OK, you're as ready as you'll ever be. Watch yourself, watch your bird. When you're ready to land, remember she comes in hot. And she'll drop like a concrete block — won't float an inch.' Then he slapped the skin and said, 'She's yours. Take 'er up.' And I was on my own. Have been ever since.

"On the ground, you can't see anything forward. Taxiing to the runway is a real kick. You know, a series of S turns. The P-47 is particularly bad. That big engine." She paused for breath. "I didn't get to fly the P-51 'til this week. It's the last one they let us in."

Then Andy rubbed a little more salt in the wound when she said, "And you should see Jo fly that 'Jug' — that's what they call the P-47. She handles it just like she says she handles the men in her life — rough and ready — and does that airplane respond to her. Whooeee! That girl is some pilot."

Lacy and Cin reported to the flight line Sunday morning for the ferrying flight. Andy and Eric were there to see them off.

At seven o'clock, they were sitting on the runway awaiting clearance from the tower. When they were cleared for takeoff, Lacy pushed the throttle forward and started the roll down the runway.

Moments later they were in the air, banking out over the ocean — much the same as Eric had that day in San Francisco when he was taking her back to Sacramento. Then they came round and set a course for Biggs by way of a refueling stop in Phoenix.

TWENTY-FOUR

The drop in rpm's caught them by surprise.

Lacy scanned the instrument panel — fuel gauge, cylinder head temperature gauge, airspeed indicator, altimeter.

"What was that?" she heard Cin say through her earphones.

"Sounds like we're getting some icing." Lacy reached for the carburetor heat knob and pulled it out. The engine returned to its complacent thrum.

They were over western Arizona. Crags of rock thrust upward like accusing fingers as the single-engine airplane droned its way aloft. Desolate valleys between those rocky promontories were no more inviting than the tops where only eagles lived. Moments earlier, Lacy had seen the sun glinting off something metallic on the valley floor. Either a piece of a downed airplane or the tin roof on some miner's hut. It was the only sign she had seen for a hundred miles that human feet had ever trod the timeless dust below.

"Strange, conditions don't seem right for icing," Cin's voice said in her ear.

"I know," Lacy responded, "but it stopped when I boosted the carb heat."

The prop was spinning the full number of rpm's pulling the low-winged aircraft through the air. The engine, once again, hummed as if nothing were amiss. Gently, Lacy waggled the stick and played the rudders. The airplane responded as it should.

An isolated cell of thunderstorms, a towering line of anvil-shaped clouds, encountered as they crossed the California-Arizona border, had sent them north of their initial course heading in order to get around the storm. Even considering the detour, Lacy figured they should land at Luke Field near Phoenix in less than an hour.

They could get a bite to eat while they refueled the airplane. An hour tops, Lacy figured, and they'd be on their way. From there, it would be an easy three-hour flight to Biggs. They should be checked in by five. Plenty of time for a shower, a leisurely dinner, then back to the barracks and hit the sack.

She would be glad to get home. Home. Amazing, she thought,

how quickly she had come to think of the base at El Paso as home. She was becoming quite adaptable.

Another scan of the horizon and of the airspace above and below — to check for other aircraft — confirmed what Lacy already knew. They were completely alone in the skies over Arizona. However, the ominous bank of black clouds appeared to be closer and moving, as they were, in an east by northeasterly direction. That, she thought, could be a problem.

At least she wasn't flying blind like she had been that other time, practicing instrument flying on a training mission while Cin dutifully watched for traffic and any signs of trouble. It had been five months — a lifetime — since it happened and Lacy had successfully buried the memory of that flight deep in the recesses of her mind, until just now when it resurfaced like a bad dream. Now, that ill-fated "buddy ride" seemed like yesterday.

Keep your mind on this flight, she chided herself.

"Those clouds are about to get between us and Phoenix. We need to go farther north. Refuel at Prescott instead."

"OK by me," Cin said.

Watching the needle on the compass, Lacy put the BT into a shallow left bank then leveled out when the new course was established. Gradually, she began to relax.

When it came, she knew instantly what it was — that small but distinct metallic rip she first heard on the training flight at Avenger when she and Cin lost their airplane. But it was louder this time because she was sitting in the front nearer what she was certain was the source of trouble and the sound wasn't distorted by her lack of visual and aural orientation under the black cotton hood.

Lacy looked down at the instrument panel again. The first dial she checked was the cylinder head temperature. She didn't have to look any further. The needle was rising. Dreading what she would see, she raised her head to look out. Sure enough, a jet of slick black oil was pulsing onto the front of her canopy.

"Oil line rupture," Lacy breathed into her microphone. Her throat was constricted and she could barely get the words out.

The smear of oil shut off her forward visibility. Then the big, 450-horsepower engine — deprived of its lubricant — seized up, coughed like a dying man, and quit. Lacy felt an awful sinking feeling in her stomach and knew instantly she had only minutes to find a place to land. Remembering the instructions in the Flight Manual as well as Shorty's and her other instructors' warnings, she reached over and turned off the gas and the ignition and lowered the nose of the airplane.

"We've got to bail." Cin's voice, through the earphones, contained the same element of terror Lacy felt.

A rush of cold air filled the airplane. Cin had opened her canopy. "Now, Lacy!"

Lacy remembered Jacqueline Cochran's words as if she had heard them just yesterday. "If you two had been more experienced pilots, you might have been able to land in a field."

She'd be damned if she'd lose a second airplane the same way without a fight. "No! I'm going to try to land it."

"You're crazy!"

"We could be killed jumping into those rocks." Lacy fought to keep reason in her voice, in her thoughts.

"We crash, we die. I'll take my chances."

The silent, powerless BT-13 had begun its gliding descent. Lacy checked again to be sure she had established the optimum angle so that it would descend slowly, but not so slowly as to stall and kick over into a spin that would mean certain death for both of them. But, ultimately, it had nowhere to go but down.

She had two choices. Jump, while she was still high enough for her chute to open, or make a deadstick landing. Right now, looking frantically out the sides of the airplane, she could see no possible place to put it down.

"I'm bailing." Cin's words came through the earphones. "I'd advise you to follow me, Lacy. Look for my orange scarf."

Lacy felt the plane tilt slightly to the left and looked back. Cin had one leg over the side. "Cin, don't."

But Cin dropped her headphones on the seat and disappeared over the side.

Lacy's frantic cry — "Wait!" — echoed in the emptiness of the rarefied air. Out of the corner of her eye, moments later, she saw Cin's chute open and hold her, suspended, as she floated downward toward some of the sharpest rock spires Lacy had ever seen.

A quick look at the chart board buckled to her right thigh confirmed that Phoenix, the destination filed on their flight plan, should be about seventy-five miles to the southeast. She checked her compass and scrawled on the chart the approximate coordinates where Cin had jumped.

By her best reckoning, she was southwest of the town of Wickenburg. Something on the map in front of her caught her eye. She looked more closely at the chart and saw the circle symbol with the R denoting a private, non-hard-surface runway. She shook her head as if clearing her vision, then looked back at the markings to verify what she saw.

Sure enough, it was there, a dirt airstrip that was part of a mining operation marked on the chart with the crossed pickax and sledge hammer symbol. Whether the mine was abandoned or still producing, she had no idea. But if her calculations were right, a slight course correction to the north should put her on the correct bearing to eventually come upon it. The question then was, could she find it before she ran out of altitude?

The airstrip might be a little overgrown if the mine was abandoned, but it was probably the flattest, longest piece of ground within a fifty-mile radius. Lacy figured it was her best hope. Her *only* hope. It could be the difference in whether both she and Cin lived or died because if she crashed out here, no one would know where to begin to look for her, let alone Cin. Gently, she put the gliding airplane in a shallow left bank and came around to a new heading of zero five eight.

Time to put out a "May Day" signal on the radio, she thought, though her remote position made it doubtful that anyone would hear her. Lacy activated the microphone button and started talking, trying to do as she had been taught — speak slowly and distinctly.

"May Day! May Day! This is Army four niner two niner out of Long Beach bound for Phoenix. Engine gone. Passenger bailed." She gave the coordinates she had written down when Cin jumped and her course heading. "I'm somewhere southwest of Wickenburg, looking for a dirt airstrip near a mine. Going down."

She held the stick to keep the airplane on the gentlest of glide paths, conserving every bit of altitude she could eke out. With no power, it was all she could do. Unable to see out the front because of the oil, she pushed her canopy back and hung first out of the left side and then the right to see where she was going. She had to shield her eyes for fear of taking a glob of hot oil in the face. At least the lower she flew, the warmer the air got.

She had no idea how long in terms of real minutes and seconds she had been flying since losing the engine. Since losing Cin. Every ounce of energy and intellect she could muster was being used to keep the airplane aloft while she searched for a place to put it down.

With Cin's weight gone, she might have bought a couple more miles of gliding time.

Scanning the rugged horizon, Lacy searched for the dirt runway shown on the chart. She also kept an eye out for any flat, open space or even a road that might be straight enough and wide enough to land on, though roads out here were probably going to be too winding and maybe even too narrow for the wingspan. She activated the radio again and sent out one more distress call.

Then, as she cleared the top of the next ridge, this time with less than a hundred feet to spare, the craggy hills fell away to a narrow valley delineated on one side by a meandering creek bed, a series of buildings with tin roofs and a telltale sluice trough. A mine!

And there, just off to her left between the creek and the beginning of the slope of the next ridge, were man-made straight lines set against nature's less stringent backdrop — a raw, narrow, smoothed out corridor of hard-packed dirt. A tethered yellow airplane stood next to a tin-roofed hangar made of two by fours. Lacy, with an almost foolish wash of relief, recognized a J-3 Cub.

She kept the nose down to keep the airplane from stalling. But she couldn't drop the nose too much because, with no power, she couldn't regain any precious altitude lost. She felt the cold sweat of fear in her armpits and beneath her parachute straps. She was now too low to jump.

Concentrating hard, her muscles cramping from the strain, Lacy put the silent BT-13 into a shallow bank to line up with the runway. A lonely orange windsock told her she was making a downwind landing. She had no choice. She didn't have power to do a one-eighty and land into the wind.

"I can do this," she said aloud through clenched teeth as she gently nursed the stick to keep her optimum angle of glide and adjusted the rudders to keep the wings level. Mentally, she pulled her feet up as if that would help her clear the stand of pale green, flowered Joshua trees on the approach to the runway. Then she was over them, watching out the side of the open canopy as the dun-colored turf rose up to meet her.

A few feet above the ground, she realized her airspeed was too slow. She felt the airplane stall and the left wing drop.

John! My God, I'm going to die like John!

Opposite rudder, Shorty's voice rang in her ears as if he was sitting behind her now. She pushed hard on the right rudder. The wing struck the runway. But at that moment, the left wheel and the ground collided. The wheel bounced once and then sank to the runway. Lacy thought the airplane was going to cartwheel, but a heart-stopping fraction of a second later, the right wheel of the BT-13 touched down and stayed down and the plane stabilized — rolling, rolling, the brisk tail wind helping to push it along.

Craning her neck out the left side to see beyond the oil-gunked windshield, Lacy watched the ground race by. The powerless BT had more roll than she thought it capable of. She toed the brakes. The tail wheel was on the runway now. Finally, the airplane spent the last of its momentum and slowed, the forward motion diminishing and finally ceasing altogether as the plane came to a standstill.

She was down.

Lacy sat for a moment, willing her heartbeat to slow down. . . willing her hands to stop shaking. . .willing her breath to come back to her lungs.

Then she rechecked the instrument panel to make sure everything was turned off and climbed out onto the left wing. As she went to step down, her legs turned to water and she sat, abruptly, on the wing.

Holding on to the booster handle below the canopy, she waited for her muscle control to return, then slid down the metallic surface until her feet touched the ground. A few more seconds and she pushed herself to a standing position. When she dared try her legs again, she began to walk slowly around the airplane and assess the damage.

The left wing was badly mangled, but otherwise the airplane seemed to have survived the landing.

A dirt road snaked away up a rise toward the buildings. Lacy started walking, figuring that whoever owned the tethered Cub wasn't too far away. A few minutes later, she saw a pickup truck appear over the rise, a roostertail of dust flying out behind it.

TWENTY-FIVE

Mining engineer Rich Cramer proved to be more help than Lacy could have hoped for. A World War I flyer, he had contacts at Luke Field and, once he heard her story during their ride back to the mine office, he called his old flying buddy, the colonel, and reported her problem. Cramer also volunteered to organize a search and rescue party of local ranchers on horseback to look for Cin.

Cramer put through a series of calls and soon had six of his friends agreeing to transport horses via trailer to a central point as near as they could get by road to the area Lacy, with his help and knowledge of the country, had pin-pointed on the map. From there, they would launch a ground search. In the meantime, Lacy and Cramer would fly his J-3 Cub back over the area where Cin had jumped and see if they could spot her from the air, thus giving better direction to the men on the ground.

Before they left the office to return to Cramer's airstrip and fire up the Cub, Lacy had two calls to make. The first was to her commanding officer, Major Clay, in El Paso. In a tight, controlled voice that masked only a fraction of her concern, she gave him the details of what had happened.

"Take care of yourself, Stearns. I hope they find Stinson quickly and that she's all right. Let us know the minute you hear something."

"Yes sir, I will. I'd like to go wherever they take her."

"With my blessing, Stearns."

"Thank you, sir."

Lacy dreaded telling Eric, but since the flight was under his command, she had to do it.

When she hung up a few minutes later, drained because of the emotion and unspoken fear that passed between them, Lacy looked up to see her rescuer setting two frosty bottles of Dr. Pepper, a slab of yellow cheese, some crackers and a knife on the top of the desk where she was sitting. He was shorter than she and stocky, with brown eyes and jet black hair streaked with silver. He was, she guessed, in his early fifties. He also walked with a limp.

"You say you were ferrying that trainer. I had heard some women pilots were ferrying airplanes, but you're the first I've met up with. Are you Army?"

She told him about the WASPs.

"Ah, would that be the Cochran woman's outfit?"

"Yes it would. Miss Cochran is CO of the program."

"I met Miss Cochran in Cleveland when she won the Bendix, back before the war. Helluva pilot!"

He gave her time to eat, then rose. "Drink up, we'd best be on our way. Incidentally, I've put together an emergency kit that we can drop to your friend when we find her."

Lacy took heart at his use of *when* not *if.*

Enroute back to the airstrip in the pickup, Lacy discovered that Cramer, born in Canada, had actually flown with the RAF in the First World War. A crack up after taking a hit from an Albatros D III had resulted in a broken leg, thus the limp. But he had dragged himself from the cockpit and walked away from the crash. Before he went down, he shot the attacking German plane out of the air.

After the war, he came to the United States to study at the Colorado School of Mines in Golden and had spent the last eight years at this copper mine in west central Arizona. But he had never lost his love of flying, kept current in his ratings and up to date on what the various new airplanes could do. He'd finally convinced the owners of the mine that a small airstrip on which he could takeoff and land a Piper J-3 Cub could be a boon to the mining operation because of the remoteness of the site.

A few minutes later, they were aloft in the Cub — Lacy reveled in the familiarity of the little airplane — and headed southwest. The storm had long since cleared the area. Lacy hoped Cin hadn't caught any of it.

By now it was afternoon and the shadows were quite different from what Lacy had seen that morning. Lacy sat in front for better visibility. As Cramer flew the reverse heading of the one she had flown a couple of hours earlier, she strained her eyes, looking for something familiar, keeping the differences of the sun position and the resulting shadows in mind and also that they were approaching from the opposite direction.

"Think we're anywhere close?" Cramer shouted over the noise of the engine.

Lacy turned to answer him. "Not yet!" She knew she hadn't flown much more than twenty-five miles once they began to have trouble.

As she strained her eyes looking, the same thought kept running through her mind. Please let me see something I remember! Something we can use as a marker. Then he can turn around. Maybe I can pick up something approaching from the west like we were flying this morning.

Back and forth, Lacy scanned the rugged terrain below her thinking that if man ever walked on the moon, it probably would look like this. Then she saw it. A flash of something metallic, something man made.

"There," she pointed out the right side of the airplane, "that reflection — over there."

"I see it," Cramer shouted.

She was sure it was the same reflection she had seen that morning. It was the only sign of humanity for miles in any direction. The trouble had started east and a little north. She remembered spotting that piece of metal just about the time the engine began to run rough the first time. Before she made the second course correction for the storm.

Cramer put the aircraft into a bank to the left and came around one hundred eighty degrees.

She turned and nodded and resumed her eyeball sweep of the ground in front of and below them. It was agonizingly slow and the shadows were different than they had been in the morning sun. Cramer began to fly back and forth on a course that intersected at right angles the heading Lacy told him she had flown that morning.

Lacy's head ached from the tension, the trauma of the deadstick landing and Cin bailing out. Her eyes burned from the long day's flying followed by the intensity the search required. She closed them for an instant, put her fingers to her brow, and kneaded the bone above her eyebrows. Then she shook her head as if to clear it and resumed scanning. Cramer flew as low as he dared above the uneven terrain.

What was it Cin had said right before she jumped? Look for the scarf. That was it! Look for the orange scarf. Cin had bought herself a bright orange silk scarf in a shop in Long Beach. She had showed it to Lacy and joked about having to use it someday if a plane she was ferrying went down.

"Look for something orange," Lacy shouted over her shoulder to Cramer.

Several minutes later, Lacy caught a movement out of the corner of her eye. Whatever had moved was bright orange. "Over there."

Cramer followed the line of her pointing finger.

"It's her," Lacy cried. Something orange was fluttering in the wind, maybe a half mile away.

Then Cramer nodded. "I see her."

Cramer swung the airplane to the right. They flew over a figure dressed in olive drab sitting in the middle of a white parachute that she had spread out between two rock outcroppings. Cin was waving the orange scarf in an arc over her head.

Cramer put the Cub into a bank to the right and held it there, circling the stranded flyer, letting her know that they were aware of her location.

Lacy watched Cin appear to struggle to get to her feet, then collapse back to the ground. "She's hurt. Where's the emergency kit?"

"Under your seat."

Lacy found the small canvas bag containing a full canteen, a First Aid kit, some chocolate bars, matches, a flashlight with extra batteries and several flares. The bag was wrapped in an old army blanket.

"Got it."

Lacy shrugged her arms and shoulders out of her flight jacket and zipped the bag and blanket inside.

"Get as close to her as you can. I don't think she can walk," Lacy shouted to Cramer, then she let down the top half of the right side door. He nodded and began a careful descent during which he tightened the circle they were flying around Cin.

Lacy scribbled a note on the back of a piece of paper torn off a chart. "Rescue by horseback on the way. Stay put. L"

"Okay, I'm ready."

When Cramer put her as close to Cin as he dared, Lacy leaned over the side of the airplane and dropped the care package. They made another circle during which Lacy observed Cin half walking, half crawling to where the package had landed. When she reached it, she waved.

"Gotta start back," Cramer shouted, pointing at the fuel gauge.

Lacy nodded. She waved to her friend as the plane climbed, turned northeast and sped away back to the mine.

"She's hurt her leg."

Cramer, who knew the ridges and valleys of the area well, assured her that he had a good fix on where Cin was. He would get word to the assembling rescue party the minute they were back at the mine and he could get on the telephone.

"It looked pretty remote," Lacy said.

"They'll find her." Cramer's voice said there was no doubt in his mind.

As the sun disappeared behind them, Lacy wished she felt as confident.

Back on the ground, Lacy had nowhere to go. She was dependent on Cramer for a way out — in the Cub or over that narrow, winding, rutted road in his pickup. Besides, she wanted to wait out the rescue attempt. The mine was closed temporarily due to a wartime shortage of manpower, but Cramer had stayed to do some additional surveying and test drilling. He and his wife, Lupe, were very much alone in the desolate landscape.

After letting the coordinator of the rescue party know by phone that they had located Cin and giving them the coordinates and information on her condition, they sat on the front porch of the small house, allocated to Cramer as supervisor of mining operations, and watched the sun sink below the ridges to the west of the mine shaft. It reminded Lacy of the night on her uncle's verandah when she first told him of her desire to fly for the WASPs.

Lupe put Lacy up in the second bedroom. The bed was soft and inviting and piled high with quilts. But Lacy slept only fitfully. Every time she dropped off, she woke in a cold sweat, her heart racing, the vestiges of a recurring dream misting at the fleeting fringes of her consciousness.

She was strapped into a sleek, form-fitting, single-seat cockpit, a stick and a control panel in front of her. She looked out through a tunnel-like window in the nose. A speck in the distance was growing larger by the heartbeat, coming closer, closer, coming straight towards her. It was another airplane. She tried to grab the stick and put her feet on the rudders to bank her craft out of its collision course, but her arms were so heavy she couldn't lift them and her legs were immobilized as if encased in quick-set cement. At first it reminded her of when she used to day dream of shooting down a German fighter plane in a dog fight, but this oncoming aircraft didn't erupt in smoke and flame and dive screaming for the ground. It kept coming — straight at her, growing larger by the split second.

Finally, afraid to sleep because of the consequences of awakening, she tried to will her eyes to stay open, her body not to sink down into sleep again for fear of waking to the terror she knew must come the instant before collision.

She was sound asleep under the pile of quilts when Lupe awakened her the next morning.

"They've found her, señora," she said in her soft Spanish lilt. "My husband will fly you to the hospital where they're taking her. He says for you to get dressed and come downstairs. Your breakfast is ready."

"Is she all right?"

"Yes, señora. My husband will tell you what he knows."

They had brought Cin down at first light, Cramer told her. She was suffering from exposure brought on by the cold and her night spent in the wilds. The only apparent injury was a broken right ankle. The rescuers got to her after midnight. She had built a fire and used the flares, sending them up periodically, and that led them to her. Otherwise, they would not have found her until well after daylight.

With help, she was able to ride out. The rescuers said that she was in good spirits. The effects of the desert at night had been minimized by the fact that, when they found her, she was wearing two flight jackets and had wrapped herself up like a cocoon in a blanket and the white silk of her parachute. Her head was wrapped in a bright orange scarf.

The doctors wanted to do some X-rays to make sure there were no internal injuries. And the ankle needed surgery to set it properly, so Cin would remain in the hospital a few days.

Later, when Lacy told Cramer goodbye at the army airfield near Phoenix, an enlisted man waiting in a Jeep to drive her to the hospital, she tried to thank him adequately for saving her friend's life as well as her own. If his makeshift airstrip hadn't been there, she surely would have crashed trying to land, probably been killed in the process, and Cin never would have been found.

"I'm eternally grateful. If she gets out of this OK, it's because of you. I don't know how to thank you."

"Just keep flying," Cramer said. And Lacy knew he meant it.

"She gave me this piece of paper," the attending nurse told Lacy. "Before she'd let me check her out, she insisted that I had to give it to a Lacy Stearns when she got here."

Now Lacy sat beside Cin's hospital bed waiting. They were preparing to take her to surgery to repair the damaged ankle.

"How the hell were you able to land that airplane?" Cin asked.

"I'll tell you all about it later. You OK?"

"Of course, I'm OK. Just a little break. God it was cold out there. Your jacket helped a lot. Kept my legs warm. I made 'em hang it up for you in the closet there. Didn't want it to get lost."

"You don't have to talk."

"But I want to. Listen, did that nurse give you my message?"

"She gave me a piece of paper."

"Look at it."

Lacy did. Scribbled there was Ashleigh's name, the names of her adoptive parents, and the town near Seattle where they lived. Lacy looked up, puzzled.

"I started thinking. I had a lot of time out there to think. You're the only one who knows about Ashleigh. What if I had bought it when I hit the ground, or died before they could rescue me? Eric would never know. Never know that he has a daughter."

"But you're all right."

"Yes, but I didn't know that then. I want you to write down those names and keep them someplace safe. Their address is in my trunk. I'll give you that too, as soon as we get back to El Paso. But, listen carefully Lacy, should anything ever happen to me, I want you to tell Eric about Ashleigh and who her adoptive parents are. He's not to try to take her away from them. I made them a promise and signed a paper. But I think he should know he has a daughter. If I'm not around for some reason, he needs to be told about her — at the right time. You'll know when that is." Cin stopped, caught her breath. Then she smiled.

"Besides, someday when she's older, she will ask questions. She has the right to know who and where she came from."

At that point, the nurse came in and shooed Lacy out. It was time to take Cin up to surgery. "I'll wait for you," she told Cin as two orderlies in white wheeled her out of the room.

The staff gave her permission to use the telephone to make some necessary calls. First she tried Major Clay at Biggs, who was in, and she gave him a full report. Then she called Eric, only to find out that he had been sent on what the voice at the other end called "an emergency mission" and could not be reached.

"Damn," Lacy said under her breath. "Will you please get word to him about Lucinda Stinson's rescue?"

They would try, but couldn't promise anything, was the curt reply. With a sigh of frustration mixed with resignation, Lacy hung up and put through a call to Andy. When Lacy had talked to Eric the day before, he had promised to call Andy to tell her what had happened. Lacy knew her friend would be worried and anxious to hear news of Cin. But Andy was out on a training mission, and so for the second time in a row, Lacy had to leave an unsatisfactory message — this one to be delivered whenever Andy returned to base and who knew when that would be.

Now Lacy sat on the unyielding institutional chair in the little cubicle next to the nurses' station contemplating her next call. She doubted her family knew anything about her emergency landing and Cin's bailout, but after what had happened, she owed them a phone call to let them know that she was all right.

Drained from the emotional rollercoaster of the last twenty-four hours, Lacy waged an internal battle with a sense of powerlessness. Inertia threatened to win out, but finally her conscience got the best of her. She hadn't spoken to anyone at home since she, Cin and Andy had driven away the morning of January 16, headed for Mather. She had wired her parents that the three of them had arrived safely in Sacramento; she had written them about her impending Permanent Change of Station to Biggs, and then of her safe arrival in El Paso.

Lacy wasn't much for writing letters, and now that things were strained she kept such contact simple, forthright and to a minimum. No pleas for understanding, no excuses, just "Hi, I'm doing fine."

She had received several letters from her mother describing how hard it was for her to deal with Kenny's death — each one ending with the same line: "Lacy, please come home."

Letters from Uncle Ike had kept Lacy going. As usual, he was supportive. She learned quickly that he had backed her decision to leave and, apparently, had raised his sister-in-law's ire by doing so.

When the call went through, it was Norman who answered and she sighed with relief.

"Hey, Sis, it's great to hear your voice."

She told him of the events of the last two days and assured him she was fine, wondering how big a lie that was. Fine physically, maybe. She wasn't sure about the rest of it right now.

"Mom's at work," Norman was saying. "Dad's gone to town for supplies. Can you call back later?"

"No, I don't know how long I'm going to be here. I have to go back to Biggs. Just wanted you to know I'm OK. Tell Mother and Daddy that I love them. Love you, too." She quickly rang off so her brother wouldn't hear the catch in her throat.

TWENTY-SIX

Lacy had just hung up from talking to Norman when a nurse appeared and handed her a message: "Call Major Clay." Again it took a few minutes for the call to go through the long distance operator, but finally she heard her CO's voice.

"I talked to your friend Cramer about the condition of the BT. Wanted to know if it was worthwhile flying a mechanic up there to work on it. He tells me you had an oil line break on a BT down at Avenger. Wish I'd known that before, Stearns. When I found out, I put out the word to check the oil line on every BT on this base. The order is being copied to every base in the country flying BTs. It's probably just a coincidence, but I don't want to take any chances."

"What's going to happen to the one we were ferrying?"

"Other than the busted oil line, the left wing is damaged and the landing gear needs a thorough inspection since you landed hard. I'll have them send a mechanic from Luke Field up to look at it. But I don't want you to hang around and wait. I need you back here. We've got an outbreak of food poisoning and I need every healthy pilot I can lay my hands on."

"What about Cin? She just went into surgery and I told her I'd be here when she woke up."

"OK. Stay there until she's safely out, then get back over to Luke and catch the first hop out that's coming this way. Tell Stinson when she's released, we'll see that she gets flown back here."

Late afternoon, Lacy told a groggy Cin that she'd see her in El Paso in a few days, repossessed her flight jacket from the closet in Cin's hospital room, and was on her way back to the airfield to find a hop to Biggs.

The next morning, April 3, she had a message that Major Clay wanted to see her.

"This just came in for you from Major Larsen at the ATC and it's marked urgent."

Lacy took the single sheet of paper from his hand and read it with a sinking heart. Eric had received orders Sunday afternoon, just before she called him about Cin. He was to be ready to move on six-hours notice. The orders were Top Secret. Since he could reveal nothing of them to her, rather than add to her worry at that critical point, he decided to wait until the emergency had passed and explain it to her then.

That was the end of the message. It contained no further explanation.

"He says he's been sent on a Top Secret mission. What's going on, or can't you tell me?" she asked Major Clay.

"He said Top Secret? I think I'd respect that, Stearns. I'm sure he hasn't been allowed to communicate any more at this time."

As Lacy turned to leave the major's office, his sergeant appeared in the doorway. Lacy sensed the man was bringing bad news from the look in his eyes and the set of his mouth. Her heart did a stutter step. Eric. Cin. Something was wrong.

"Yes, Sergeant," Major Clay said.

"This just came in, Sir," and he handed the major a message off the wire.

Lacy watched and held her breath. Then Major Clay looked up at her, a sorrowful expression washing over his face.

"One of your WASPs, an Evelyn Sharp from the 6th Ferrying Group in Long Beach, died this morning when one of the engines on the P-38 she was ferrying to Newark quit on takeoff in Pennsylvania. Did you know Miss Sharp?"

Lacy felt the air go out of her lungs. Andy had spoken of Evelyn when they were all together the previous Saturday. Evelyn had just left for the east, Andy said, ferrying her first twin-engine P-38 Lightning, a plane Andy very much wanted to get checked out in. Evelyn, Andy said, was one of "The Originals" — one of the first twenty-eight women pilots recruited by Nancy Love for the WAFS.

"She's one of the best." Coming from Andy, Lacy knew that was high praise. Now she was dead.

"I know who she was," Lacy said, the weight of that statement hanging in the air between them.

The following afternoon, when she returned from her target towing assignment and checked her mail, there was an Air Mail letter from Eric saying that the emergency had not passed. He was, and would remain, incommunicado and could tell her nothing other than he would not see her for awhile. He would write when he could. And, yes, he had been notified of Cin's rescue and was, of course, greatly relieved to hear that she was all right.

He promised he would contact her the minute it was allowed. Remember, he said, "I love you."

As Lacy settled back into the routine in El Paso, she began to hear some disturbing news and pieced the story together from gossip and from newspaper clippings posted on the Ready Room bulletin board.

On March 22, General Hap Arnold had gone before the eighteen-member House Committee on Military Affairs in Washington D.C. and asked Congress to militarize the Women Airforce Service Pilots. Lacy had been vaguely aware of this, but with the excitement over the upcoming trip to Long Beach, hadn't paid much attention. Now, depending on who she talked to, she got conflicting reports.

Some said that it was only a matter of days until the bill — H.R. 4219 — was passed by an overwhelmingly positive majority in Congress, led by Los Angeles Representative John Costello. Others said the bill was in trouble. That the Chairman of the Civil Service Committee, Robert J. Ramspeck from Georgia, had decided to conduct an investigation of the WASP program.

"See if the citizens of the United States are getting their money's worth," growled Lacy's 43-9 classmate Ronda Reeves.

Lacy knew the war had turned in the Allies' favor. Losses by the bomber and fighter squadrons abroad had proved to be much lower than anticipated. The Army no longer needed the plethora of pilots it had initially set out to train. Young men slated for flight training were now being sent, instead, to the infantry. They and their families were not happy about that turn of events.

But the controversy had really begun, one of the other WASPs told Lacy, early in January when the Army's civilian-run and staffed primary flight training schools around the country were closed and the male flight instructors who had been teaching cadets — future fighter and bomber pilots — to fly were out of a job. With that, they lost their deferments and were eligible to be drafted into the infantry. The men began to write their congressmen. They were being denied employment.

"They want our jobs," wailed 43-8 Martha Ware.

"God forbid, one of 'em might have to carry a rifle and fire a shot in anger," said 43-6 Joan Lawrence.

"I think you girls are being too hard on these men," Joanna Wright, another 43-8, said. "Most of them have families to support and if they can't get jobs because of us, then we need to step aside.

It's only fair."

"But we're doing the job they trained us for. I don't think it's fair to replace us with men. They can do a lot of things we can't, like fight overseas," Martha persisted. "I thought that was the point. We perform duties stateside to release more men to fight overseas."

"Well, I sure can't blame some guy for not wanting to be drafted into the infantry," Jessica Alexander, 43-5, said. "But I don't think they ought to take our jobs away."

Then someone got hold of a national magazine and passed around the week's hottest story. The WASPs were labeled "Jackie Cochran's glamour girls" and referred to as "35-hour female wonders." By now, the requirement for acceptance into the training program at Avenger was a private pilots' license and that required a minimum of thirty-five hours.

The story went on to suggest that these "pseudo pilots swap their flying togs for nurses uniforms and do some REAL work!" The WASPs were characterized as a glamorous publicity ploy designed to "promote undeserving women at the expense of deserving men."

Lacy thought she was going to be sick when she read that one. She much preferred the article that claimed the WASPs were the country's "best kept secret weapon."

On April 10, Cin arrived back at Biggs, her leg in a cast to the knee.

"I'm grounded 'til this ankle heals. I'll be flying a goddamn desk!" she grumbled. "Major Clay's idea of limited active duty is to have me scheduling the aircraft available to fly and who flies 'em, sending the planes that need repairs to the shop, and the ones beyond repair to the graveyard."

Over coffee in the mess hall two weeks later, Major Clay confided in Lacy that Cin had proved so good at this, he had given her complete authority over when a plane was declared ready for the scrap heap, how many parts could be salvaged from it, where a replacement might be found, and who was available to ferry the dying bird to the graveyard in Oklahoma.

But as Cin's ankle began to heal, and boredom set in, she began to schedule herself to fly the graveyard duty.

"Is your ankle really up to working the rudders on those sick airplanes?" Lacy asked.

"Don't you start on me."

"I'm not starting on you, I'm worried about you."

"I want to go back to towing targets, but they won't let me. Probably afraid I'll foul up and crash, wiping out a few of their precious gunnery recruits in the process."

"They want to be sure your ankle is strong enough to handle the rudders. That's why I don't understand you wanting to fly redliners."

"It's very simple, Lacy. It isn't just the ankle that's keeping me out of the rotation — out of the cockpit. Right now, I've got a reputation for being too quick to jump — unwilling to stick with a stricken aircraft and fly it down. In other words, I'll save my own skin rather than trying to put the bird down in some farmer's field."

"Cin, that's not true!"

"Are you sure? After all, I was the first one out back at Avenger when our trainer crashed. And I skipped out on you in Arizona, leaving you to fly that sick BT down alone."

"But I jumped the first time too, and it was pure luck I didn't crash in Arizona."

"I beg to differ. That was skill, my friend. You stuck around and proved your could do some really nifty flying. I didn't. Anyway, nothing's been said to me directly. I just feel the current in the air. Major Clay is being real good about it. He's giving me free rein. I can fly as much as I want as long as it's dogs headed for the boneyard. But they're not about to put me in something valuable.

"Redliners, throwaways — they're my ticket to proving myself. I gotta show them that I can fly anything — even a really sick bird — back to the ground intact."

TWENTY-SEVEN

"Stearns, it's come to my attention that you've requested a transfer to pursuit school. That right?" Major Clay asked.

Her CO's eyes were fixed on her like she was a truant from school, not a qualified military pilot. Lacy raised her chin and answered. "No sir. I mean, not a transfer from here. I requested pursuits way back at Avenger and also while I was at B-25 training."

"Well, it looks like somebody has decided to give you a trial run."

"What do you mean, sir?"

"I have here a specific request for you to proceed, immediately, to Romulus, Michigan. They've got a P-47 up there that they need delivered to Newark, and they seem to think you're the one to do it."

"A P-47!" Lacy couldn't believe her ears. "But I'm not checked out in one, sir."

"Well, it looks like you're gonna be. The orders say 'transition P-47, then proceed with aircraft to embarkation point'. — It's a rush job, Stearns. That Jug is due to leave for England in four days."

"I don't understand," Lacy stammered, competing emotions warring within — finally the chance to fly pursuit versus leaving Cin when she was still vulnerable and in need of support. And what about Eric?

"Don't ask me why the army does what it does. This couldn't have come at a worse time, ya' know. I'm short on pilots here. I can't put Stinson back on active duty yet and who knows how long you'll be gone." He looked up at her. "The orders give me the option of saying no if it creates a hardship on the command."

Lacy knew Major Clay always complained of being short of pilots. She held her breath, and then he added, "But if the army says it wants you, who am I to stand in the way. Get your bag packed!"

"Yes, Sir!"

Cin was in a redliner on her way to the graveyard in Oklahoma, so Lacy left her a note and told her she'd explain when she got back, whenever that was.

"Somebody up there likes you, Stearns," said the lieutenant in charge of operations at Biggs Field when she reported to catch a hop for Detroit, her B-4 bag in hand. "Though I'm not sure where you're gonna put that in a P-47," he said, pointing to her luggage.

It turned out that the male ferry pilot taking a newly modified P-47 from the modification center in Evansville, Indiana, to Newark had diverted to Romulus to avoid weather and ended up being grounded in Michigan with an ear infection. The ship the pursuit was supposed to be on was scheduled to leave the docks for England in a few days and they had to get that airplane to the east coast. All the Romulus ferry pilots were out delivering or otherwise tied up. She was to spend two days getting up to speed in the big pursuit and take off the third day for the docks in New Jersey.

Barbara Donahue, the WASP squadron commander at Romulus — home of the 3rd Ferrying Group — sent Lacy to the flight line the minute she reported in. "Our quarters are the other side of the airport, more than a half mile from here," Donnie said. "We have to hop buses driven by Red Cross volunteers to get anywhere on base. So make yourself at home here in my office for now and we'll set you up with a room in the barracks after dinner."

They put her in the back seat of an AT-6 and Lacy spent two days looking around the instructor's broad back, taking off, landing, and taking off again and reading tech orders for the P-47. The 12,500-pound Thunderbolt, or Jug as it was nicknamed by the combat pilots who flew the bottle-shaped aircraft, was by far the heaviest single-engine fighter the Army had. Its 2,400-horsepower engine drove a thirteen-foot, four-bladed prop that loomed in front of Lacy's eyes as she climbed in for her first flight on her third day in Michigan. Since all the pursuits were single seaters, the first flight in the real thing was a solo. As she sat in the cockpit of the P-47, Lacy remembered Andy's words. "You'd better do it right the first time."

Wedged down in that cockpit, with her instructor squatting on the wing beside her, Lacy thought about the 65-horsepower engine in the little Cub at Shorty's and wondered how she had ever got up the nerve to move from there to here. Her instructor, whose name was Cliff, had grilled her on the Jug's flight characteristics and now he waited for her to give the word that she was ready to try it.

She looked up at him and nodded. "There's a ship waiting in the harbor. I guess I'd better see if I can fly this thing."

He jumped off and a mechanic stuck a battery charger into the side of the engine. Lacy pressed the starter button and activated the throttle. The engine roared to life. She pushed the button on the stick to activate her throat mike and called the tower. She was ready.

Gently working the rudders, she made a series of S-turns down the taxiway — the massive engine cowling blocked any view straight in front of her. When she reached the end of the runway, she ran the checklist once more — magnetos, manifold pressure, rpms. When everything checked out, she sat for half a minute and wondered if maybe she should pray. She figured the gods of aviation were already lined up for or against her at this point, but she harkened back to the Methodist Sunday School teachers of her childhood and offered up a last minute plea.

"I think I may need some help here, Lord. If you can see your way clear, I'd appreciate any you can spare. Amen." She pressed the mike button on the throttle, called the tower and was cleared for takeoff.

Lacy pushed the throttle all the way forward, felt the airplane surge down the runway, and watched the airspeed indicator climb. The noise was deafening, the airplane shook, and her body was pressed back against the seat. But before she knew it, she was off the ground and climbing. Soon, she was soaring over the western end of Lake Erie at an altitude of ten thousand feet at nearly three hundred miles per hour. She moved the stick, very delicately, ever so slightly, and banked to the right. Then she moved it in the opposite direction and banked to the left. The response was immediate and sweet.

"This is some airplane!" she said, exultantly.

For half an hour she played with the fastest aircraft she had ever flown, getting the feel of its flight characteristics. Then, satisfied she knew what she was doing, Lacy called the Romulus tower. Though she wanted to fly on forever, she told them she was ready to bring it in. Moments later, she entered the pattern for her first landing in a P-47.

As she set it down on the runway, she remembered what Andy said about landing pursuits: "She comes in hot and she'll drop like a concrete block — won't float an inch." Lacy put her first pursuit down easy and triumphantly rode the ship back to the hangar and cut the switches.

"Everything check out OK?" Cliff asked, climbing back up on the wing.

"Yep. She's a sweet one."

"Well, then, as soon as the gas truck tops you off, you're cleared to take it to Newark. Here's your papers." Cliff handed her the official documents that said the Army owned the airplane and she was ferrying it to its debarkation point. Then he hopped off the wing and went to supervise the gassing up. A few minutes later, he was back to give her the OK.

"Tell 'em I'm on my way," Lacy said, and closed the canopy.

She taxied back out, again with a series of S-curves, called the tower and, once cleared, pushed the throttle in full and, again, felt the big plane hurtle down the runway and into the air. Soon as she reached cruising altitude, she set her course for the docks in New Jersey and settled back to enjoy the ride.

Lacy, who had never flown east of the Mississippi River until three days earlier, got her first birds-eye view of the Atlantic Coast as she guided the P-47 into the flight pattern and prepared to land on the runway next to the docks. She never had flown in this kind of murk before — never seen so much smoke belching from factory chimneys, even in Detroit where she had just come from.

She bounced the wheels when she set the big pursuit down. "Not pretty, Stearns," she growled out loud, remembering Shorty's admonition. "You bounce the Army's planes and they'll wash you out faster than piss out of a chamber pot."

Lacy ran the plane straight down the runway, gradually slowing, until the tail wheel settled. Then she began the zig zags so she could see where she was going as she turned off the runway and onto the taxiway. A member of the ground crew directed her to the designated parking spot on the tarmac and she finally shut everything down. The last thing she did before climbing out was to grab her briefcase and the slender overnight kit that she had wedged behind the seat. There hadn't been room for her B-4, so she rigged a small overnighter that would carry her toiletries, a change of underwear and socks and a clean blouse.

As she waited in Operations to sign the aircraft in, she wondered if she would have time for a shower, a meal, and a night's sleep before heading back to El Paso.

"Stearns?" the young officer behind the desk said when she handed him the aircraft's papers. "You just got out of that Jug that came in, right?" His interest increased as he eyed her flight coveralls and jacket with the WASP insignia.

"Yes," she said. "Flew it in from Detroit."

"I hear you gals may be out of a job if some ol' guy in the

government gets his way."

Lacy looked steadily at the young man who wore the single gold bar of a second lieutenant. "There's all sorts of rumors flying around, if you'll pardon the pun. That must be today's take by some yellow Eastern journalist. In Romulus this morning, I heard we were set to get our commissions," she lied. Tired of hearing all the negatives, she decided to give the rumor mill a positive tidbit to toss around.

I can hear it now, she thought. This peach fuzz shavetail will be telling his buddies over a beer tonight, "Some WASP dame flew a P-47 in from Detroit today. Said they were gonna be commissioned. Shazzamm! Just like that." Nothing wrong with a good offense. Lacy smiled at that thought.

"Orders." He handed her an official looking communiqué and a voucher for a train ticket. She was to catch a train to New Castle Army Air Base in Delaware and report by oh-eighteen-hundred hours that evening to Betty Gillies, WASP squadron commander, 2nd Ferrying Group.

"What?" Lacy asked, not fully understanding the orders.

Patiently, he explained where the train station was and how to get there.

"Are you sure you've got the right person?"

The officer checked her name again. "WASP Lacy Stearns?"

She nodded.

"Yep. Those are your orders."

"Okay," she said, doubtfully.

"If you hurry, you can catch the one-oh-four, I mean the thirteen-oh-four," he said.

She digested that for a minute and tried to remember back to fourth grade geography and how close New Jersey was to Delaware and whether or not they touched. "How long does it take to get to New Castle from here?"

"You'll be there for dinner."

Lacy shook her head. A born and bred Westerner, she was more attuned to the notion that it took a couple of days to cross a state, not a couple of hours.

Hoisting her bag, thankful it was light since she was going to have to carry it who knew how far, she wondered when she would get back to El Paso. She headed for the door and in the direction the lieutenant had told her to go to reach the train station.

TWENTY-EIGHT

Lacy had seen pictures of petite Betty Huyler Gillies and was well aware of her flying exploits. Gillies had been one of the founders, along with Amelia Earhart, of the women pilots organization known as the Ninety-Nines. She also had been named second in command to Nancy Harkness Love, the woman who organized the WAFS in 1942 while Jackie Cochran was still in England with the Air Transport Auxiliary formulating her plans to establish what had become the WASPs. When the WAFS and WASP were combined into one organization with Cochran as Director of Women Pilots, Love had been named Executive in charge of the women ferry pilots. She was now headquartered in Cincinnati and Gillies was in command of the WASP squadron that was part of the 2nd Ferrying Group stationed at New Castle.

A tall, lanky sergeant told Lacy that Gillies was at dinner in the officers' mess. "Go on over. You'll see her. She and the others are all over there. She'll be the littlest one you see, but she's the boss."

Lacy nodded and thanked him. She recognized the five-foot-one-inch Gillies immediately and approached the table where the blue-eyed squadron leader was seated with four other women all dressed in the uniform of the off-duty WASP, khaki slacks and a white blouse.

"Mrs. Gillies? I'm Lacy Stearns. I'm to report to you."

"It's Betty, and, yes I've been expecting you. Welcome, Lacy. Have a seat. Have you eaten?"

Lacy shook her head. In minutes, she had a tray full of food in front of her and had met the other four seated at the table. The conversation ranged from a front — that promised to bring rain to the Eastern seaboard tomorrow and the accompanying fog that could play havoc with the flight schedules — to gossip out of nearby Washington, D.C.

"No more offers to fly the Pond, eh Betty?" one of the WASPs said. "You've heard about Betty's brush with fame, haven't you, Lacy?"

Lacy nodded.

On September 5, 1943, Betty and Nancy Love had been scheduled to ferry a B-17 "across the pond" to England. The two, pilot and copilot with an otherwise male crew, had been ready to depart Goose Bay, Labrador, when Air Forces commander General Hap Arnold got wind of the mission and stopped it. He didn't want women pilots ferrying airplanes into the war zone.

Gillies waved her hand. "Enough. That's ancient history. What has anybody heard about the invasion that no one is supposed to know about or talk about?" And she effectively turned the conversation away from herself and on to the topic on everyone's mind and lips.

When dinner was over, Betty showed Lacy to her room in BOQ 14 where the WASPs lived, told her to get some sleep and report in the morning. She'd fill her in on her orders then.

"One question," Lacy said, hesitating.

"What's that?"

"How close are we to Baltimore, Maryland, and what would be my chances of getting a pass to go down there tomorrow?"

Gillies laughed. "First time east, right? Baltimore is a mere ninety miles by train. And if you want to go down there and visit someone, I'll arrange a pass. Boy friend?"

"His father, actually. We've never met. But Eric, Major Larsen, is on a classified assignment somewhere. I don't know when I'll see him, and this is probably the only time I'll be far enough east to meet his father."

"You're a war widow, aren't you Lacy?"

"Yes ma'am." The inquisitive blue eyes seemed, to Lacy, to see into her soul — behind the protective mask she put on for the outside world. "I met Eric while I was training at Avenger, long after John's death."

"Oh, please, that's not why I asked. If you've found someone else, you're very lucky. It's just that I pride myself in knowing the women serving in the WASP and I thought I had seen a gold star by your name. He was a pilot too, was he not?"

"Yes, ma'am, B-24. He's been gone since January 1943."

"Too bad." Gillies shook her head. "So many of the girls, like you, have lost someone. I'm lucky. My husband is safe at home. In fact, the U.S. government requires that he stay on duty as a civilian executive at Grumman Aircraft. He and his mother are taking care of our children so I can serve here. I guess you'd say I'm doubly blessed. You find out if the gentleman can see you and what time tomorrow and I'll see that you get that pass."

That night, Lacy sat down and wrote a long letter home,

concluding with: *You won't believe this, but today I flew a P-47 from Detroit to Newark, New Jersey. Not bad for your little girl, Lacy, don't you think! First B-25s, now a P-47. I'm climbing the warplane ladder.*

The next morning, Lacy boarded the nine-fifteen train for Baltimore. She was to meet Olaaf Walther Larsen, bank executive, at the Baltimore Athletic Club at noon.

When she talked to him the previous evening, she told him, simply, that she was a friend of Eric's, that she had ferried an airplane into Newark and was staying over at New Castle pending further assignment. Immediately, he had invited her to come to Baltimore for lunch the next day, but his voice and his response to her call gave her no clue as to whether Eric had ever mentioned her.

Since she had no clothes with her other than her flying garb, she borrowed a WASP dress uniform from one of the women pilots who was close to her size. Considering where she was lunching and with whom, she opted for the skirt rather than the trousers. Besides, the skirt length was a little easier to deal with since the other girl was two inches shorter and the legs of the trousers hit Lacy mid shin.

They'd had their uniforms but a short time, and not much opportunity to wear them and show them off. But Lacy felt it made her look official. And it gave her confidence. Meeting with Eric's father, she was convinced she would need every bit of confidence she could muster.

As she set the borrowed WASP beret on her short brown hair, worn so as to affect a carefree attitude she didn't really feel, Lacy eyed herself in the mirror. What would Eric's father see in her face? Would he simply see a young woman serving her country, doing a job she loved? Or would he see behind the civilized mask she kept carefully in place to hide the increasing fear of loss she couldn't escape? To lose her beloved brother, Kenny, just when she had learned to deal with John's death and move beyond it, had been unbearable. Then, when she thought she might have lost Cin as well, Lacy began to wonder if she was truly dealing with the reality of war or if she was playing a losing game in her mind. And now she had no idea where Eric was.

Would Eric's father see how much she had come to care for his son? How much did she really want him to see? And, darn it all, why had she let herself become vulnerable again? Why hadn't she shut Eric out like she intended to in the first place. She didn't have the strength to "care" about anyone any more.

Seated in the elegant restaurant, a bastion of male privilege with dark wood, plush red velvet draperies, heavy silverware, white linen tablecloths, and a colored waiter in a starched white jacket, Lacy sized up Olaaf Larsen knowing he was doing the same with her. What she saw was an older version of Eric.

His hair was iron gray, but still thick like Eric's, a preview of what the son would look like in late mid-life. He had the same dark blue eyes, but they lacked the riveting depth she had seen in Eric's. Maybe the weight of the years had stolen from him the capacity to feel, to care, the things Lacy had been surprised to find in Eric once she got beyond the brashness that he used to shield himself from his inner feelings. Olaaf was almost as tall as Eric and had the same erect carriage, but his manner bespoke a man worn out by life.

"I know you're a flyer, Miss Stearns, but how do you know my son?"

"It's Mrs. Stearns, sir."

His eyes registered a flicker of surprise. He glanced at her left hand where she no longer wore a wedding ring. "I'm sorry."

"Don't be sorry, sir." And she told him about John.

When she had finished, he said, "You're wrong, Mrs. Stearns, to tell me not to be sorry. I most certainly am sorry to hear of your husband's death. Too many young men have met a similar fate. And there will be more."

The waiter appeared with a bottle of Sauvignon Blanc, presented it to Mr. Larsen and, at his nod, opened it and poured a small amount of the pale gold liquid carefully into his glass. Mr. Larsen paused to taste the wine. "Excellent," he said, nodding to the waiter. When both their glasses had been filled, he picked up the conversation but changed the subject. "Do you have children, Mrs. Stearns? I understand that some of the WASPs have left their children home with the grandparents in order to fly."

"No, John and I had no children. Sometimes I regret that, but other times I think it's probably better this way." She hesitated, took a sip of the delicious, mildly chilled wine. "Besides, I didn't learn to fly until after John's death. I was afraid of flying at first. If I'd had children, I could never have taken that kind of chance."

"Eric is my only son, my only child. His mother died more than twenty years ago when Eric was only eight. It has always been my fervent wish to have grandchildren some day."

Lacy felt her breath catch as she remembered Cin's words. "If something should happen to me, when the time is right, tell Eric he has a daughter." She wondered if Eric would, someday, tell his father that there was a granddaughter, but that she belonged to someone else.

Mr. Larsen continued. "Eric, however, seems disinclined that way — at least so far."

Lacy wondered if he was leading up to asking her what exactly her relationship with Eric was.

"Have you heard from Eric, sir, recently that is?"

"No. I was hoping maybe you had and that you brought some word. He sent a wire saying he was off on some hush-hush mission, would be out of communication for awhile and not to worry."

"That's basically the same message I received," she admitted.

"I see," he was saying. "So you have no idea where he is either?"

No, sir, I don't. I was hoping maybe you did."

They sat in stalemated silence for a moment. Finally, Olaaf broke the silence. "My son and I have never been close. He says I shut him out as a boy because I was too busy making money. As a young man and now as an adult, it is he who has shut me out. I condoned the flying only because it was something he wanted badly enough that I could use it as a lever to get him to finish school first.

"When he graduated from Princeton, I wanted him to come into the banking business with me, but, no, he had it in his mind to go out to Montana for graduate school. Told me he wanted to teach mathematics and be of some use to society."

"He also taught flying."

"Did he teach you to fly, Mrs. Stearns? He once mentioned teaching a young woman to fly."

"No," Lacy said, sure that the woman he referred to was Cin. "An old bush pilot in Lamar, Colorado, by the name of Shorty McDermott, taught me to fly."

"How did you meet my son, Mrs. Stearns?" It was the second time he had asked her that question. She had to answer him.

"A mutual friend introduced us, another WASP. The woman he taught to fly in Montana, as a matter of fact . . . Lucinda Stinson."

Lacy watched closely for a reaction, but Cin's name seemed not to mean anything to Larsen. "He ran into the two of us at a dance in Texas last fall, while we were in training at Avenger Field near Sweetwater."

She stopped as, suddenly, the whole thing sounded cheap and tawdry, as if she had told him they had met in some cowtown dance hall in the middle of nowhere. But, in truth, it was what happened. And it was the story of many wartime relationships.

Eric's father looked steadily at her. "I seldom hear from my son, Mrs. Stearns. And in his rare letters, he has not mentioned you. Do you mind if I ask if you are just casual friends or, perhaps, is it something more?"

There it was. Lacy didn't hesitate.

"More than just casual friends, sir." She looked directly into his eyes when she said it.

"Are you engaged to marry my son?"

"No sir, and he hasn't asked me. Even if he had, I would have said no. I cannot plan ahead until this war is over. I did it once. I will not do it again."

"What about after the war?"

"I can't see that far now, Mr. Larsen. My life revolves around the next flight I'm asked to make. I think no further ahead than that."

"I want my son back, Mrs. Stearns. I want a chance to make up to him what I didn't, maybe couldn't, give him when he was growing up. If his mother hadn't died ..." His eyes held hers. "I hope you never have to look back and regret something you didn't do when you had the chance, my dear."

"I think, sir, that if you try to see Eric's life from his perspective rather than your own, that you might gain the insight you need. I asked my mother to do the same thing for me when I left to join the WASPs and was unsuccessful. Maybe you and Eric will have better luck."

He sighed. "I sympathize as well as empathize with your mother. Children can be very trying." He almost smiled. "I hope, someday, you will have the opportunity to find out for yourself."

"So do I, Mr. Larsen, so do I."

He insisted on taking her to the train station in a taxi. "Where are you stationed, Mrs. Stearns? I would like to keep in touch."

"I wish you'd call me Lacy."

She wrote out her military address and the family address in Two Buttes and handed it to him. Then she leaned over and kissed him on the cheek. "Eric has both of us to come home to, Mr. Larsen. The sooner, the better. Take care of yourself."

She climbed from the cab and headed into the train station for the trip back to New Castle.

TWENTY-NINE

"You're going to pursuit transition school."

Lacy stared, unbelieving, into Betty Gillies' smiling blue eyes. Had she heard correctly? The woman seemed to be waiting for a response, but Lacy was speechless.

"Pursuit production is way up. Deliveries are behind. We need more pursuit pilots. It means picking up the airplane at the factory and taking it to the shipyard." Betty paused, then continued. "It can be dangerous. But your handling of the two BT incidents proved you were capable of thinking quickly in an emergency. Your quick study and skillful handling of the P-47 the other day got you the final nod."

"It's what I've been wanting," Lacy finally spoke, finally found her tongue.

"You've earned it. You know, of course, pursuit training has moved from Palm Springs to Brownsville, Texas. Your orders are to be there in time for the next class. It starts in three days."

Lacy nodded, her mind racing. "Betty, I want to ask you something."

"Go ahead."

"You say there's a need for additional pilots to ferry pursuits?"

"I'd call it a critical need at this point."

"My friend from Avenger days, Lucinda Stinson, is as good a pilot as anyone around. But, right now, she's sidelined. She broke her ankle in the jump from the sick BT we were flying in Arizona. Major Clay has put her in charge of logistics for his target towing squadron at Biggs while she heals. She's so good at it, he's kept her there. To get flight time, she's flying redliners to the graveyard."

Lacy felt Gillies' eyes boring into her.

"She's really down about it. Thinks she's going to spend the rest of the war, as she puts it, 'flying a desk' and an occasional war weary to the boneyard. It's not what she joined the WASPs to do."

"There are a lot of jobs to be done out there, Lacy. Not everyone is guaranteed they will get the one they want. Many, unfortunately, have gotten jobs they absolutely hate. But the good ones grit their teeth and do it to the best of their abilities."

"And that is exactly what Cin — Lucinda — is doing right now. But she's capable of so much more. If the Army truly is looking for good, reliable pursuit pilots, you won't do any better." Lacy paused. "Think about it?"

Betty looked at Lacy for a moment, her gaze level, a slight frown creasing her brow, obviously weighing the request and the woman making it. For an instant, Lacy was back in Jacqueline Cochran's presence at Lowry Field in Denver — the interview that got her accepted into the WASP, the questions that powerful woman had asked her, and the answers she had given. A lot had hung in the balance for her that day. A lot hung in the balance for her friend today.

Then the squadron commander seemed to come to a decision because she relaxed and the smile reappeared. "OK, Lacy. On your recommendation, I'll take a look at Miss Stinson's record. I promise to give her a full measure. If she qualifies in our eyes, she'll get her chance to fly pursuits."

"Thanks, Betty. You won't regret it."

"I'm sure I won't, Lacy. Now get out of here and do us proud in Brownsville."

With those words ringing in her ears, Lacy was on her way back to Texas, but her final destination was the opposite end of the state from El Paso.

Again, Lacy began training in the backseat of an AT-6. The whole process appeared to be designed to wash out as many potential pursuit pilots as possible, which, if they were so badly needed, didn't make a lot of sense to her. But then she had learned that the Army didn't always make sense.

Lacy took to pursuits like an eaglet to flight. She quickly mastered the continuous descending turn — the prelude to landing that meant a pilot could always make the runway in case of a loss of power. And she executed with aplomb all of the required maneuvers with a delight and abandon that gave at least one of her instructors near heart failure.

Somehow, the flight in the BT in the skies over Arizona had forever altered Lacy's handling of an airplane. In those awful moments, when her own survival depended on it, she had learned how to take charge of stick and rudder and what it meant to fly by the seat of her pants. That flight, for all the fear it engendered at the time, had boosted her confidence level to new heights — something she had begun to realize in the last few weeks while doing her routine towing of the target sleeves over the Rio Grand valley with artillery shells pursuing her across the sky.

The flight in the P-47 from Detroit to Newark had sealed it for her. She had only a short amount of time to master the peculiarities of that airplane — worth $68,000 in wartime dollars — or both she and the government's money might burn up in a fiery heap. Lacy had flown that airplane for all it was worth.

Two weeks into her pursuit training, she got a phone call from Cin. "Lacy, you won't believe this but I'm being transferred to Brownsville, to pursuit school. I have to pass a medical to be sure my ankle is properly healed. But Major Clay has had me doing therapy. It's almost as good as new. I'll be there in time to see you graduate."

Lacy could hardly contain her delight for her friend, and her relief that her gamble in taking Cin's case to Betty Gillies had paid off.

In her final week in Brownsville, Lacy went aloft in a P-51 for only the third time and was drawn into a mock air battle. She had watched the other pilots, mostly male, dogfight for fun in the air over the Gulf of Mexico. She knew that a couple of the WASPs had taken part as well, but she had stayed away, preferring to learn each plane's characteristics in her own way.

But today, she was challenged by a Navy pilot in a P-40 Warhawk and, with a surge of adrenaline, took him on. A few minutes later, victorious in her faster aircraft, she lowered her flaps to slow down a bit so her victim could catch up with her and give her the customary salute from the cockpit. She thought he took a little longer at it than necessary, but returned the snappy salute in kind.

That night, she was called to the phone.

"Miz Stearns," a southern voice drawled, "this is Ensign Robert Faircloth Sutherland, uh, Baker Delta Charlie One One Two. I was flying the Warhawk you, uh, shot down this morning. I wonder if you'd like to go out to dinner with me?"

Lacy decided she had been working much too hard and her life was entirely devoid of play. She accepted and proceeded to drink too much, dance too much, and talk too much — by her own admission to Cin later. She even let twenty-one-year-old Ensign Sutherland kiss her goodnight. In the morning, she regretted only the overindulgence in the good Tennessee sour mash whiskey the young man had a newly acquired penchant for.

* * *

D-Day hit the pursuit school at Brownsville like a summer storm when it finally breaks after a long build up of heat and humidity. Rumors of invasion had been flying for weeks. Lacy had wondered if the rumored invasion had something to do with Eric's disappearance and long absence.

When word reached the base the morning of June 6, the news was greeted with a resounding celebration. By the time graduation arrived, the news had fueled the fire that already burned inside all of them, male and female alike.

Most of the men, including Ensign Sutherland, were going off to that war to fly combat in the fast little planes they had been learning about for the last month. The six women in the class were assigned to the Ferrying Division. Lacy got word that she was being sent to Long Beach where Andy was stationed. Now, if only Cin — a few weeks behind her in training — was sent there too, the three of them would be together again. Just like at Avenger. Just like Mather Field.

No sooner was Lacy settled at Long Beach, in a room down the hall from Andy, when a letter dated June 10 arrived from Eric explaining his part in the D-Day invasion and the preparation for it. Having already committed himself to take part, he'd been notified on April 1 to fly immediately to New York. There, he joined an AAF command team that was to oversee the flotilla of airplanes that dropped paratroopers on the European continent prior to the sea invasion and those that flew the bombing and strafing missions that "softened up" the area for the invading troops.

None of the team was allowed to notify any loved ones as to where they were going, when or why, he explained. It was part of the cloak of secrecy around the D-Day landing. He wrote:

> Dearest Lacy,
>
> First of all, I am relieved Cin was found safe and relatively unharmed. I'm sorry I couldn't be there with you when you needed me. That the airplane was one under my command and that it was found to be defective — something that should have been caught — has caused me to launch an inquiry into maintenance at Long Beach and other bases as well. We've heard about far too many

of these incidents, several involving WASPs, but many involving our male pilots as well.

Now, as for my sudden disappearance. We were sworn to secrecy. I had no choice in the matter. Besides, I wouldn't have missed Operation Overlord for anything.

I don't know when I will get back stateside. Remember what you are doing is important to the war effort. Until such time as we can be together again, I love you. Please don't ever forget that.

Eric

Lacy, who had been writing him letters all along, sending them to his APO address and hoping they were being delivered, immediately sat down and wrote a long letter telling him about her reassignment to Long Beach. She also wrote Mr. Larsen, just in case Eric had neglected to write his father, again.

Then she settled down into the routine of delivering P-51s and P-38s to the East Coast and bringing P-47s back to California, to be shipped to the Pacific Theater of the war, or taking P-39s or P-63s to Great Falls, Montana. Ultimately, those airplanes were destined for the Soviet Union via Alaska, but the women were only allowed to ferry them as far as Great Falls. It was far different from the daily regimen of towing targets and there was far more freedom. You never knew from one day to the next where you'd be.

Then word came from Cin that she was being assigned to Long Beach. The three friends were together again, along with Jo Bertelli. Andy, in her separation from Cin and Lacy, had grown considerably closer to the abrasive easterner.

One night in early August, when all four of them were on base at the same time, they went to a movie and stopped for a beer after.

"So, Stearns, Stinson, how does it feel to be among the elite?" Jo said, downing her third beer and signaling for a fourth while the other three nursed their second. "Took you long enough to get here."

"Is that what we are, Jo, elite? I thought we were just doing our job," Lacy said.

"Oh, we are doing that, all right. We're fine-tuned air jockeys flying the top o' the line, the screamin' pursuits. The fastest, the hottest thing goin' in this man's, pardon me, this woman's army. Aren't you glad you finally made it up here in the rarefied atmosphere — up here with Andy and me? I know for a fact, Stearns, you were jealous as hell when we got this assignment back in February and you didn't."

"Hey, Jo, take it easy," Cin said.

"No, Cin, let her say what she's trying to say," Lacy said. "Get it off her chest. You got some problem with me being here, Bertelli?"

"It's not me that's got the problem. Until Stinson got here, you sure as hell did your best to avoid me and Andy. Now I don't mind gettin' the cold shoulder from you, but your little friend here minds."

"Jo!" Andy interrupted.

But Jo waved her hand and swayed slightly in her chair. "She's been spillin' her guts to me, Stearns, 'bout how worried she is about you," Jo continued. "She doesn't need anything else to worry her, see. She's got enough on her mind with her fella over there killin' Jerries and gettin' shot at. So, be a little nicer to her. Got it?!"

"You're drunk, Jo, and you're disgusting," Lacy said.

"Please!" Andy glowered at both of them. "Both of you. Be quiet. I can take care of myself. What I don't need is my best friends shouting at each other. Can't you two try to get along?"

That night, lying on her cot, Lacy vowed she wouldn't let Jo come between her and Andy. That she would make a greater effort as long as Jo and Andy had gotten to be such good friends.

The next day, Lacy was in the midst of writing to Bob Sutherland aboard his aircraft carrier when she got a letter from his bunk mate that the young pursuit pilot had been shot down in the South Pacific. The bunk mate thought Lacy was Sutherland's girlfriend and he wanted her to know, as gently as he could break the news, what had happened. He enclosed the photograph taken of the two of them the night they went to dinner at the Officers Club. Apparently it had graced the front of Sutherland's locker.

Lacy sat on her cot, alternately staring into the middle distance and looking into the laughing brown eyes of the young man she had "shot" out of the air over the blue waters of the Gulf and who had saluted her, toasted her with Jack Daniel Black Label, and kissed her, oh so hopefully, on that warm June night — not so long ago.

She wished, fervently, that Eric was back on U.S. soil, safe. Preferably in her arms.

THIRTY

A telegram caught up with Lacy when she made delivery of her twentieth P-51 in Newark, New Jersey, a week later.

> August 25, 1944
> Coming home. Will be in Long Beach August 26.
> Love, Eric

Lacy went in search of a phone immediately. Every one she could find was in use. She sought out the Operations Officer. "What's going on. I need a telephone."

"Haven't you heard?" he said. "Our troops marched into Paris this morning!"

No, Lacy hadn't heard. She had just gotten out of the cockpit of a P-51 she'd flown in from the West Coast.

When she finally got possession of a phone, she had the operator call Long Beach. It took nearly an hour for the call to go through to the WASP living quarters. Finally she got a connection and asked for Cin or Andy, praying one of them would be there. She explained to the off-duty WASP who answered who she wanted to talk to.

"Just a sec, Stearns. I'll see if I can find one of 'em."

Lacy imagined the receiver left dangling off the hook — or maybe propped on top of the call box — useless now to anyone else. Dead space existed over three thousand miles of phone wire, she at one end of it and, right now, no one at the other. Anxious, yet powerless to do anything else, Lacy waited some more.

After what seemed an eternity, Cin's voice came on the line.

"Cin, Eric is due in Long Beach tomorrow. I'm stuck on the East Coast, I don't know for how long. Depends on the next delivery they have planned for me. Are you going to be there tomorrow?"

"Looks like I should be. I've been taking A-20s up to Daggot this week. That's a day trip. You want me to waylay him for you?"

"Please. Tell you what — soon as I can get my orders here, I'll call you back and give you some idea where I'll be and when I'm due back. OK?"

When she hung up, Lacy was struck by the unreality of it all. American troops were, at this very minute, marching triumphantly through Paris. The Allies had more than a foothold now on European soil and Eric had played an important part in getting that foothold established.

But she didn't even care. All she truly cared about, at this very moment, was that she was going to see him in a couple of days, and that realization surprised her. Until right then, Lacy realized, she hadn't understood quite how much she missed him — how much she loved him. She had spent so long denying feelings for him and then enduring this long, forced separation, Eric had taken on an almost dream-like quality with her — like he wasn't real. Like he was a figment of her imagination. Someone she had conjured up to take John's place in her needy subconscious.

But he was real. And unlike the hapless boy pilot she had befriended briefly at pursuit school, he was coming home to her.

When Lacy got back to Long Beach, via Brownsville where she had delivered a P-47 to be used as a trainer, Eric was waiting for her.

She went to Colonel Ashworth to ask for a three-day pass.

He scowled at her and shifted his cigar to the other side of his mouth. "I need you to take a delivery to Newark day after tomorrow. How is Larsen, anyway? You gonna be asking to be relieved of duty so you two can get married?"

Colonel Ashworth had been at Brax Thompson's wedding. He had seen them arrive together, late, just in time for Eric to perform his duties as a groomsman at the 11 a.m. nuptials. He had seen, she was sure, how they only had eyes for each other after the ceremony and at the reception, unabashedly telegraphing to the entire wedding party that they now were lovers. What he couldn't have seen, during the exchange of vows, was how she imagined herself and Eric to be standing there instead. Not Lacy and John. Lacy and Eric.

Colonel Ashworth was waiting for an answer to his insinuation. Lacy pulled her thoughts together. "I wouldn't do that to you, sir. It's just that Major Larsen and I haven't seen each other since the end of March. He's been in England. So much has happened since. I must see him. Otherwise, I wouldn't ask."

He relaxed the scowl and Lacy swore she saw a twinkle in his eyes. "Twenty-four hours, Stearns. That's it! Should be enough to get done what you need to get done, say what you need to say. I want you back here by twenty-hundred hours tomorrow and in condition to fly that Mustang to Newark the next morning. I want you in that cockpit at oh-seven-hundred, ready to go the minute the fog clears enough for you to get off."

Lacy knew that probably meant oh-thirteen-hundred hours because the scud cloud overcast in Long Beach had a way of hanging around until after noon, but she didn't mention that. "Thank you, Colonel." She had been holding her breath and now released it in a smothered sigh of relief.

"All right, Stearns. Get outta here. You're old enough to know what you're doing. I don't suppose your mother is expecting me to treat you like an eighteen-year-old recruit. But behave yourself and at least be careful."

It was all Lacy could do to keep a straight face. "Yes SIR!"

Lacy smiled, stretched, and came slowly awake to the sound of running water. The bathroom door was partially open and she could hear Eric singing softly in the shower.

The smell of fresh coffee close by caught her attention. A room service tray with a large pewter pot and two white china cups and saucers sat on the bedside table. Lacy pulled herself up to a sitting position, poured herself a cup and added cream until the dark liquid turned the right shade of light brown. She pulled the sheet up, covering her bare breasts, tucked it under her arms, then wrapped her hands around the cup letting the warmth seep in through her fingers. She shivered with pleasure, then took a sip and felt it trickle pleasantly down her throat into her stomach, slowly waking her from her early morning torpor.

As she drank, the cobwebs of sleep fell away and she thought of Eric standing naked in the shower, needles of hot water from the spray playing on his bare skin. Lacy set the cup on the tray, rose and, her bare feet sinking sensuously into the thick pile of the plush champagne carpet, walked across the room and through the bathroom door. Steam was rising from the shower and she could see the flesh pink of his body through the filmy curtain.

With a shiver of anticipation, she reached out and pulled it aside.

He turned, hearing the metallic chink of the rings moving on the rod, saw her and smiled. He took her hand and drew her under the spray with him. Gently, he tilted her chin upwards and kissed her, the water running in rivulets over their shoulders and down their bodies.

His arms went around her, pulling her close. They stood locked together, quietly, for a few moments, letting the hot spray soak both their bodies. He took the bar of soap and slowly moved it over her back, her shoulders, her breasts and down her body in gentle circular motions, letting the water rinse away the lather.

Then she took the soap from him and repeated the lathering motions, watching the thick mat of black chest hair curl wetly under her soapy fingers.

Finally, Eric turned off the water and pushed the curtain back. Taking turns, they toweled droplets of water from each other's skin and kissed again. Then Eric led her back to bed.

They ate breakfast on their balcony and watched the mid-morning tide roll in. Lacy thought she had never been happier.

"I have been asked to head up the same kind of detail for the Pacific Theater as I did for D-Day," Eric said, setting his coffee cup on the table. "Incidentally, you're now speaking to Lieutenant Colonel Larsen."

"Oh Eric, that's wonderful. You deserve it. So, tell me, what exactly does that mean?"

"It means that I'm in Long Beach to recruit my operations team. From here, I fly to Honolulu where I will be stationed as long as my command is in effect — which is probably until the war with Japan is over. I'll be leaving in about three weeks." He paused, then added, "Who knows, before it's all over in the Pacific, I might even get my chance to fly a little combat."

Lacy stared at him, unbelieving. "Oh Eric, no!"

"I just want one chance, Lace. Just once, I want to see what it feels like. You should understand. You've flown the pursuits. Bomber, fighter, I don't care which. I just want to be able to say I did it. Tell our children that daddy flew combat in The Big War."

At the same time she heard the "our children," John's words came back to her, as clear as if he had said them yesterday. "I'm not one of these guys who has to come home and brag about how many Germans he's killed in hand-to-hand combat. I'm interested in the mechanics of what it will take to get this war won. I'd be happy to stay behind and work on this side of the Atlantic, if that's what it takes."

Eric had the kind of job John would have been happy to have and now he wanted to go put his life on the line, just like John had, doing the very same thing. John had no choice. Eric did! Already

184

reeling from the thought of him going to Hawaii for what could amount to a couple of years, now Lacy heard the word combat and felt like he had stuck a shaft of ice in her heart.

"Combat? You're a trained, skilled ferry pilot and a commander. You, of all people, know you don't have to be a fighter jockey with a P-51 stick in your hand to prove you're a man."

"I don't understand, Lacy."

"What don't you understand?"

This wasn't happening. Not to her. Not again. Once was enough. And it wasn't once anymore. It wasn't just John. It was Kenny, who wasn't just a brother but a friend, as good and understanding a friend as she had ever had, and poor, sweet, young Bob Sutherland.

"I've lost enough people to this war already. I'm not going to lose any more."

He smiled, took her hands, leaned over and kissed her gently. "Lacy, forget it. It was just an off-hand comment. And you made me forget what I really meant to say the very first thing. I want you to marry me, now, and come to Honolulu with me. As a lieutenant colonel, I can take you along."

"And leave the WASPs?" Lacy was surprised at the shrillness in her voice.

"I think Jackie Cochran can get along without you now," she heard Eric saying. "You've done your part. Besides, from what I'm hearing, the WASPs are going to be disbanded soon."

"Where did you hear that!" Now her voice was really on edge, though she knew very well where he had heard it. It was being bandied about on every base. Everywhere she delivered an airplane, she ran into the same insidious rumor.

"It's common knowledge in most of the commands now. They've stopped taking trainees at Avenger Field. You know that. The last three classes are being allowed to finish training, but by the end of the year, the WASPs will be no more."

"How dare you say that. How dare you say that what we all sweat blood to achieve and some even died for is being swept under the carpet like so much dust."

"Lacy . . ."

"I waited five months for you to come back from England. I didn't know where you were half of that time. I thought one of the vows I took as a WASP was to uphold the Constitution of the United States and keep its military secrets. I think I deserved the common courtesy of being told where you had gone and why. Who was I going to blab it to anyway?"

"No family was told."

"I'm not family. I'm a member of the same military establishment you are!"

"We were told that to tell anyone was a court martialable offense. Please listen, Lacy . . ."

"No, you listen to me. No, I will not marry you and go to Hawaii and leave Colonel Ashworth and Betty Gillies and the others in the lurch here just when I'm needed most. I waited for this job. They finally saw fit to train me to fly pursuits — a highly specialized kind of flying. They did it because they have a lot of pursuits to deliver to the docks and need more qualified pilots to do it. I will not walk out on that.

"I also waited, patiently, for you to come back from England because it was your job. Well, this is my job and you'll wait while I finish what I started out to do. I'm not leaving here until they tell me we're no longer needed. Besides, I'm not so sure I want to marry someone so egotistical as to think that his needs are the only ones important enough to consider."

Eric was now looking totally dumbfounded. He tried again. "But I've already put in the request for you to come to Hawaii. It takes awhile for that to come through."

"You've put the wheels in motion, as if I had already said yes?"

A puzzled frown creased Eric's forehead. "Well, I thought you would. We love each other. We've been apart for five months. We're looking at another long separation. I thought you'd jump at the chance."

"Jump at the chance to leave work that I think is important — that I *love* — to go sit with the other officers' wives, serve tea on the verandah, and twiddle my thumbs. No! You go organize your command and you go fly your missions, but count me out."

In a calm, rational tone that contrasted markedly with the strain in her high, tight voice, he said, "Well then, we can be married now and you can go on flying as long as the program is operational. Then, when you're disbanded, you can follow me to Hawaii. A lot of the women are married and still flying for the WASPs."

"Oh, thank you very much for reminding me of that."

But Lacy knew what he said was true. It was what she, in truth, wanted. They could marry and have a short but real honeymoon. Then he could go on to Hawaii for his assignment and she could continue to deliver pursuits either until the war was over or the WASP program was shut down. Then she could join him.

It made sense. It's what most women in love did now in order to spend as much time as possible with their soldier-lovers. It was being handed to her on a silver platter. But Lacy, already on the edge emotionally, saw only the worst set of consequences. She saw only his desire to fly combat.

Granted, he said he only wanted to fly one mission — just to say he'd done it — but Lacy knew the odds of a pilot dying on his first mission. That's what happened to Bob Sutherland. And maybe one wouldn't be enough for Eric. It might get in his blood like it did so many combat pilots. He'd feel the tug to go out again. Kill again. Always the potential for glory. It was a seductive mistress.

Lacy couldn't stand the thought of losing Eric like she lost John. The only way was to break it off now. Then she wouldn't have to think about it. She'd be free to do her job unencumbered. Live her life unencumbered. Pain free. That was it. No more pain.

She knew she was lying to herself. It could be her last chance for happiness. Few got a second chance. She had loved and been loved by two good men. But she couldn't face, again, what she had faced with John. No, she would not take that kind of risk again.

"Lacy, I know you're overwrought now . . ."

"I'm not overwrought. I've never thought clearer in my life."

"OK, I know you're unhappy with me. I'm sorry, I didn't realize the depth of your feelings or how left out you felt when I was in England. I should have guessed. I've learned a little about you and your dedication and your deep feelings. Cin warned me. I was a dolt and I'm sorry."

"When did you talk to Cin?"

"Night before last, before you got in."

"And did you have a nice reunion with your former girlfriend?"

"Lacy, that's not fair."

She heard the anguish, the hurt in his voice.

"You know Cin and I are old friends, good friends. Besides that, she's the best friend you've got."

Lacy was mollified. She knew she had lashed out unfairly, but she also knew she had set her course and now, having done so, must stick to it.

"Eric, feelings come and go. Feelings I can handle. An argument I can handle. What I can't handle is the thought of you going into combat and me not knowing again for weeks — maybe months —

where you are, whether you are alive or dead."

"Lacy . . ."

She reached over and put her fingers to his lips, silencing him.

"I cannot live through another loss. I'd rather know right now that it's over than string out my feelings over several months and then learn that you, like John and my brother, are dead.

"If you can be content with your obviously very important command position in Hawaii, we may still have some future. But if you insist on foolishly risking your life and our future by going into combat when you don't have to, then our whole relationship is at risk."

Eric was silent for what seemed, to her, a very long time. "Lacy, I'm the commander of this mission. I must be willing to take the same kind of chances I ask my men to take, otherwise I'm no good to them. I'm not in a position, at this time, to make the promise you ask."

"Then I cannot marry you, Eric. And I'm sorry."

"So am I, Lacy . . . so am I."

THIRTY-ONE

"Notice of permanent change of station, effective 9-5-44," said the orders that awaited Lacy when she returned to base from delivering the P-51 to Newark. She was being transferred, on Betty Gillies' request, to the 2nd Ferrying Group in Wilmington. From there, Lacy would join the all-woman ferrying operation at Republic Aviation in Farmingdale, New York, whose duty it was to take P-47s from Long Island across New York harbor to Newark on a daily basis.

Betty's prediction of too many planes and not enough personnel to fly them was coming true.

A hand scrawled note from Colonel Ashworth attached to her orders told her to get her necessary belongings together to be forwarded on the next transport heading for New York. He added that the chances of some of her fellow WASPs from Long Beach joining her there was a distinct possibility. "I tell you this, Stearns, so that you won't think I'm picking on you alone."

The realization that she would be permanently across the continent from Eric, from Cin, from Andy, was more than she could handle at the moment. She needed to talk to someone, now.

Eric was at Mather Field on a recruiting mission. Cin had left for the east coast the previous day with a P-51. She wouldn't be back until after Lacy had left for the East. Their flight paths would cross mid-continent. She found Andy in her room and all her unhappiness over Eric and the added shock of the transfer across country came tumbling out.

"I think you need to have your head examined," Andy said. "The man loves you. You love him. He wants to marry you, Lacy."

"Yes, and take me away with him to Hawaii where I'll never see the inside of an airplane cockpit again."

"You said he was willing to let you stay here and continue flying."

"Only after I told him I wouldn't follow him to Hawaii."

"Well, what's wrong with that? A lot of the girls do it."

"Not me. I don't want that kind of married life."

"What's different about it from the way you're living now, except that you wouldn't have to sneak around to sleep together?"

"You wouldn't marry Pink for the same reason."

"Yeah, and I think I was wrong. I thought it was the brave, honorable thing to do. Besides, I saw what losing your husband did to you. Now, I wish I had opted for the momentary happiness because I miss him so terribly and live in fear of his not coming back to me."

"That's what I face with Eric. It's easier this way. I did it the other way with John and got hurt."

"I think you'll be hurt either way if something happens to Eric. I think you'll regret for the rest of your life not spending what time you could with him. You're running away from something, Lacy. You're probably better off in New York. That ought to make it easier."

"I've had enough of this conversation," Lacy said. She stood up abruptly and stalked out of Andy's room.

She ran into Jo Bertelli in the hallway.

"Well, our heroine is off for Long Island."

"Word gets around fast, doesn't it, Bertelli."

"I'd write the guys I know back home and tell 'em that you're coming, but I don't think they'd find an Ice Queen very interesting."

Lacy slammed the door to her room, shutting out the rest of what Jo said to her.

She agonized over a note to leave for Cin and finally settled for: *I've broken with Eric. It was wrong from the start. Maybe the two of you should give it another try. I'm transferred to Long Island.*

A P-51 — her transportation cross country — was waiting for her the next morning. She had simply to get in, start it up, do the checklist and run up, fly off east, and deliver the airplane in Newark. The perfect solution, she thought, to the deep depression into which she felt herself sinking. Of course, hanging in the air for the eight to ten hours it took to fly from the West to the East Coast would give her ample time to think about what she preferred not to think about, everything that had happened between her and Eric.

Two weeks later, Cin, too, arrived in Farmingdale. "That was some note you left me, Stearns!" she said, storming into Lacy's room at the Huntington Hotel that served as WASP living quarters.

"What are you doing here?"

"I convinced Ashworth that I was the one to send."

"What happened with Eric? Why didn't you stay with him? I gave you free rein. I wanted the two of you to have a chance to put something back together."

"Oh, Lacy, will you live in the *real* world?"

"What do you mean?"

"Won't you ever get it through your head that Eric and I are no longer lovers, will not be lovers again, don't want to be lovers. We are friends. Friends, Lacy, just like you and I are friends. At least I think we are. But the way you've been acting lately, I'm beginning to wonder — on your part, not mine."

"I don't know what you're talking about."

"Oh yes you do. Andy said the same thing. She couldn't talk sense into you. She said you dumped Eric because you didn't want to give up your precious job — a job that, in a few weeks, may not exist any more. That's pretty stupid, Lacy!"

"It's not the job," Lacy cried out. "I could have married him and stayed here and finished the job — gone to Hawaii when and if we're released from duty."

"Then why didn't you?"

"He wants to fly combat."

"So, how many guys are there flying combat in Europe and the Pacific? Thousands, ten thousands. He's only one more."

"Not if he gets killed. Then he's 'my' one and I've already had more than my one. When John died, I thought I was going to die. But I lived. Then my brother died. And I thought I was going to die all over again. But I lived. Then that young pilot I went out with a couple of times died."

"You hardly knew him, Lacy," Cin interrupted her, then added with a grin, "unless you slept with him and didn't tell me."

"No, I didn't sleep with him. But I liked him. People I get attached to die. Now Eric wants to go out and notch a Zero so he can tell his children how he helped keep the world safe for democracy in The Big War."

"Eric doesn't know he has a child, unless you told him," Cin said quietly.

"He was talking about our kids, the children he wants us to have, together, after the war is over."

"Well, what's wrong with that?"

"If he gets himself killed, there won't be any kids. There won't be any us."

"I'm confused. Do you or do you not love Eric? And don't try to lie to me. First, I lived with your agonizing over his interest in you when you said you didn't want a romantic entanglement. Then I lived with your mooning over him after you realized you did care. I'm not blind. Did you or did you not, at least up until a couple of weeks ago, plan to spend the rest of your life with him?"

Lacy hung her head. She could not meet the intensity in Cin's eyes. "Yes," she said, barely above a whisper.

Cin sank down in the spare chair.

"I'm sorry Lacy, I don't understand."

"I don't fully understand it either, Cin."

"What are you going to do — when the war is over, I mean? If you don't marry Eric, will you go back home to Colorado? Somehow I don't see you being happy there now. Will you go back to teaching?"

"I hadn't really thought about it. Since John died, I've just wanted two things. One, to be a WASP and two. . .well, I wanted Eric. I got them both, and now it looks like I'm going to lose them both."

"Eric and I did have a few beers together the other night after you left. Of course, we talked about you. I told him what I thought made you tick. I think the thing that puzzled him the most was when I tried to explain to him your pride in conquering your fear of flying and going on to becoming one of the most talented and versatile pilots in the WASP corps. When I reminded him to look within himself for some clues, he looked like he had been struck by lightning."

"Poor Eric," Lacy murmured.

"Give him time, Lacy. If he wants you badly enough, which I'm sure he does, he'll meet your terms. It's you I'm worried about. Now come on, let's go get a beer. I want to tell you about my plans for after the war. One of the other WASP ferry pilots and I are talking about setting up a flying service in Long Beach. If things don't work out with Eric, or even if they do, maybe you'd like to join us."

On September 20, 1944, the WASP P-47 squadron gathered at Republic on Long Island to celebrate the 10,000ᵗʰ Thunderbolt produced at the factory in two and a half years. Lacy and Cin watched as WASP Teresa James climbed into the one christened *Ten Grand* and took off. She had been the lucky one to draw the longest straw.

Lacy and Cin were between flights in Farmingdale on Tuesday, October 3, when they, like some eight hundred other WASPs stationed at ninety bases scattered across the United States, received envelopes addressed to them from the AAF Headquarters in Washington, D.C. It contained a letter from Jacqueline Cochran who was writing to let each and every one of them know that the program would be deactivated on December 20, 1944. A second letter, from General Hap Arnold, explained the decision.

They were devastated, even though the rumors had been rampant for months. All the WASPs at Farmingdale sat around that night and drowned their sorrows in the champagne they had been cooling in a toilet tank, waiting for a victory celebration that would mark the end of the war.

"To the end of 'our' war," Cin shouted, as they all toasted their demise.

The next morning, miraculously stone sober and meeting the eight-hour-from-bottle-to-throttle dictum, they flew. That night they congregated again and discussed what, if anything, they could do about the decision. The consensus was, they had two choices. They could either quit and prove that their detractors were right all along and that they were only in it for the glory and the glamour, or they could keep flying, doing their jobs to the best of their abilities — at peak performance — until December 20. And so they flew.

Another telegram caught up with Lacy on October 30, as she returned to Farmingdale after delivering her eighty-seventh P-47 to the docks in Newark: *Come home immediately. Your father has suffered a heart attack. Ike*

Lacy ran to the phone booth outside Operations and put in a call for home. Typically, it took awhile to get through. Finally, Norman answered.

"How's Dad?" she asked, skipping the "hi, how are you" first.

"Where are you?" he breathed into the receiver.

"Farmingdale. I just got the telegram. How is he?"

"Not good, but he's alive. How soon can you get here?"

"I'll have to find a hop that's coming someplace close. I'll go talk to the Operations Chief and see what he can do for me. Where is he?"

"At the hospital in La Junta. Mom's there now. I'm going back tomorrow."

"I'll call you back as soon as I know something." She hesitated. "Norman?"

"Yeah."

"Tell Dad to hang on. I'm on my way. And . . . tell him I love him."

"I will, Lace. But hurry!"

She hung up and ran back to Operations.

Four hours later, she was on a transport headed for Scott Air Field outside St. Louis. With any luck at all, she could catch a hop from there to Lowry Air Field in Denver. From there, she would have to wait for transport to the B-25 base in La Junta. She was to call Norman or Uncle Ike at the hospital when she got in. Someone would pick her up.

If the cross-country weather cooperated — fortunately, late October in the mid-section of the country was unlikely to have too much brewing in the way of bad weather — she would be home within twenty-four hours.

Sitting bundled up in her fleece-lined flight suit, Lacy looked around the cargo bay of the C-47. There was no comfort here, only that which was utilitarian. The seat pack of her parachute kept her from having to sit on the hard metal buckets that served as seats. The bleakness matched her mood.

Death loomed on her horizon again and this time is was her father who was in peril. Her dear, caring, supportive father who had been no closer to the shooting war than the VFW hall in Lamar and the stories told by the World War I vets. Still, by being deprived of the physical presence and support of his two eldest sons at a time when he, himself, was beginning to wear down, Jared Jernigan Sr. could very well become a casualty of war. Would it ever end?

Lacy turned and looked out the window. They were headed into the setting sun. The Allegheny Mountains lay below. Only a faded remnant remained of their so recent resplendent autumn shades of gold, red, russet and brown. Now the evergreens alternated with the buff and gray of approaching winter.

She had gotten up early that morning and delivered two airplanes before the telegram came and, once again, changed her life. Now the worry and the strain of the last few hours were beginning to tell on her. But she was on her way home. She closed her eyes and drifted.

THIRTY-TWO

Lacy couldn't believe her rugged, rawboned father could look so small lying there in the hospital bed, eyes closed, covered to his armpits by a white sheet, his chest and upper arms encased in a hospital gown. A nurse in a starched white uniform was leaning over him removing a blood pressure cuff from his right arm. Janice sat erect in a straight-backed chair next to the bed. When Lacy pushed the door open, her mother looked up, stood, her face contorting into a silent sob, and held out her long thin arms. Lacy crossed the room quickly and embraced her mother.

"Oh, Lacy, you've come home."

"Lacy . . ." her father's deep voice, almost unrecognizable it was so weak, caught her heart. Gently she extricated herself from her mother's firm grasp, leaned down and kissed him on the forehead. Then she put her arms around her father, and buried her face where his leathery, lined neck and the pillow met.

For an instant, she thought she was going to lose her well-honed, tightly held self control. Now was not the time. She took a deep breath as she felt her father's roughened hand stroking her hair, and raised her face, her gray eyes shining as they looked into his.

"Hi, Daddy."

The nurse wouldn't let the family reunion last long for fear of tiring the patient. One visitor at a time, she said. Janice glowered at the woman when she said that Mrs. Jernigan would have to leave in order to let the daughter have a few minutes with her father, but, finally she consented and moved out into the hallway.

"You've come home," her father rasped. An oxygen tent stood sentinel nearby.

"I had to see how you were, Daddy."

"Sorry I let you down, when you were home last January."

"Sssshh, Daddy, it's OK. I understand."

But her father gripped her hand hard. "No, not OK. You did what you had to do. That's how we raised you. Should have stood up for you. Proud of you. Flyin' B-25s, P-47s."

"Thank you, Daddy. I needed to hear that."

When the nurse reappeared a few minutes later, she informed Lacy that she would have to let her father rest now. Reluctantly, Lacy let go of his hand. "I'll be right outside." And she backed out of the room, his eyes following her until the door swung shut cutting off her view of him. She walked toward the waiting area where her mother and Norman had been joined by Ike and Virginia.

When Ike saw Lacy, he heaved himself out of the institutional chair and wrapped her in his arms. As Lacy was kissing her aunt's cheek, Doc Barrows appeared.

"A minor miracle," he said, "though he's not out of the woods yet. Jared has the constitution of a horse, otherwise he'd be a goner. The problem is, he's so used to acting like a horse, we've got to get him to slow down to a walk in order to let the healing take place."

A few minutes later, he took Lacy aside. "Your father's not going to be much help on the ranch for a long time. He's going to have to take it easy, and he's not going to like that. How long are you going to be here?"

"Until Sunday."

Doc shook his head. "Norman's going to need help."

"As of December 20, I'll be back here for good," Lacy said. It was out before she realized what she was saying, so she went on to tell the old family friend of the WASP's coming demise. "But until then, I have a job to do," she added.

"We might try to bring Jared Jr. home from the war — on an emergency leave. I'll sign whatever government papers are necessary."

Lacy had been home less than two days when her mother brought up the same subject. "I know you don't want to hear this Lacy, but I think it's your duty to stay home now and help Norman."

"I've been thinking about it, Mother. Don't think I haven't. The problem is, he needs another man around here."

"Well! I never thought I'd hear those words from you. You're the one who always claimed she could do as much as any man."

"That's not exactly what I said, Mother. I have learned to do a man's work. I'm not afraid of riding the range all day or getting my hands dirty. But I'll be the first one to admit I think this ranch needs at least two men in addition to the help you or I can give."

"So what do you propose to do about it?"

"I'm going over to talk to Uncle Ike tomorrow. See if he has any suggestions."

* * *

"I'm willing to offer my WASP salary — $250 a month — to pay a ranch hand until December 20," Lacy told her uncle. "At that point, I'll come back and work side by side with Norman. Doc Barrows also suggested that we try petitioning the government to get Jared Jr. released or even discharged due to a "home emergency." I've written to him, explained the situation, and asked him to consider it. But even if they let him come home, it won't be for several weeks and by that time I'll be released. Of course, we're probably going to need Jared worse anyway come spring. But right now, the key is covering Norman until I come home."

Her uncle sat, smoking his pipe, drawing on it, making it glow that red orange that resembled the fire of the setting sun. "Could you get an early release?"

Lacy sighed. "Possibly, except that they need every ferry pilot they can get their hands on. If I were still towing targets down in El Paso, there would be less of a problem."

"I've been trying to think who around here might be out of work, or looking for something to tide him over because the war's hurt his business," Ike said. "The load isn't as heavy this time of year. It wouldn't take someone highly skilled at ranching, just somebody dependable and willing to work."

"That's it!" Lacy said. "Shorty. Shorty McDermott! He can't be busy flight instructing now. Too many out-of-work pilots out there looking for jobs. That's why the WASPs are being let go. Make room for all those male pilots who can't get hired. Nobody is learning how to fly right now unless they're wealthy and have nothing else to do. Nobody like that around here. He probably doesn't have more than a couple of students, if that."

She called the airport in Lamar. Shorty answered the phone himself. That was a good sign. He wasn't out flying.

"Not a one right now," he laughed, when she asked him about his students. "And not a one in sight. Since I sent you away to the WASPs, students have been as rare as whiskey bottles at a Temperance meeting. As for crop dusting, the season's over 'til spring."

Quickly, she told him what she needed.

The line was silent for a second or two. Lacy imagined her flight instructor rubbing his chin, mulling over the commitment in his mind. Commitments had never bothered Shorty. Neither had hard work, she knew. What probably was bothering him was having to swallow that regret all pilots had to swallow when they knew they were going to be out of the cockpit for any length of time.

When he spoke, his voice was positive, almost buoyant. "You got yourself a hired hand, Lacy. I'll help Norman out 'til you get home in December. Clara will be glad to see me doing what she calls honest work again."

"Shorty, you're not only the best flight instructor I ever had, you're a life saver and a very good friend." She hung up brightened by the first inkling of hope she had felt in some time.

"It's a temporary solution at best, darlin', and it's gonna be hard on you when you do get home," Ike reminded her.

"I know, Uncle Ike. But it buys us time. And when I do come back, I'll need hard work to make me forget what I'm missing."

The eastbound C-47 Lacy boarded in La Junta developed a hydraulic problem and had to land at Lockbourne Army Air Base in Columbus, Ohio. With the plane grounded over night, Lacy phoned Andy's mother whom she had met at graduation at Avenger the previous January. An hour later, Connie Sellers picked her up at the airfield. Mrs. Sellers promised the Operations Officer and the transport pilot that she would have their passenger back by seven in the morning.

Lacy immediately felt at home with the very pretty, petite lady who, with her blonde bobbed hair and blue eyes, not the least bit dimmed by a pair of bifocals, was an older version of Andy. Al Sellers reminded Lacy of a teddy bear. He was shorter than her five feet ten inches and round, with marble green eyes, red cheeks, a merry smile, and a brown crew cut that was frosted with silver at the temples.

Andy's parents, to Lacy, seemed much younger than her own parents, though there probably was less than a five-year age difference. Lacy was sure that the city dwelling Sellers — Andy's father was the owner and president of a manufacturing firm — had lived an easier life than had her parents who had barely kept body and soul as well as their land together during the Depression, the Dust Bowl, and even during the Twenties when life was more affluent back east than in southeastern Colorado.

The Sellers were much more like John's parents, Augusta and Joseph Stearns — upper middle class, both college educated, belonging to the second oldest country club in town.

"Have you heard from Andy, recently," Lacy asked, remembering that Andy wrote home every other day without fail.

"A letter just came today." Connie handed Lacy a letter containing Andy's familiar scrawl. "The third paragraph should be of particular interest to you."

Lacy skipped to the bottom of the page.

> The Ferrying Division, in all its wisdom, wants two more pursuit pilots to ferry P-47s from Long Island to Newark and the two picked are Jo Bertelli and me. We are due in Farmingdale, Long Island, November 14.
>
> Jo has already extended an invitation to join her family in Bayonne for Thanksgiving. She says its right across the Hudson River from New York City. She's absolutely thrilled at the prospect of being home. Lacy and Cin are invited too. I've already accepted, as there is no chance of me getting to Ohio, particularly with our demob less than four weeks afterwards.
>
> I look forward to meeting Jo's family, but, even better, this means we will all be together again, just like at Avenger.

"So we'll all be together again," Lacy echoed, smiling as she handed the letter back to Andy's mother.

"Andrea has told me so much about all of you. Her letters are full of the flying you all are doing, and some of your off duty adventures as well." Her blue eyes, behind the lenses that slightly enlarged them, twinkled at that. "It sounds like you've all been good for each other. I know you've been good for my daughter."

Dinner was served at seven in the elegant dining room of the Sellers' home on Dunedin Road in the Northmoor Park area of Columbus. Lacy was sure the massive mahogany table, sideboard and china hutch had been handed down through several generations. They looked old, expensive, and were polished to a sheen. The silver, crystal and good china gleamed in the festive candlelight, giving the entire room a warm, soft glow as the Sellers had gone all out for their dinner guest.

In spite of the war, they had kept the services of a housekeeper-cook. Hattie was a big boned, heavy set Negro woman who had worked for the family since Andy was born. She and Connie obviously knew how to make wartime rations go a long way, Lacy realized, when she tasted the delicious stew they had concocted. What was probably the last of the vegetables from their 1944 Victory Garden had been combined with a small piece of beef and bone and seasoned admirably with herbs and spices probably hoarded for some time. Homemade apple pie topped off the dinner, and Lacy wondered how much of the family monthly sugar ration that had cost.

Al Sellers excused himself after dinner. His presence was required to check on the second shift at the plant. Al Jr. was on an aircraft carrier in the Pacific. Sixteen-year-old Bruce, claimed homework. He was medium height, skinny, all arms and legs, with a brown crew cut that matched his father's, minus the silver. He also had Al Sr.'s red cheeks, but he definitely had his mother's and Andy's blue eyes.

"I've taken a lot of criticism from my friends for letting Andrea go off and join the WASPs," Connie said, when she and Lacy were settled in the library with their coffee and tiny silver cordials filled with after dinner brandy. "They think I've let her go wild. That she will forget everything of social value she ever learned. That she has been thrown with coarse women who have no morals and that she will end up dead or, worse, degraded."

"My mother used similar arguments on me when I told her I wanted to join the WASPs," Lacy said.

"I led a very sheltered life," Connie continued. "Young women before the First World War did not have the kind of freedom they've been permitted since. I, for instance, begged my mother to let me go join the volunteer nursing corps. It was 1917 and I had just turned nineteen. I was entering my sophomore year in college. My fiancé, Harry Caldwell, was shipped to France that summer with the first of the Allied Expeditionary Forces.

"Patriotic romantic that I was, I wanted to do my part, too. If I couldn't serve at his side, at least I could do something for the war effort. But my mother wouldn't hear of it. She trotted out the same arguments my friends have used against me and my liberal raising of Andrea. *Ruin, degradation!*

"She dangled in front of me the possibility that Harry might come home and disown me if he found out I had done such an unthinkable thing as go into a hospital and hold dying men's hands or, heaven forbid, give one of them a bath."

She shook her head and sadness filled her eyes.

"Well, Harry was killed at Belleau Wood in June 1918."

"Oh, Connie." Lacy felt the other woman's loss, all these years later. It was a bridge, a kinship they shared.

"Oh, yes, Lacy, we, too, lost loved ones in the First War. Andrea's father was not my first love, but he is my best love. I have no idea what would have happened if Harry had come home and we had married as planned. Possibly, we would have lived happily ever after like the fairy tales say, but I doubt it. We were too much alike. Whereas Alan, whom I met on the campus at Ohio State when he returned to college after the Armistice, and I are exact opposites. But we seem to prove that opposites attract. At least we've kept life interesting for each other. Never a dull moment."

And suddenly Lacy saw, in the older woman, the woman she could be twenty-five years from now, remembering John and her own wartime loss. Would she be as positive, as at home with her various competing emotions as Andy's mother was? Or would she, by then, be lost, and bitter, and lonely?

"When Harry died, I fought harder to go, but Mother upped the ante: 'Your reputation will be forever ruined and no other man will look at you . . . you'll die a spinster.'

"So, I did not join the nurse corps and I have regretted it the rest of my life. It is, in fact, the only thing I truly regret in my forty-six years. We have to be true to ourselves first, then we are free to love others and to forgive them their faults. I did forgive my mother, you see. She was a child of her times, and I a child of mine. But I swore that when I had a daughter, I would not stand in the way of her being and doing that which she passionately wanted."

That night, flushed from the after dinner brandy and the glow from her warm, intimate conversation with Andy's mother, Lacy snuggled under a bright yellow and white quilted coverlet in Andy's fourposter bed and wrote to Eric.

Dearest One,

I was wrong. You probably never thought you'd hear me say that. But a sweet, wonderful, incredibly strong woman — Andy's mother — helped me see what I was blind to before.

I've spent the last week with my family. My father had a heart attack. When I saw him in that hospital bed, I was overcome by love and wanted to protect him. But I know now that I can't do that. We can love with all our hearts, but we cannot protect those we love from harm.

Your job is to make decisions that sometimes put people in jeopardy — including yourself. If you need to fly a combat mission in order to get the job done, then you will, of course, have to do just that. My insistence that you not do it compromised your ability to do that job. I know that now.

My darling, I love you very much. If you will still have me, I'll marry you at the earliest possible date. The WASPs will be disbanded December 20. I would give anything to fly to you that very day, but I cannot. We have one more impediment that will keep us apart a little longer. My father will be incapacitated for some time. I must go home and help my brother run the ranch until my older brother is allowed emergency leave or released from the Marines. If you still want me, I'll come to you the minute I am no longer needed there.

Lacy

She asked Connie Sellers to mail the letter for her after she dropped her at Lockbourne the next morning.

THIRTY-THREE

Back on Long Island, Lacy watched November deepen on an alien landscape of concrete and steel. Used to the open country of southeastern Colorado, where sky and prairie melded at a distance farther than the eye could comprehend, she found this a harsh, hostile territory. Blue sky was a rare luxury with gray overcast the norm.

She had yet to hear from Eric, but told herself that, under the best of circumstances, the letter had not had time to get to Honolulu and for a reply to come back to her. And, if he was off base for any length of time at all, he might not even have seen her letter yet.

Cin, in whom she had confided everything — from her talk with Andy's mother to the letter she had written to Eric afterwards — reminded her of that daily when she walked away from mail call dejected.

"It'll come, Lacy. It will come."

If it hadn't been for Cin, Lacy thought she would have gone mad by now.

Thanksgiving was two weeks away. In spite of the fact that she would be with Andy and Cin again, and surrounded by the warmth that was sure to be pervasive with Jo's big Italian family, Lacy was homesick. But for where, she wasn't sure. The previous year, she had spent the holiday at Avenger Field with Cin and Andy and the rest the WASP trainees. The year prior to that, she had been home with her family in Two Buttes because John, by then, was overseas. The year before that, 1941, right before Pearl Harbor, she and John had been living in Boulder. She was teaching while he worked on his masters in education at the university. Thanksgiving dinner had been eaten with his family.

Where is home now? The ranch with Mother and Daddy and Norman? Certainly it would be after December 20. It's where I'm needed now. Daddy's heart attack made sure of that. But is it home? Is home merely where you're needed? Where will home be next year? Will Eric and I be together? In Hawaii? In Two Buttes? In Baltimore with his father? Or will he be somewhere out there in the Pacific on an island directing the pre-invasion bombing of Japan? Or will the war be over by then? And what if he doesn't want me now?

I'm twenty-five-years old and single again. I've served my country for a year and a half, but in six more weeks I won't be needed anymore. I'm dispensable and I'll be on my own.

If I hadn't been so stubborn, so idealistic, I could be in Hawaii right now. Oh, Eric, why didn't I wise up sooner? You warned me. You knew the WASP was doomed. So did I, but I wouldn't admit it. Now you're alone over there and I'm alone here. What have I done?

Andy and Jo were on their way to the modification plant in Evansville and from there to Long Beach to deliver P-47s destined for the Pacific Theater of the war. They weren't due back for three days.

The letter from Eric beat them there by a day. The first paragraph told Lacy all she needed to know: *I love you. How could you ever doubt that? I want you here as soon as you can come. But I understand about your father. I will make the arrangements from this end the minute you tell me you're ready.*

The rest, Lacy read through a mist that settled over her eyes after the first three words. When Cin came in the room they shared at the Huntington Hotel, Lacy was sitting on her bed holding the letter in both hands, staring off into space.

"Lacy, what's wrong?"

She couldn't speak. She shook her head and tried again. All that came out was a croaked "Eric."

Cin's eyes widened. "Oh, no, Lacy, he's not . . .?"

"No," Lacy finally got her voice to work. "He's fine. He still loves me."

"Well of course he does," Cin said, a sigh escaping as she said it. "I told you that!"

"But he'd had a couple of months to change his mind."

Cin sat down on her own bed and leaned toward her friend. "Lacy, I talked to him after you left to come east. I know how deeply he feels for you. That's what I've been trying to tell you these last few weeks while you've been moping around like a love-sick teenager."

Thanksgiving 1944 found Lacy, Cin and Andy seated at the Bertelli family dinner table — a Ping-Pong table in the basement of their crowded home was brought upstairs and converted for the occasion to accommodate all the people in Jo's family.

Because she and Jo had antagonized each other from the beginning, Lacy still was surprised at how easily Andy had taken to her.

But then Andy, Lacy told herself, got along with everybody. She and Cin, who was an only child with a built-in prickly personality, had been the ones to raise porcupine quills at the perceived slights and digs that were part of a big group of young women living together in close quarters. Now, through Jo's big, boisterous, demonstrative family, so different from the reserve of her own family, Lacy was seeing her classmate from Avenger in a different light.

"Josephine, now that girl knows how to handle herself," Jo's stocky, florid-faced father confided in Lacy, as he drank deeply from his goblet of red wine. She was seated on his right and Cin on his left, the places of honor at the table. Andy and Jo, similarly, were seated at Mama Bertelli's right and left elbow. "The boys used to tease her in junior high because she was so much taller than they were. My big, beautiful girl there could beat 'em all up — Guiseppe, Antony, Lucca, all those boys. When they got in high school they kept comin' around here, followin' her around like puppies." He laughed, his black eyes twinkling, and took another swallow of his wine.

"Here's to my girl, the best pursuit pilot in the WASPs," he said, toasting his dark-haired daughter. Then he looked at the other three young women, laughed heartily, and added "along with her friends Lacy, Lucinda and Andrea."

And everybody at the table drank to the four women pilots in their midst.

"She earned every penny it took her to learn to fly," Mr. Bertelli told them in what, with him, passed for a whisper. "I was my pig-headed self about it when she came to me her senior year in high school and told me she wanted to learn to fly. 'Flying is for men, Josephina,' I said. 'You go have babies like your sisters.'

"Well, she proved me wrong. She went to work at Woolworth's and saved her money, got a second job waiting tables at Caravino's restaurant weekends. She started spending all her spare time at the airport. Before I knew it, she had her license. Pretty soon she was teaching the boys she had gone to school with. The only way they could impress her was to take flying lessons. She could hardly wait to turn twenty-one so she could get in the WASPs."

Lying awake that night in her small room in the WASP quarters, Lacy conceded that Jo Bertelli was OK. You just had to know how to take her.

The next day they were flying again.

As they moved further and further into December and closer to deactivation, Lacy, Cin and Andy began to make preparations to return to their home base at New Castle, official deactivation, and to leave for home. Cin had even decided to spend Christmas with her mother and try to work things out.

On December 16, the three of them and Jo sat in the Ready Room at Republic waiting for the ground crew to do a final check on four P-47s scheduled to go to the docks that morning. They drew straws for order of takeoff. Andy pulled the first position, Jo and Cin the middle two. Lacy would bring up the rear.

They weren't needed back in Farmingdale until mid afternoon. "Let's rendezvous in the Ready Room at Newark and head over to my Mom's for lunch," Jo said. "She's invited you three over one more time. She likes you guys."

A few minutes later, the Operations officer came to the door and hollered, "They're ready." The friends grabbed their parachutes, slipped them on, and headed for the flight line. Lacy was conscious of her parachute straps between her legs and wondered how many more times in the next three days she would feel that particular sensation.

She was beginning to notice little things like that and mentally jot them down with the same question. How many more times? How many more times would she feel the awesome power of a U.S. Army pursuit as it streaked down the runway and hurtled into the air while her heart soared with it. She knew she would never again fly an aircraft with anything near that kind of speed and power.

She hesitated as Cin, who was walking in front, stopped, opened the door and held it for the other three of them. "Got your lucky coin, Stearns?" she asked, an impish grin on her face.

"What do you think?" Lacy laughed.

A few minutes later Lacy sat in the cockpit of the last of the four P-47s lined up on the taxiway. She listened as Andy called the tower and moved into position for takeoff. Seconds later, the big Thunderbolt was roaring down the runway and lifting off.

"See you in Newark," Lacy said into her mike, and she watched as Andy cleared the low building at the end of the runway, climbed for altitude, and disappeared into the haze. When she looked back, Jo was moving her pursuit into takeoff position on the runway. While Lacy waited on the taxiway behind Cin, she reran everything in the cockpit again and was satisfied when it all checked out.

She heard Jo call the tower and, moments later, she, too, was in the air climbing out and disappearing into the ever-present haze.

Two down, two to go, Lacy thought. She watched Cin taxi her Jug into position. Cin's call to the tower came over the earphones and Lacy heard the words "cleared for takeoff" followed by Cin's "Roger."

The aircraft started its takeoff roll. Seconds later, Cin lifted off.

Lacy started to move up into takeoff position. Her crew chief Randy, who had been watching Cin's airplane, turned and abruptly signaled her to hold her position on the taxiway. Lacy throttled back, toed the brakes, and held.

Then she saw why Randy had stopped her. The engine of Cin's P-47 was belching black smoke and the aircraft was not climbing.

Mesmerized, Lacy watched as Cin — up there alone in an ailing aircraft — fought to control a power source gone haywire. She banked the faltering silver pursuit to the left. Lacy knew what she was trying to do. Cin was going to try to bring the aircraft around one hundred and eighty degrees to land on the runway from which she had just taken off — going in the opposite direction.

Lacy cut her engine. In the sudden quiet, she could hear the sound of Cin's powerful pursuit choking to death. Now she was not much more than skimming treetops.

Following procedure, Cin had pulled up the landing gear the minute she left the ground. Now her airplane, the wheels miraculously back down and locked in place, was aimed straight for the runway. But for Randy's quick thinking, Lacy and her P-47 would be sitting right in the path of Cin's oncoming airplane.

The engine of the stricken plane coughed one more time and quit just as Cin made the far end of the runway, maybe fifty feet off the ground. The 12,500-pound pursuit, true to its reputation, dropped like a rock. The landing gear collapsed on impact. The heavy nose slammed into the runway, the massive four-bladed propeller digging a trench in the concrete, sparks flying everywhere. The plane skidded, turned sideways, and seemed to slide for an eternity until it came to a screaming stop directly across from where Lacy sat rooted to her seat in the cockpit of her P-47.

Silence. For a heartbeat, nothing moved.

Lacy held her breath for fear the airplane would burst into flames. Already a fire truck was racing toward the crash site. Ground crewmen ran in the direction of the stricken aircraft. From her high vantage point in the cockpit, sitting at a ninety-degree angle from the wreckage,

Lacy could see that the canopy of Cin's pursuit was intact. All that armor plating around the cockpit was supposed to protect the pilot.

"Get out, Cin," Lacy implored her friend, speaking out loud even though she was alone. She waited for the canopy to open and her friend to climb out. But nothing moved.

The first crewman to reach the wreck scrambled up on the wing.

"Get out, Cin," Lacy repeated through clenched teeth.

The man got the canopy open and leaned down to talk to the pilot. Then he straightened up and hollered something. Lacy couldn't hear what. Two crewmen carrying a stretcher and two more carrying fire extinguishers approached. The fire truck pulled to a stop and the firefighters leaped for the hose.

"Cin!" Lacy started to climb from the cockpit, but Randy looked up and signaled her to stay put. So she sat, helpless, impotent, as she watched several men lift Cin from the wreckage.

They laid Cin's still form on the stretcher and, for safety in case of explosion and fire, carried it some distance from the airplane. A wail in the distance signaled the approach of an ambulance. Moments later it appeared on the taxiway and was waved in. Two men got out and ran to the stretcher. One examined the inert figure. After what seemed like an eternity, Lacy saw one of the men shake his head and put away his stethoscope.

"No!" she screamed.

Randy jumped up on the wing. "Take it easy, Lacy."

"I want to know what has happened to my friend. Is she dead? She can't be dead!"

"You stay in the cockpit. I'll find out what I can." He jumped down and took off, running.

Lacy watched another fire truck pull up. The men were loading Cin's stretcher in the ambulance. Firefighters were spraying water on the wounded aircraft. Then several men swarmed over its exposed metallic surfaces.

Her crew chief came back and, from his face, she knew the news was bad. Lacy bit back the sob that clawed at her throat. She clamped her jaws shut and swallowed hard. She would not cry. She had learned not to cry.

"Lacy . . ." Randy shook his head and tried to talk, but he couldn't seem to find his voice.

"Tell me!" Lacy screamed.

"They think she died on impact."

Lacy took a deep breath, "I want to see her."

"The ambulance is taking her to the hospital."

"But you said she was dead."

"Well, yes, but . . ."

"I want to see her." And Lacy was climbing out of the cockpit onto the wing before he could stop her.

Randy jumped to the ground and they both sprinted toward the ambulance, Lacy weighted down by full flying gear. The driver was climbing in the front seat. The other man had crawled into the rear with the stretcher.

"Wait!" Lacy shouted. She climbed in the back of the ambulance before the attendant could shut the door. "She's my best friend," she said, pleadingly.

The man shook his head and said nothing.

"She's dead?" Lacy asked. "You're sure?"

The man nodded. "That kind of blow to the head is usually fatal. She has no vital signs. But a doc has to pronounce her dead. We can't."

Cin still wore her flight helmet, but the leather had been sliced by the blow and gaped open. A deep, bloody gash extended across her cheek, past her ear, and into the temple.

Lacy stared, transfixed. John, she thought. Just like John. A simple blow to the head.

But instead of the face of death, Lacy saw the impish grin when Cin asked about her lucky coin, the compassionate face that had so recently assured her of Eric's love, and, lastly, the heart-catching pride in a mother's face looking at a photograph of the daughter forever lost to her.

Lacy reached forward and gently touched her friend's unshattered cheek. "I'll tell Eric about his daughter, Cin, I promise," she murmured.

She rejoined her crew chief outside the ambulance and, together, they walked back to her aircraft. Several crew members already were checking it out. When they were finished, the Operations chief came over to her.

"What happened?" she asked.

"We still aren't sure. The engine was cutting out and finally quit, but it'll take days to determine what really happened. At least the plane didn't burn up so they can go over it."

"What about mine?"

"Your aircraft checks out, Stearns. We'll get someone else to fly it over to the docks."

"How long before I can take off?"

He looked at her, surprise written on his face. "You're cleared for takeoff — but don't try it. With what you've seen, you've got no business flying that airplane. Let somebody else deliver it. Nobody is going to think less of you if you don't."

Lacy gave the man a level look. "If I was a man, you wouldn't say that. It's my responsibility and I'm ready." And she climbed onto the wing of the waiting P-47 and back in the cockpit.

"You'll need to stay to the right side of the runway."

Lacy nodded and closed the canopy.

She followed the directions of the ground crew and got her P-47 lined up to the right of center on the runway in order to avoid the crippled plane that now lay like a wounded bird, blocking the far left side.

When she was satisfied, she called the tower. Then she focused on the narrow corridor down the runway, just as she had once sighted down the barrel of her rifle and caught the rattlesnake's head in the crosshairs. She eased the throttle in full and felt the might of that 2,400 horsepower engine as she hurtled down the runway and into the air.

Lacy saw Andy and Jo watching with the rest of the crew when she taxied the P-47 in to the docks at Newark, again following the directions of the ground crew. When she had pushed the canopy back and started to climb out, she heard Andy's voice. "Lacy!" And Andy and Jo were running towards her.

Moments later she and Andy were hugging and Andy was crying.

THIRTY-FOUR

The following afternoon, December 17, Lacy boarded the train bound for Missoula via Chicago. She refused to ride in the coach car, insisting that she stay in the baggage car with Cin's coffin. A sympathetic conductor helped her make up a cot and saw to it that she had a chair on which to sit.

Lacy felt suddenly very tired, very war weary. From a young woman who, just six weeks ago, burned to get back in the cockpit of those captivating airplanes — so much so that she refused to stay home and help her brother run the family ranch — she had, by her own reckoning, gone from glory-seeking warrior to shell-shocked victim of war in two short days. Or was it simply the culmination of two years of combined elation and sorrow that was finally getting to her. How many rollercoasters could she ride?

As the taxi drew up in front of Cin's childhood home, a one-story frame house on a rundown street, Lacy steeled herself. Peeling paint marred the shutters and the down spout to the left of the front door was broken. One pane of glass in the front door was cracked and taped with adhesive tape.

The woman who opened the door was tall and slender with straight iron gray hair pulled back in a bun.

"Mrs. Stinson?"

The woman stared at Lacy's WASP dress uniform of Santiago blue serge. Lacy had gone to a local dry cleaners enroute to the house and waited while they steam pressed the skirt and jacket, ridding the uniform of the wrinkles of traveling.

"I'm Lacy Stearns, Lucinda's friend from the WASPs."

The woman nodded and held the door open so Lacy might enter.

The resemblance between mother and daughter was striking, including the ruddy complexion and black-brown eyes that bespoke the Sioux blood Cin often bragged on. However, a permanent scowl had etched itself on Elvira Stinson's face whereas Cin usually wore a look of amused skepticism.

Lacy sensed that, had her friend not escaped the circumstances that surrounded Mrs. Stinson in middle age, she, too, might have, one day, worn that same scowl. But the daughter had combined a god-given skill to fly airplanes with an insatiable drive and made herself part of the juggernaut that was rolling through history seeking victory in the world's most widely-contested war.

"So you brought my daughter back, eh," Mrs. Stinson was saying as Lacy seated herself on a frayed brown fabric couch in the cramped living room.

"Yes ma'am. The army and the WASPs feel she belongs with her family."

"What do you know? What do any of them know? She was a wild one, was Lucinda. Never listened to me or her father. She had her eye out for the boys way too early, and they knew she was looking. Couldn't stay away from them, she couldn't. Got herself in trouble, too. Had to have an abortion. Shameful!" She paused and fixed Lacy with a penetrating stare. "You know 'bout that?"

"Yes ma'am, she told me. I've met the father. She was going to marry him."

"Marry, my foot," she spat out. "He was a skirt-chasing flyboy who deserted her. No better than those cowboys she used to take up with. Drove her father to an early grave."

"Mrs. Stinson, she was a grown woman when she met Eric. . ."

"Don't speak that name in this house! No good S.O.B."

Lacy caught her breath and tried another tack. "Do you know what Lucinda was doing with the WASPs? She was flying highly complex pursuit airplanes and she was headed for even better things after the war . . ."

"AFTER THE WAR! The girl's dead! There is no *after the war* for her. You killed her — you and all those other people down there in Texas and California and that den of sin New York City."

Ice water ran through Lacy's veins. "Mrs. Stinson, Cin was a good friend, my best friend. She was a dear, caring person and a very brave woman . . ."

"And it got her dead!"

Lacy was silent for minute, picking her way through the mental mine field the woman had thrown up in front of her. She decided to be diplomatic. "We want to have the graveside service tomorrow morning at ten in Evergreen Cemetery, if that's all right with you."

Cin's mother glowered at her. "I told that Cochran woman when she called two days ago. You people took her. You keep her. You bury her when and where you want."

Lacy was prepared for this. Jacqueline Cochran, having gotten nowhere with Mrs. Stinson, had given Lacy authority to make the funeral arrangements. And Cochran had told Lacy to have the bill sent to her, that she would pay the expenses out of her own pocket. Still, Lacy couldn't believe the mother wanted nothing to do with her own daughter.

"I checked with the Baptist church listed as Lucinda's church of record," she continued, ignoring what the woman had said. "They told me that her father was buried at Evergreen. We were able to secure a plot on one side of him. I hope that's agreeable with you. If it isn't, it's not too late to change. We want to abide by your wishes."

Silence hung over them for a moment, then the woman stirred and said, "Do what you will. I don't care. I want no part of it."

"But Mrs. Stinson, you will come, won't you?"

"Get out, get out of my house, and out of my life and take that woman my daughter became with you. I don't ever want to see you again and I sure as hell won't see her again in this life — or the next either most likely. Now go!"

Lacy rose and walked to the door. She took a deep breath, turned to try one more time but the woman was standing, looking at her, eyes blazing. She tried anyway. "Ten a.m. tomorrow." And then she opened the door, walked outside, and closed the door behind her.

She heard a muffled cry and a crash as something hit either the floor or the door through which she had just exited. The darkness of early winter had crept up the street while Lacy was in the house. Thank goodness she had asked the taxi to wait, figuring it would be difficult to get another this late out in this part of town. She climbed into the backseat, sank back, took a deep breath, and waited for the tears to come. But they didn't.

"Miss, is something wrong?" The cab driver turned and looked at her. "Is there anything I can do?"

"No, thank you though. I think everything that can be done has already been done." And she gave the driver the name of the hotel downtown where Cochran had booked her a room.

At 9:45 the next morning, Lacy was at the cemetery. The cold, pale sunshine glinted off the snow on the higher peaks that surrounded Missoula. The winter solstice was only a day away. Her months back east had taught Lacy an even greater appreciation of the west she called home. She gloried in the blue mountain sky, the morning sun on her face, the crisp cold of the air that stung her eyes and her cheeks and caused her breath to form in clouds about her mouth and nose, and then felt guilty that she should feel pleasure at a time like this.

Reverend Tyler Phillips from the Missionary Baptist Church met her there. The portly man with receding blond hair and glasses looked older from a distance than he did up close. When Lacy first saw him, she would have put his age at fifty. But now, as he took her hand, she swore that he was barely past forty. He had sparkling light blue eyes and a blonde mustache. A smile lurked behind the funereal expression she guessed he had donned just for the occasion.

He had been in Missoula only three years and hadn't known Lucinda or her father. When Lacy told her of her encounter with Mrs. Stinson, he shook his head. "Sad case," he said. "But tell me about Miss Stinson — Lucinda, or Cin as you called her. And tell me about the WASPs."

By ten, a handful of people had entered the graveyard and made their way toward Lacy and the preacher. Lacy was, once again, in uniform and she introduced herself to each of the mourners. One drew her aside.

"I'm Carol Anderson Collins, the one Cin lived with the last month of our senior year in high school. She wrote me about you. She really loved you. And she loved the WASPs."

Reverend Phillips delivered a short, well-spoken, surprisingly insightful eulogy lauding Lucinda as a local war hero. Lacy wondered how many war dead he had buried in the last three years. He read telegrams of condolence from Cin's closest military friends who could not be there — Lt. Col. Eric Larsen, WASP classmates Andrea Sellers, Josephine Bertelli and Karen Richardson Wilson, and Major Clay, her former commanding officer at Biggs. Mrs. Deaton had sent what was now the traditional WASP wreath of yellow and blue flowers and WASP Commanding Officer Jacqueline Cochran sent her personal condolences.

Then Reverend Phillips recognized Lucinda's best friend, WASP Lacy Jernigan Stearns, who had accompanied her friend home to her final resting place. While the pastor spoke, Lacy couldn't help but remember another memorial service — nearly two years earlier.

The non-denominational chapel near the University of Colorado campus was bathed in the refracted light produced by the millions of tiny pieces of leaded glass needed to make stained glass windows. John's picture was on the altar. A copy of the one Lacy had kept in her bedroom. The U.S. flag and the state flag of Colorado — with its red C and golden sun in the center — stood to the left and right of the altar, respectively. The Episcopal priest who had known John since he was a boy delivered the eulogy.

At the last minute, before the Jernigan family was to leave the Boulderado Hotel for the memorial service, Lacy had broken down. "I can't go. I can't go. I can't face his family. I can't face their friends, my friends, our friends," she wailed. "Oh please, don't make me go," she sobbed.

It was her Uncle Ike who took her in his arms and soothed her and talked low into her ear. "Lacy. There aren't a lot of things in life you have to do, but this is one of them. You can't let John's folks down. You can't let yourself down. You're made of tougher stuff than that. Go in there and show them just how tough you can be."

She listened. She sighed. The sobs began to diminish. Then she excused herself, went into the bathroom, alternately considered fleeing through the window and slashing her wrists with the razor her father had carelessly left lying on the sink. Then, calmly, she splashed water on her face, blotted it dry, repaired the little makeup she used, and walked back out into the sitting room to join the rest of the family. She did insist on wearing her dark glasses to hide her now puffy, red-rimmed eyes.

But she was dry-eyed as she listened to the eulogy. The portrait offered by Father Elgar sounded reasonably like John. She wished she could have given him a few insights that would have made John sound less stuffy, less serious. But she realized that she had seen a side of him no one else ever had or ever would. The side a wife and lover sees. And she would never see it again.

Now, at Cin's funeral, Lacy hardly recognized the memory of the girl she had been two short years ago.

WASPs were not permitted to have an official American flag draped over their coffins. But Lacy had purchased one on her own and, in open defiance of protocol, laid the Stars and Stripes over the top of Cin's casket. When Reverend Phillips concluded his remarks, he and Lacy took the flag and folded it with the military precision of a full honor guard, crisp corners and triangular in shape. Lacy glanced once more at the mourners, hoping that Mrs. Stinson had come at the last minute.

Originally she planned, as tradition would have it, to offer the flag to the fallen warrior's mother. But Mrs. Stinson had not come. Lacy clutched the flag to her WASP uniform jacket and bowed her head. Reverend Phillips said a brief prayer and it was all over.

Lacy waited after everyone else had left the cemetery. Deep inside, she felt she still had to say goodbye to Cin in private.

The groundskeepers had already lowered the coffin. They were eyeing her and obviously waiting to toss the clods of dirt back into the hole. "Want us to hold up a minute more, miss?" one asked. She nodded. They moved a distance away, but continued to stare at her.

Lacy wondered if women in uniform were that rare in this remote part of Montana, or all over the country for that matter. On her way west, she had drawn several stares and looks of disbelief when she got off the train to stretch her legs. One man had asked her if she was a WAC or a WAVE. When she answered that she was a WASP and that she flew for the Army, the man had looked at her with great disdain then walked off, shaking his head, mumbling to himself about women not knowing their place, war or no war.

Because they spent most of their time flying, they hadn't had a lot of occasions to wear their dress uniforms — the trim jacket with matching skirt and trousers. Today, both she and Cin were wearing their uniforms and their silver wings — Cin to be buried in and Lacy as her chief and official mourner. Cin would wear hers into eternity. Lacy was wearing hers, officially, for the last time.

Now she stood at the side of the open grave and the words of her own thoughts about her friend formed in her mind and spilled over in an eloquent, personal eulogy.

"Well, Cin, it's over. I never in a million years thought it would end like this. Because we were so close, I got the job of burying you. I wouldn't have had it any other way. I wish Eric and Andy and Jo and Karen, all of them could have been here but, as you know, there's a war on. And I will tell Eric about his daughter — like you said 'when the time is right.'

"The groundskeepers are waiting to fill in your grave. It's December 20, deactivation day, and when I leave here, my last WASP duty is done. I'll get on a train and head for Colorado — for home." She felt the sting of dammed up tears. "Hopefully, before I lose it here in front of strangers.

"I'm sorry your mother didn't come, but I think you must have known that she wouldn't. Now I know why you left home so early and, as you so often put it, 'never looked back.' Well, none of us can look back now, Cin. Too much has happened. I'm just glad that we happened. We fought a good war and we fought it our way. I'll never forget you, friend."

Lacy turned and pulled a single blossom from the floral arrangement with the card that said 43-W-9 and tossed it into the grave. She broke off one more and placed it in her lapel. Then she turned and walked away.

THIRTY-FIVE

Far from the somber affair Lacy expected, Christmas at home turned out to be a gay holiday. The family not only was celebrating her homecoming but also the word that Jared would be granted emergency family leave and would be home in early January. Her father had been released from the hospital in nearly record time and was making a quicker-than-expected recovery.

Even the word filtering through on the radio of the U.S. troops in danger of being cut off in the Battle of the Bulge, coupled with Lacy's loss of her close friend Cin, couldn't dampen the spirits of the Jernigan clan. They saw too many other positives in the current chain of events.

This year, Shorty and Clara joined Ike and Virginia and Lacy and her family for the traditional Jernigan family Christmas Eve dinner, after which they all adjourned to the tiny Methodist Church in Two Buttes for the midnight candle lighting service.

Lacy had received a fat letter from Eric that morning, telling her of the plans he was making in preparation for her arrival. The biggest news was that he had rented a house for them and was to move in the day after Christmas. At dinner, she told the gathering of her plans to marry Lt. Col. Eric Larsen, USAAF, in Honolulu, as soon as possible after Jared's return home. That capped off the festive mood of the evening in spite of her mother's response.

"Don't you think it's a little soon after John's death, Lacy? You haven't told us hardly anything about this young man. What about his family?"

"I've met his father. He's the president of a bank in Baltimore. He's the only family Eric has and he loves his son very much."

Her mother sniffed. "You have no business running off and leaving Jared with no help."

"He'll have me, Mother," Norman protested.

"Lacy, that's wonderful," Aunt Virginia said, and got up from her chair to go hug her niece.

"John's been gone almost two years, Janny," Lacy's father said. "This war has played havoc with the old traditions. People gettin' married a couple of months after losing someone. I'd say two years, in this case, is a long time. You love this Larsen fellow, daughter?"

"Yes, Daddy, very much."

"Then you have our blessing. I'm just sorry the wedding has to take place so far away. But, from what you've said of his job, it makes sense."

A couple of mornings later, Lacy had trouble getting out of bed. With the high of the festive holidays over and the isolation brought on by the short gray days of winter, Lacy's mind continually returned to her last days as a WASP and the injustice of the demise of the program. Inertia gripped her. Though the duties of running the ranch pulled at her, relative inactivity — the loss of the grueling flight schedule she had grown used to and loved — stifled her. Though she had set her foot to the path she wanted to follow and, within weeks would be with Eric, doubt about the meaning of it all assailed her. And above all, she agonized over the futility of Cin's death. But, still, she could not cry.

Engine failure, the accident investigation team had ruled.

The four of them had drawn straws for order of takeoff that morning in the Ready Room at Republic. She could have drawn the third, not the fourth slot. What had spared her, and Andy, and Jo, and not Cin? Why? Why Cin?

Lacy knew she could have bailed out over Arizona with Cin. If she had, they both might have died before they could find their way out. But because she had stayed with the stricken plane, landed it, and helped launch a ground and air rescue, she was alive today and Cin was dead anyway. Lacy shook her head, turned over, curled up in a ball, and pulled the covers over her head.

Her mother found her that way an hour later.

"Your brother needs you," she said, her tone of voice implied an order that Lacy should get her lazy body out of bed.

"In a minute, mother," she said and pulled the covers back over her ears.

Janice stomped out of the room.

On the afternoon of January 2, 1945, her father was taking a nap, Norman was out in the barn mending a broken halter, Lacy — who hadn't gotten out of bed until eleven — was going over the ranch accounts at the dining room table, and her mother was seated across from her doing some mending. They both heard the car.

Because of a New Year's Day snowstorm, not much traffic was moving around Baca County and they weren't expecting company of any kind. Lacy got up and looked out the window. Her heart lodged in her throat. A military staff car was making its way slowly through the icy ruts on the road to the house. Her mother moved up behind her, gasped, and grabbed Lacy's arm, her long, work-toughened fingers locked in a vise that hurt. For Lacy, it was a replay of two years earlier when the telegram about John had come. For both of them, it was a replay of last year when word of Kenny had come.

Lacy's immediate thought was of Eric. He had asked that she, not his father, be notified as next of kin should anything happen to him.

"Jared!" her mother breathed.

That it could be Jared crossed Lacy's mind, but he was supposed to be on his way home. "No, mother, I don't think it's Jared. I think this one, like John's, is meant for me."

Her mother looked at her, her eyebrows raised in an unspoken question.

"It may be Eric," Lacy said from between clenched teeth.

Again Lacy watched the drab green staff car draw to a halt in front of their house. The time warp was back and the present and the past began to merge in her mind. An Army Air Forces major got out and stared for a moment at the house. Jared was a Marine. Lacy shook off her mother's hand and, holding her breath, walked to the front door and opened it wide to the stranger. She stood at attention, just as she had learned to do in the early morning PT and marching sessions at Avenger. The control she had exerted graveside in Montana a few days earlier, took over once again.

"Lacy Jernigan Stearns?" the officer asked.

She nodded.

He handed her the telegram.

She thought she was going to die on the spot. Twice, when two different airplanes had stopped flying with her at the controls, she had looked death in the face and survived. Then she had looked death in the face again when she watched as Cin pancaked the P-47 on the runway in Farmingdale and, for all her skill at handling an airplane, had died, like John, of a blow to the head. Now Lacy wanted to die rather than open that envelope. But she opened it anyway with cold, stiff, trembling fingers.

Once again the words "The army regrets to inform you" burned themselves into the back of her brain like the branding iron used by ranch hands to sear the flesh of the hapless cattle in their charge. But this time the message was different. Instead of "Killed in action" it said *"Missing."*

"There's more, ma'am," the granite-faced young major said. He handed her an official Army communiqué.

Her mother appeared behind her in the door. "Lacy, where are your manners, letting that young man stand on the porch and freeze. Come in, Major, and have some coffee. You must have had a long drive."

"Yes ma'am," he said, "from La Junta." And he stepped across the threshold.

Seated in the living room balancing a cup of coffee on his knee, he related to Lacy and her mother what else he knew. Ordinarily the officers who delivered these messages were merely bearers of bad news. But before he had left for the journey to Two Buttes, he had received a dispatch from Col. Larsen's second in command in Honolulu. Considering Col. Larsen's rank and standing — and because of the contents of the dispatch and because this was not the standard next of kin notification — he was ordered to be more forthcoming with information. The message read:

Dear Mrs. Stearns,

This is to inform you that Lt. Col. Larsen was NOT — I repeat, NOT — flying combat when his plane disappeared over the Pacific.

Lt. Col. Larsen was on a simple reconnaissance flight when his airplane disappeared. It is quite possible that he was forced down on an island somewhere, most likely by bad weather. There were squalls in the area. We don't think the Japs have anything flying in the zone where he was. We are holding out all possible hope that he is safe and dry and will be picked up. He had a good supply of rations. Don't give up hope, Mrs. Stearns.

He asked me, some time ago, to contact you personally if he should not return from one of these flights and to give you as exact details as the military censors would allow. Please feel free to contact me if you have further questions. We will be sure to notify you the minute we learn of Lt. Col. Larsen's whereabouts and condition. He asked that you relay this message to his father.

Yours, Major William "Bill" Forbes

"But he also could have gone down in the ocean," Lacy said, dead voiced, after reading the dispatch. She didn't dare allow herself the slightest bit of hope because there was none. Not in this war.

"Yes ma'am," the young major sitting in front of her now said. "He could have done that, but his staff doesn't believe that's what happened.

"Don't give up hope, Mrs. Stearns," were his parting words a few minutes later.

Just like the other times, Lacy watched the car turn right onto the highway, head west into the snow covered fields of winter wheat and disappear in the Colorado sunshine. The ache had returned — the balloon that grew bigger and rounder and tighter in her chest until it felt like it was about to burst inside her. She had felt it when John died, again when Kenny died, and again when Cin died. Now it was back at the news that Eric, too, could be dead.

Somewhere in a fog that was the present, Lacy heard her mother on the telephone. She was talking to Aunt Virginia.

"Yes, missing," she heard her mother saying.

Norman had come in from the barn when he saw the car. Her father, who awoke from his nap to hear a strange voice coming from the living room, had come downstairs. He read the two pieces of paper Lacy handed to him, then took her in his arms.

Tears burned her eyes, but the carefully constructed floodgates held firm.

Late that night, Lacy, dry eyed, unable to sleep, once again sat on the couch staring into the pot bellied stove thinking about John, and Cin, and Kenny, but mostly about Eric. Her mother came in the room, dressed in her flannel nightgown, robe and slippers. She had released her gray streaked hair from the bun she always wore in the daytime and it hung long down her back, almost to her waist.

Janice sat down in the chair directly across from Lacy.

"Lacy, I don't know this young man Eric Larsen and I had some misgivings at your announcement the other night. Now you may think I'm old and beyond understanding, but I'm not that old. I've watched you as you've lost one after another to the war and you seem to grow stronger with each loss, but you also are becoming more remote. That, Lacy, is not like you. The strength I can understand and appreciate. Though you've never chosen to talk to me, I know you used to talk to your father and your Uncle Ike and to Kenny. But now you aren't talking to anybody.

"Why don't you tell me about him."

Lacy looked at her mother. Her eyes burned like someone had applied a hot poker to them, but still there were no tears. It was like when the well dried up back in '34 when the Dust Bowl drought gripped the land and all the moisture was sapped from the earth and the air.

She began to talk. She told her mother of meeting Eric and about Cin, about how she had fought not to fall in love with him, and how he had pursued her and broken through all the barriers she had thrown up. She told how she had turned down his marriage proposal, but, after a couple of months and her father's illness, had come to her senses. How he wanted her to come to Hawaii just as soon as she could be spared from the ranch.

Her mother reached over and took her hand. The touch of her mother's rough, red hand was gentle. Suddenly Lacy felt like a dam was bursting inside her. She gripped her mother's hand and let go of all the hurt and sorrow and fear and loss.

And the tears came.

Lacy didn't know how long she sat there sobbing. She realized that her mother had moved over by her on the couch and had taken her in her arms. Janice stroked her hair.

"It will be all right. Believe me, it will be all right, dear daughter. You've already found out that time can heal."

Lacy sobbed even harder.

They sat like that until some of the tears and sobs subsided and Lacy began to gain control again. Then she moved away and blew her nose and wiped her eyes. She smiled a weak smile at her mother. "Thank you," she said softly.

"Lacy, I know you won't believe this, but I never opposed you doing the things you wanted to do. Your father was so willing to let you do anything and everything, I thought you needed a leavening influence. I know now that I was wrong. I should have treated you the same way I treated the boys. That's what he did, and look how good you've turned out. The only problem is, I made you think I didn't care, but I did.

"When I was a girl, I was just like you. Out there on the western plains in Kansas, I was free as a bird and my daddy let me have my head, too. But then my mother died, and because I was the eldest, I was left to raise the rest of the children. That was the end of my freedom. I became Daddy's little mama and though I wasn't ready, wasn't prepared, I learned to think and act like a grown up.

"I married your father and it began all over again as you kids came along. I forgot what it was like to be a little girl with little girl feelings. When you came, I had already lost my first baby girl, Jana, and I thought I had to make a mother out of you, too. Prepare you. That was wrong. Now I realize, when the time comes for you to be a mother — and I hope it does come for you — that it will come naturally. So if you can forgive me for seeming not to care, maybe it's not too late to start again."

Lacy leaned over and hugged her mother.

"Janny? Lacy?" Her father called from upstairs. A minute later, he had joined them and Janice was telling him, with Lacy's nod of approval, all about Eric.

"Well, daughter, he's only missing. That means he may be alive. I think I'd try to hold on to a little hope."

"I'll try, Daddy. But I'm just about out of hope."

THIRTY-SIX

The next day, Jared came home.

Almost overnight, Lacy felt left out, useless. She stayed in bed later and later in the morning and had daily bouts of uncontrollable crying. The tears — dammed up for so long — now that they were let loose, would not quit flowing.

She wrote to Andy about Eric and asked her to pass the word to the rest of their WASP friends. "I don't think I can face putting the words on paper again," Lacy wrote.

A few days later, she received a letter from Andy.

> I'm bored. Nobody's home. Everybody's married or off fighting the war or doing something useful. I miss you. I miss Pink even worse. After the awful news about the Battle of the Bulge, I'm convinced this terrible war will never end and that he will never come home to me. And now Eric.

Could Lacy get away from the ranch now and would she like to come to Columbus for a visit? Or would she, Andy, be welcome at the Jernigan ranch? She closed with: *I've got to talk to somebody who understands!*

Lacy was still trying to decide whether she could get away from the ranch and go to Ohio or to invite Andy to Colorado when she got another letter — this one from Karen Richardson Wilson.

After her recuperation period was over, Karen had gone back on active duty with the WASPs. She served with the tow target squadron at March Army Air Base in Riverside, California, and married Bob Wilson before he left for overseas after D-Day.

Now, Bob was in France with the 12th Armored Division, her father was busy in the legislature, she was footloose and, like Andy and Lacy, bored. Next week, she was leaving Phoenix in her yellow convertible and coming through Two Buttes on her way to St. Louis to meet up with Lacy's former baymate Arabella Sanders. They were going in search of the "WASP nests" they had heard about — apartment complexes in Florida and California where WASPs were congregating to live and hunt for flying jobs. Would Lacy like to join them?

That night, as usual, Lacy couldn't sleep. As had become her habit, she went downstairs to read by the stove and found Jared sitting at the dining room table going over the ranch accounts.

"Can you decipher what I've done there?" she asked

He looked up, seemingly surprised to see her. "Yeah, it's pretty cut and dried." He looked back down at the ledger he had been studying.

Lacy curled up on the couch, turned on the light and tried to read a paperback novel. After she had read the same paragraph three times, she sighed and put the book down, got up, walked to the dining room table, and sat down. "Jared, can we talk for a minute?

Her brother looked up. What appeared to Lacy to be a fleeting look of annoyance crossed his rugged features. He had their mother's piercing blue eyes, her tall, rangy frame. Though he was only thirty, deep lines, put there in his youth by Colorado wind and sun and more recently by the jungles of the South Pacific, already creased his face. His hair was black, but it wouldn't be long before it began to show signs of gray, Lacy thought.

He dropped his pencil, clasped his hands and stretched his long arms, yawning. "What's on your mind?" He sounded very much the older brother, remote, almost judgmental, not at all like Kenny.

"I know we WASPs weren't in combat, but, still, we were living in military quarters, under military discipline, flying military airplanes, meeting military schedules. I wonder if you're having some of the same difficulty I am adjusting to civilian life?"

Jared stared at her for what seemed like a full minute, but probably wasn't more than a few seconds. Then he snorted. "Let me get this straight. You think that the conditions you were living under were even remotely like what I faced out there in the jungle?"

"No, no Jared, that's not what I meant. I know the physical conditions were vastly different. It's the attitudes I'm talking about and how civilians have no concept of what we were really doing. I'm talking about feeling like you're part of a team. We were doing something important. Something that made a difference. Now I feel like I'm cut off from everything that's real — everything that matters."

"Lacy, if you think for one moment that tea party you call active duty with Hot Shot Cochran's girly flying review has even the remotest connection to bushwhacking your way through a jungle with Japs shooting at you, you've lost more of your mind than mother thinks you have."

Lacy gasped. "Mother said that?"

"Well, not in so many words. But she's worried about you, moping around here, staying in bed all morning, staying up until all hours of the night. And you've really got to get a grip on that crying jag."

Lacy stared at him now, thoroughly chagrined. But she had one more question. "What about your buddies?"

"What about them?"

"Don't you miss them? I know you're probably glad to be home, but don't you miss the closeness — being there with them and in on the action?"

Jared was shaking his head. "You just don't get it, do you Lacy. I'm outta there and I'm glad. When I raise my head now, I don't have to worry about some Nip sniper blowing a hole in it. Miss my buddies? Not really. We had nothin' in common other than just trying to stay alive and I don't have to worry about that anymore."

He stood up and stretched. "I'm going to bed. I'd advise you to do the same. Get yourself back on a normal schedule like everybody else in this house."

After he had climbed the stairs to the room he used to share with Kenny, Lacy sat for a long time and stared at the fire in the pot bellied stove.

The next morning, she did the unthinkable. She picked up the phone and called Karen long distance. "Count me in. What about Andy?"

"I've already written her. The more the merrier," Karen said. "I just heard from a friend living in a nest down in Miami who says 'come on down'."

Between Andy's letter and her phone conversation with Karen, Lacy realized that she was not alone in her feelings of having been used up and thrown aside. Most of the young women who had served felt cast adrift by the sudden lack of something meaningful to do — that specific something being flying airplanes. Less concrete, but nevertheless a factor, was the knowledge that the war they had tried to help win still went on without them.

Now, with the initial shock of deactivation and separation over and the Christmas holidays and the need to see their families out of the way, they were flocking to those WASP nests in order to be together. It was a natural enough phenomenon. They had trained together, lived together, worked so closely together, often under such grueling conditions, that they shared a bond that was rare among women.

Lacy called Andy and within a couple of days, they had it all put together. Andy would meet them in St. Louis at Arabella's.

Karen's roadster pulled into the yard in front of the ranch house on January 23, 1945. She spent the night and, once again, was treated to a home-cooked meal courtesy of Janice Jernigan. The following morning she left, taking Lacy with her.

This time, her father and Norman were on the porch to wave goodbye. Her mother didn't approve of young girls going off and living on their own with no visible discipline or supervision and Jared resented losing the good help his sister could provide around the ranch.

They camped one night with Arabella's family, picked up Andy in St. Louis as well as Karen's old baymate Anne Rogers and Patty Arthur, 44-1, and struck out, wedged into the convertible, each carrying one small bag.

The six of them came from diverse backgrounds. Karen was a rich girl whose daddy was a politician in Arizona. Lacy was a rancher's daughter/school teacher from the high plains of southeastern Colorado. Andy had been a college coed, from an upper middle class family, with a liberal arts education and a lot of prospects. That she also turned out to be a crack stunt pilot had surprised everyone but her.

Arabella had been a dance hall girl before joining the WASPs. She learned to fly because one of her boyfriends taught her. Pretty, petite, brown-haired, brown-eyed Anne Rogers was a secretary for an air service before she got the urge to fly those airplanes and join the WASP.

Patty Arthur was a rodeo rider from Oklahoma — a barrel racer — and one of the few women earning a living at that before the war. The black-haired girl with stunning green eyes figured if she could rope and throw steer, she could handle an airplane. She ended up parlaying her rodeo-honed nerves of steel into a test pilot job with the WASPs.

They pooled their money to buy gas and food and spent their nights on the road south with friends or relatives, often driving out of the way in order to do that and save the cost of lodging.

But Miami was their destination.

THIRTY-SEVEN

The six were able to rent a furnished, two-bedroom, ground floor apartment in a Miami complex where several other WASPs were living. Given their living quarters at Avenger, they were confident that, by adding two cots, they could sleep three to a room and deal with a single shower and bathroom.

"We're together," Andy said during a bull session the day after they moved in. She was, at that moment, waiting for the hot water heater to recycle so she could take her shower.

"Did the rest of you find you didn't fit in at home any more?" Anne asked. "At first, I thought it was those I'd left at home who'd changed. Finally I realized it was me. Nobody understood what I had been doing for a year and a half. Nobody cared."

"One day we were a group of women with an identity — pilots flying for the Army. The next day, we're civilians and about as necessary as yesterday's garbage," Patty said.

"The looks I got," Arabella chimed in. "The 'oh, sure' attitude when I tried to explain what I had been doing to help win the war."

"When I flew home to Phoenix on December 20, I wore my uniform," Karen said. "Since it took me so long to get back on duty after my accident, I hadn't had it long. Had only worn it one time. I was proud of it and wanted to wear it home. A woman in the airport had the nerve to ask me if I was a stewardess."

Andy summed it up. "The hardest part for me was going, overnight, from living on the edge — flying P-47s one day and a redlined wreck destined for the boneyard the next, and constantly facing the danger of the unknown — to living in my parents' house in Columbus, Ohio. I give my mom and dad credit. They understood pretty well and left me alone. But my mother's friends all had that 'isn't it nice dear, you did your part for your country, but now you're safe and sound at home' attitude. And my own friends, those who'd listen, didn't believe half what I told them."

"Has it occurred to you girls that what we did was . . . well, revolutionary?" Lacy asked.

"What do you mean revolutionary?" Anne said.

"I don't think a group of women like us has ever before been brought together and given this kind of opportunity to fight for a common cause. It happens to men through sports and war experiences. You've seen how these guys become buddies. They love each other — with the possible exception of my big brother, who seems to have been immune to feelings of any kind while overseas," Lacy laughed. "They live and die for each other. But it doesn't happen to women, at least it hasn't until now. We're the first. What we did was important."

"Aw, come on Lacy," Patty said. "Most of the country never knew we existed. Those who did could care less or have already forgotten us."

"Men write the history books," Karen said. "And they don't write about what women do."

"Then women need to start writing history books," Andy said.

"It took a particular set of circumstances and pressures for the WASP program to happen in the first place. Unfortunately, I don't think that kind of opportunity will come around again for women for a long time," Lacy said.

"It took a woman like Cochran to bring it off," Karen said. "A woman with vision, connections, and most of all guts."

That brought nods from the others.

"Don't laugh," Andy said. "Fifty years from now, the men who survive this war are going to be getting together, sitting around re-telling their war stories to each other for the umpteenth time. Look at the Spanish American War and the World War I veterans. They turn out, in uniform, for every Decoration Day and Fourth of July parade."

"We've got to do the same thing," Lacy said. "We've got to make sure the WASPs never die. . .keep what we did *alive*."

"How?" Arabella asked.

"Stay in touch. Have reunions. Talk and write about our experiences, share them with anyone who will listen," Lacy said. "Like Andy said, we women need to write some history books."

The others laughed.

"No, I'm serious. Don't you see? We're part of a finite group. There are roughly a thousand of us. There will never be any more WASPs. We're it. We got to do something women rarely get to do. We got to put our lives on the line in service to our country. None of us will ever forget Cin and the others who gave their lives — Cornelia Fort, Evelyn Sharp, Helen Jo and Peggy, all of them. It's not so much patriotism as it is making a statement, taking a position, and wanting to make a contribution. It's up to us to keep that alive. To make sure that they didn't die in vain."

"Tall order, Lacy," Patty said. "Right now, I'd settle for a job."

With the same determination they had used to learn to fly for the Army, the six tackled the Miami job market. Lacy took a waitressing job and made the rounds of the elementary schools to see how far a Colorado teaching certificate and two years classroom experience would get her. But February was the wrong time to find a teaching job, she was told. Right now, because of a glut of teachers, they couldn't even offer substitute teacher work. They all took her application, looked at her credentials, and told her they would consider her come summer when they were looking to fill any vacancies before school started in the fall.

Andy got a receptionist's job at a small airport. Her two years experience at the airport in Columbus, before joining the WASPs, helped secure that. The minute she was hired, she told her employer about Lacy and the others and made sure that all of them had applications on file in case anything turned up.

Arabella found a nightclub that was happy to have her dancing talents. Karen resurrected her haughty debutante air and was offered a hostessing job in an exclusive Miami restaurant. Anne, with her skills, secured a secretarial job. Patty went to work at a local horseback riding establishment as an instructor and stablehand. But none of them could find a flying job.

Then the flight service Andy worked for offered to hire a couple of the girls to sew wings on some of the J-3 Cubs and other trainers they were reconditioning. The owner was getting ready for what he expected to be a post war boom in general aviation flying. Andy was small enough to get back into the tight places and do that kind of work, as was Anne. So they took those duties on in addition to their day jobs.

None of them had their flight instructor's rating, so each of them began to scrape together money for flight time figuring that would boost their salability in the tight aviation market. They all did just fine on the written test, but for some reason they ran into trouble when it came time to take their flight tests. Karen was the first one to try. Because of her father, she had more ready cash than the rest of them and could afford to get her hours out of the way sooner. But she flunked the flight test, much to everybody's surprise. Then a few days later, Patty, even with her test pilot experience, flunked as well.

"Something's wrong," Andy told Lacy. "I did some sleuthing. Found out why they failed. What you need to do is tell your instructor you're going back to Colorado. They're flunking people they think want to stay in Florida and fly. Too many pilots down here already. But if they think you're leaving, they'll pass you."

A few days later, Lacy flew. With a straight face, she told her instructor that she planned to go back to Colorado and work once she had her rating. He passed her. She put in an application for an instructor's job the next day.

"I thought you were going back to Colorado, Stearns?"

"I am. Just not ready to go yet," she said with a big smile. "Probably in the fall." She also put in an application to teach ground school. Though it wasn't flying, it was one step closer. A lot closer than waiting on tables.

Parties became the best way to unwind.

Karen's twenty-fifth birthday was April 12 and a party was planned for that night. As Karen and Lacy made last minute preparations that afternoon, they heard over the radio that President Roosevelt had died in Warm Springs, Georgia.

"Should we cancel out of respect?" Lacy asked. Franklin Delano Roosevelt had been president for the second half of her twenty-five years. She couldn't imagine anyone else in the job. "President Roosevelt" sounded right. "President Truman" had an odd ring to it.

"How are we going to get word to everybody this late?" Karen said. "Besides, the food's bought."

"Why not make it a wake?" said Anne, who had just come in. "My mother's Irish. Her side of the family always has a big blow-out party when there's a death in the family. It's their way of showing how much they loved the deceased and of saying goodbye."

The party went on. Midway through the evening they toasted the memory of the late president and drank to the health of the new one, Harry S Truman.

"I just want to remind everyone," Arabella said, as they raised their glasses and beer bottles for the toast. "President Truman is from Missouri!"

When VE Day arrived May 7, they threw an impromptu victory party and invited every WASP in Miami and any friends, particularly male, that they might like to bring.

* * *

Two weeks later a V-mail letter arrived for Andy. The girl lay on her bunk completely absorbed in the contents — a lot of very cramped writing on the tissue-thin paper.

Lacy was propped up on her bunk studying a ground school manual. She noticed that her friend was awfully quiet while she read the letter. Lacy assumed it was from Pink, though she knew Andy corresponded with several young men who were overseas. It could have been from any one of them. She hoped it wasn't bad news and waited, knowing Andy would eventually share whatever news there was. Finally she looked up. There were tears in Andy's eyes but a strange smile on her face.

"Pink's coming home. Now that the war in Europe is over, they're sending the pilots home. He wants me to meet him in New York. He's got five days leave. He wants to get married on June 6, the anniversary of D-Day."

"What are you going to do?" Lacy asked.

"I'm going to New York to get married June 6 — and I want you to be my matron of honor." And with that, Andy, grinning broadly, leaped off her bed, grabbed Lacy, pulled her up and began to waltz her around the small room they shared with Karen.

That night, Lacy lay on her narrow bunk, unable to sleep.

The current rumor was that experienced pilots from the European theater would be sent on to the Pacific. That meant Pink could, after a few weeks of R and R, be sent to fight the Japanese. The future continued to be murky. But one thing was for sure. Andy was leaving the nest in Miami. Karen might not be far behind. Bob certainly would be sent stateside soon. Lacy suddenly felt very much alone. She also recognized a gnawing envy. She remembered all too well what it was like to be a newlywed.

Married just before the fall term of their senior year in college, she and John had been the campus lovebirds — living in a tiny apartment, studying together, getting sidetracked, making love, and then having to get up in the wee hours to finish reading or writing a paper left unfinished in the wake of their passion. Now, as she thought about it, they were more like children playing house.

Then John decided, at his father's urging, to go on to graduate school and get his masters in education, putting him on a good solid career path to go into school administration once he got his feet sufficiently wet in the classroom.

They moved to Boulder, John began classes at the university in the fall of 1941, and Lacy went to work teaching at Elmdale Elementary. She still had the class picture with the names of all twenty-two students in her fourth grade class inscribed on the back. Yes, she and John had their life all planned and in front of them.

Lacy pulled the shade on that memory. Too painful.

She turned over on her back and stared at the ceiling.

Where are you, Eric? Are you alive? It's been five months. No trace of you or your plane. Logic says you're as dead as John. So why do I keep having this day dream, right before I drop off to sleep, that you've been found — alive?

She closed her eyes again and willed sleep to come.

The night of June 4, Lacy packed her bag for the trip to New York.

"I've got a line on a ground school job that may lead to some flight instructing," Lacy told Karen, as she slipped the ground school manual into her suitcase. "I figure I can bone up on it on the airplane flying back after the wedding. If any word comes through while I'm gone, tell 'em I'll take it. And don't take the job away from me."

Karen had mysteriously passed her flight instructor's test after declaring her intention to return to Arizona the minute her husband came back from overseas.

"I'll be back after I get our little friend here married off."

THIRTY-EIGHT

After the brief wedding ceremony, June 6, First Lieutenant Charles
W. "Pink" Fletcher kissed his bride and then the wedding party — the
bride and groom, Lacy, and Pink's best man, fellow P-47 pilot First
Lieutenant Jim Allen — went out on the town looking for a couple of
bars they had been told they had to visit while in New York City. A
wedding dinner at Sardi's in the theater district topped off the evening.

At eleven o'clock, the four arrived back at the Biltmore Hotel.
Grinning, Pink and Andy hopped an elevator and left Jim and Lacy
standing in the lobby staring after them.

"One for the road?" Jim said. He was tall and gangly like John,
with freckles and a carrot-red crew cut.

Lacy sensed the appeal for company written on the young man's
face and in his soft brown eyes and shook off the feeling of tiredness
that threatened to engulf her. "Sure, just let me check for messages.
I'm hoping to have a ground school job waiting when I get back to
Miami."

There were two messages for her. One, a phone message from
Karen taken by the hotel operator, said, "The job is yours. Report
Monday." The other was a telegram from Two Buttes. Oh my God,
she thought. Daddy? She stood for a moment staring at it.

"Anything wrong, Miss?" the desk clerk asked.

Lacy looked up. "I hope not."

She joined Jim at a small table in the bar and ordered a Tom
Collins. "I got the job," she said, smiling.

"Congratulations." He raised his glass of beer in a toast.

"This is from home." She waved the telegram in front of him.
"I'm afraid to open it. I've had pretty bad luck with telegrams."

"Want me to open it for you?" he asked.

"Yes." She handed it to him.

He tore it open, read it, then looked up at her. "Shall I read it out
loud?"

"Please." She could tell nothing from his expression.

"It says 'Eric alive. Sends his love. Call home.'"

Jim hesitated. "It's signed, Dad."

Lacy didn't move. She had closed her eyes when she heard the words "Eric alive." But her brain was not processing the information her ears had just heard. She opened her eyes and silently reached for the telegram.

"It's good news, Lacy," he said quietly.

She read it over again and again, the words, in all capitals, awash on the yellow page. She looked up and Jim's earnest young face was blurred. Her cheeks were wet and she realized it was from her own tears.

He patted her shoulder, awkwardly, then when she reached out to him, he put his arms around her. She clung to him, her whole body shaking with silent sobs.

"It's OK. It's OK, Lacy. He's alive."

Realizing Jim was holding her, and that people were looking at them, she pulled herself together and sat back.

"Thank you." She dabbed at her eyes with a tissue then blew her nose.

"I take it Eric is someone special?"

Lacy nodded. "My fiancé. He's been missing since January."

"Well, he's been found. And he loves you." Then Jim grinned and added, "Can't say I blame him."

Lacy looked at the earnest young man, nearly four years her junior. He probably had been hoping for a more interesting evening than holding her hand and telling her that her lover was alive and had come back to her. She smiled at her thought and at him.

"I need to put through a long distance call," she said, regaining some bit of composure.

"I'll help you. Come on." And he found an empty booth, deposited her there and started checking his pockets for coins.

"Here, I have some," she said, opening her purse and extracting her coin purse. Soon they had a series of quarters, dimes and nickels lined up on the platform in front of her. Then she lifted the receiver, dropped in a nickel and asked for the long distance operator.

It took about a half an hour, but because of the lateness of the hour, the circuits weren't busy. Finally, she heard Norman's voice on the phone.

"Norman, it's Lacy."

She heard a whoop from the other end of the line. "Hold on, Sis, lemme get Dad. He's alive. Eric's alive!"

"I know," she answered.

"Lacy?" Her father's deep voice came on the line.

"Daddy! How is he?"

"He's fine, darlin'. He's all right. We've talked to him. All the way from Honolulu. He called here this afternoon. I didn't know they could do that. He's got a nice voice. Won your mother over right away."

"What did he say, Daddy?"

"Well, now, here. First let me read the message that nice young officer from La Junta brought earlier today from Major Forbes.

Lt. Col. Eric Larsen was found, alive, June 3, 1945, on a small island in the South Pacific. His plane went down near the island January 1, 1945. The natives there rescued him, unconscious, from the surf. All communications equipment was lost, so he had no way of notifying the Army as to his whereabouts. He was suffering from a broken right leg and contusions about the head. The natives set the leg and nursed him back to health. A mine sweeper on reconnaissance happened to send a party ashore there three days ago and found Lt. Col. Larsen alive, in good health, and in good spirits. He's being flown to the hospital at Hickam Field, Honolulu, for observation.

"Oh, Daddy." Lacy realized she had been holding her breath.

"Now, here's what Eric said, and I'm quoting him word-for-word because I wrote it down for you. 'Tell her the house is still ours, even though we will be a little late moving in. All systems go from this end.' He left instructions for you to call him through a military operator. Get a pencil and write down what I tell you. He says he wants you to call no matter what time we got hold of you. He also said 'tell her I love her'."

Later, in her room, Lacy remembered the message from Karen, pulled it from her purse where she had stuffed it and reread it.

During the months in Miami, Lacy felt she had begun to find an inner strength she didn't know she had. What her Uncle Ike had said to her, the night they learned of her brother Kenny's death, had stayed with her: *You're not the same young woman you were a year ago. You were so fragile after the news came about John. I worried about you. I sensed some deeper despair in you. For a long time, I was afraid you weren't going to come out of it. That you were going to be one of those ghost-like widows, wrecks left in the wake of wars. It happens to some women, you know. But the day you told me you wanted to join the WASPs and fly, I knew you had turned the corner.*

Because of her uncle and his faith in her, Lacy, who had encountered several more corners since then, now believed that things were coming together for her. She had made choices, lived with them, and would do so again.

Just as she had once resigned herself to a life without John, Lacy had begun, slowly, to resign herself to a life without Eric. Her longterm goal was to become the country's foremost advocate of women's role in aviation. This was a role she was convinced would grow with the years. She would follow in Amelia Earhart's and Jackie Cochran's footsteps and pick up where they left off.

Lacy felt she was in control of her life and her destiny.

And now that destiny was turning yet another corner. Eric was alive. Safe!

She wanted badly to talk to Andy right now, to tell her what all had happened. But it was her friend's wedding night. The news would have to wait until morning.

If only Cin were here.

Cin! At some point she would make good on her promise to her best friend — when the time was right she would tell Eric about his daughter. Right now, she just wanted to hear his voice. She picked up the phone and asked for the long distance operator.

At two in the afternoon, June 7, 1945, Andy, Pink and Jim put Lacy on Pan Am flight 245 for Chicago and San Francisco, where she would catch a military transport bound for Honolulu. Major Forbes was taking care of those arrangements. She had sent telegrams to Karen, telling her the job in Miami was hers if she wanted it, and to her parents, telling them she was on her way to Hawaii.

"Have you got your lucky coin, Lacy?" Andy said, grinning with tears in her eyes.

"On a gold chain around my neck," Lacy said, hugging her friend.

For once the visibility in and around New York City was crystal clear. As the airliner took off from Idlewild, Lacy spotted the runway at Republic Aviation in the distance and thought of Cin. Then as the plane banked out over Long Island Sound, it made a 180-degree climbing turn and she could see the Statue of Liberty. She, Cin, Andy, and Jo used to fly their P-47s over the lady and her torch on their way from Republic to Newark.

Then the pilot up front completed the airliner's turn out and set his course for Chicago. For Lacy, too, it was a new course and a new beginning.

Acknowledgment

On June 20, 1996, I sat in Caro Bayley Bosca's living room in Springfield, Ohio and listened to Caro, Katherine (Kaddy) Landry Steele and Nadine Canfield Nagle talk about their days as WASPs during World War II. A fourth WASP, though not in the room, was "with us" in absentia. Caro and Kaddy told a series of hilarious stories that included their good friend Emma Coulter Ware. From what I learned that June day came the seeds for this book. Though *Flight From Fear* is NOT the story of these four women, elements of the characters and stories in this book were generated by what I heard and saw and felt while talking to them.

Nadine, a teacher, did lose her first husband early in 1943. The copilot of a B-24, he died in a crash landing in England returning from a bombing mission. Nadine did learn to fly after his death — because she wanted to fly in his place. When she read about the Women's Flying Training Detachment, she knew what she had to do.

Caro, from the beginning, was a natural at aerobatic flying. After the war, she went on to become the U.S. Women's aerobatic champion. Her letters home — carefully preserved by her mother — provided several descriptions of WASP life at Avenger Field.

Caro and Kaddy were sent to B-25 school in California and then on to Biggs Field in El Paso where they met Emma and established a rollicking lifelong friendship. Caro and Kaddy were classmates — 43-W-7; Emma graduated earlier, 43-W-3, and Nadine later, 44-W-9.

The five female characters in *Flight From Fear* are all members of 43-W-9. There was no such class. It exists only for the purpose of this story.

Sarah Byrn Rickman
Centerville, Ohio
June 6, 2002

Photo: Daniel Cleary

Sarah Byrn Rickman attended the Pikes Peak Writers Conference in 1996 immeditely after completing her Master of Arts in Creative Writing at Antioch University McGregor in Yellow Springs, Ohio. Sessions presented by members of Women Writing the West inspired her to turn her fledgling idea of a WASP-based story into a female quest novel. Three years later, *Flight From Fear* won First Place in the historical fiction competition at PPWC. The following year, the sequel *Flight To Destiny* won First Place. Although Sarah's heroines are women of "airplanes" rather than the Great Plains, the pioneer spirit lives in them nevertheless.

In 2001, Disc-Us Books published *The Originals: The Women's Auxiliary Ferrying Squadron of World War II*, Sarah's non-fiction book about the women pilots who preceded the WASPs.

Sarah and her husband, Richard, live in Centerville, Ohio, and have two grown sons. Her actual aviation experience is 22 hours in a Cessna 152. But she also grew up riding horses in Denver and at Cheley Camps outside Estes Park, which helped with the mostly western setting of *Flight From Fear.*